driving lessons

Also by Zoe Fishman

Saving Ruth
Balancing Acts

driving lessons

ZOE FISHMAN

WILLIAM MORROW
An Imprint of HarperCollins*Publishers*

This is a work of fiction. Names, characters, places, and incidents are products of the author's imagination or are used fictitiously and are not to be construed as real. Any resemblance to actual events, locales, organizations, or persons, living or dead, is entirely coincidental.

HarperCollins books may be purchased for educational, business, or sales promotional use. For information please e-mail the Special Markets Department at SPsales@harpercollins.com.

FIRST EDITION

Designed by Diahann Sturge

Library of Congress Cataloging-in-Publication Data

Fishman, Zoe.
Driving lessons / Zoe Fishman.
pages cm
ISBN 978-0-06-205982-6
1. Pregnancy—Fiction. 2. Cervix uteri—Cancer—Fiction.
3. Friendship—Fiction. 4. Life change events—Fiction.
5. Domestic fiction. I. Title.
PS3606.I85D7 2013
813'.6—dc23

2013017389

---

14 15 16 17 18 OV/RRD 10 9 8 7 6 5 4 3 2 1

In memory of Barbara Morace

Acknowledgments

Thank you to my muse, Ari Shacham. Being his mother is a gift for which my gratefulness cannot be measured. Thank you to my husband, Ronen Shacham, for supporting and encouraging me, always. Thank you to my parents, Sue and Ethan Fishman; my brother, Brenner Fishman; and my aunt Alice Fishman for believing in me.

Thank you to Mollie Glick, for being a great, honest agent. Thank you to Jeanette Perez, for her wisdom and insight over the years, and to Amanda Bergeron for carrying *Driving Lessons* over the finish line with such grace and smarts. Thanks to my production editor, Laura Cherkas; my copyeditor, Aja Pollock; and both my former and current publicists, Katie Steinberg and Joanne Minutillo, for setting their respective bars so high.

Thank you to Dr. Chad Levitt for sharing his wisdom and knowledge. Thanks to Nurit Shacham, Karen Shacham, Michelle Putnam, Arin Tritt, Andrea Neiman, and Joel Murovitz for making Atlanta feel like home. Thank you to Lauren Gottlieb, for being my Mona.

And finally, thank you to Hilda Queiroz and Ashley Graham. I could not have written this book without your help.

driving lessons

1

Intersection: any place where one line of roadway meets another.

Sarah, what the hell?"

From above, I peered down the three flights of stairs to Josh below. He stood over the flattened cardboard box filled with now-broken picture frames. Even as I had balanced that box on the banister for just one second—*just one second!*—while I knelt to retrieve what looked like an integral screw from the bed frame that Josh and Ben had just hauled down the stairs, I had known that the aforementioned second would be its last. Still, I did it—tempting fate and physics out of sheer exhaustion. Naturally, the box had toppled over almost immediately, and I had watched its graceful descent with surprising ease.

"Sorry!" I yelled down. Josh gazed up at me, his face an accordion of annoyance. "That was stupid."

"What was in here?"

"Picture frames, I think?"

"Great." He sighed heavily. "Are you okay?"

"Yeah. I'll come down there and clean it up." I wiped my sweaty brow with my sweaty forearm. It was August in Brooklyn, and boy, was it hot. So hot that my bra had become a medieval torture device as far as I was concerned. I descended the stairs carefully, hugging the wall at the second flight in order to let Josh and Ben by.

"You sure you're okay?" asked Josh, grabbing my hand. I nodded.

"Yeah. Just clumsy."

He smiled and kissed me with lips that tasted like salt before continuing on.

After I had moved into Josh's apartment five years earlier, we had made a pact never to move without enlisting professional help ever again. And yet here we were, lugging our boxes of pots, pans, utensils, appliances, books, clothes, and miscellaneous crap and our heavy furniture up and down three—four, including the stoop—flights of stairs in ninety-degree heat. The fact that we had gotten the couch out without filing for divorce was no small miracle.

At the bottom of the stairs I surveyed the sad, flattened box. FRAGILE, it read on its side, in wobbly black letters. I picked it up gingerly, cringing at the sound of broken glass inside. So much for the newspaper I had wrapped each frame in. I could either just load the box on the truck and deal with it in Virginia, or duck out of further work by sitting on the floor and dealing with it now. Now sounded good.

I moved over to the opposite wall and sat down, feeling only a remote pinch of guilt as Ben stumbled by under the weight of a giant box of books. Ben was Josh's younger brother, and they were ridiculously close. Like *The Waltons* close, except the Jewish version. His wife, Kate, and I were friendly but far from tight. She was someone to roll eyes with at our husbands' and their family's expense whenever we went out to dinner or gathered around a holiday table together, but that was about the extent of our relationship. To be honest, she intimidated me. Someone four years younger with her own catering business and a baby on the way could do that to a person with neither of those things on her résumé.

My best friend was Mona, who was nowhere to be found. I couldn't blame her. When I'd told her that we were handling all of the moving ourselves she had shaken her head in disbelief.

"How come you're willing to spend two hundred bucks on a pair of jeans, but you can't spring for some burly Russians?" she had asked. It was a valid question that I had no answer for.

I opened the box and pulled out a photo of Josh and me from our very early days of dating, marveling at our youth. When my friend Betsy's wedding invitation had arrived in my mailbox, I had begged shamelessly for a plus one, even though Josh had not yet earned his plus-one rights. The thought of attending another wedding alone was enough to drive me into the East River. She had mercifully agreed, and here we were at our table, me with my head thrown back and laughing, and Josh grinning beside me. It represented so much to me, this picture. Us before us.

I was thirty when we met. At thirty-two, we were married, and now here I was at thirty-six—moving to Farmwood, Virginia, of all places. Not three months prior, I had fought through the predictable end-of-workday subway mob; picked up my and Josh's dry cleaning as well as toilet paper, beer, and Thai food; hauled it home like the urban pack mule that I was; dumped it on the kitchen table; and promptly burst into tears.

"I can't do this anymore," I had said to Josh, who watched me with alarm from the couch. "I hate New York."

"Me too," he'd replied, and promised to look around for professorships out of state. I nodded absently, dried my eyes, drank my beer, and felt a little bit better but no less trapped. We both wanted to leave, but for some reason an escape seemed out of the question, as though beyond New York City's borders was nothing but sky.

And then, impossibly, a job offer from a small liberal arts college in Virginia had landed in Josh's lap. A friend of a friend knew someone who knew a sabbatical-bound mathematics professor whose planned fill-in had bailed last-minute. Voilà—a job for Josh and the escape we had been pining for. We had hemmed and hawed about whether I should come with him—after all, the job was only guaranteed for a year, and my job in New York, although mind-numbingly uninspiring, was stable and lucrative—but when I had asked my boss about the possibility of working long-distance, she had literally laughed in my face.

"You're going to run the marketing division of a makeup empire remotely?" she had cackled. "That's like Biden working from Spain. All due respect, Sarah, but no dice."

The liberty she took in comparing my job to that of the vice president was beyond delusional but, in my world—as the second-in-command to a lunatic—unfortunately, not that far off. I was on call twenty-four/seven to make decisions about bronzer packaging. Somehow, despite the fact that my personal face prep involved only lip balm at best, I had become, over the course of thirteen years in the business, a big shot. My life was consumed by my job, or at least it had been. Until now. Now we were moving to a town called Farmwood, and I was unemployed. You couldn't get farther from New York than that.

"Hey, Sar, c'mon. You can sort through that later," yelled Josh over his shoulder. "Let's get this over with."

"Why would we haul a box of broken glass to Virginia? I'm just going to rescue the photos real quick and dump the box. It'll take two seconds."

I slipped the remaining photos out of the rubble with minimal fanfare, miraculously managing to avoid slicing my fingers open. As I transferred the box to the garbage and the photos to my back pocket, I kept a close watch out for our landlord, Denise, who lived next door. Her maniacal attention to our refuse had given me heart palpitations on countless occasions.

"You can't put Tupperware in the recycling can," she would yell when I begrudgingly answered her phone call only moments after putting our bag out.

"But it's plastic, I thought that—"

"No!"

It went on and on:

"Are those your empty boxes downstairs?"

"Is that your old air conditioner on the curb?"

We had gotten to the point where we only took our garbage out under the cover of night. She was watching now, I knew it. *Glass in the recycling bin or no because it's broken? What to do?* My heart began to race. *Screw it.* I dumped the whole thing—box and all—into the can and exhaled deeply. A point for Farmwood: no Denise.

I headed back up the stairs slowly. Our apartment was nearly empty. Five years of cohabitation all packed up and shipped out. In Farmwood, there would be no more bathroom attached to the kitchen, no more dust balls the size of cats, no more onion apartment smell weeks after cooking something that involved onions, and no more listening to our middle-aged downstairs neighbor rapping in his makeshift studio.

Who would I be without those things to complain about? Sure, I would find new things to complain about—I had a natural talent for that sort of thing—but it wouldn't be the same. These were New York complaints, which by context alone made me cool. Farmwood complaints were not going to be cool. And what about the fact that I had no job? Who was I without that to complain about? What if all of the free soul-searching time that Farmwood was going to provide me with fulfilled my deepest fear—that I had no passion? What if there was no career option that excited me? I grabbed one of the last boxes and made my way back down to the street.

"Hellooooo!" Mona's familiar, raspy voice shrilly pierced the air just outside my building's front door. "Sarah?"

"I'm here! You're just in time to help with nothing," I yelled back from inside, smiling behind my box as I stepped blindly over the brownstone's threshold. Mona had been in denial about my leaving ever since I had announced it two months earlier. I had been afraid she wouldn't show up.

"Oh, that's too bad," she answered. "I was hoping to help schlep your armoire down four flights of stairs this morning. So sorry I missed it." I put the box down on the stoop and stuck my tongue out at her.

"I can't believe you're really leaving, Sarah. Can't you change your mind?" She picked up the box and we walked down the stoop stairs together to the truck below. "Here ya go, Josh." She handed it to him and he nestled it into our beige mass of belongings.

"Thanks. Anything else in the apartment?" he asked.

"One or two more boxes, I think, but that's it," I answered.

He looked at his watch. "Cool. I'll take a shower, we'll grab some lunch, and then we'll hit the road. Sound good?" I nodded.

"Hey, Ben, call Kate and tell her to start making her way over," he yelled. Across the street, Ben looked up from his phone.

"Nah, I'll go get her. She'll appreciate an escort. We'll meet you at Bodega." Kate was eight months pregnant—much to the overwhelming delight of Josh and Ben's family, who had been eyeing my empty uterus with contempt as each year crept by—and painfully candid about the entire experience. Over chips and guacamole a few nights before, she'd told me that her labia were blue. *Smurf blue*, she had added for emphasis, before asking me to pass the hot sauce.

Josh disappeared indoors, and Mona I and walked back over to the stoop and took a seat.

"I'm not going to shower," I announced. "It's too much work."

"Agreed," said Mona. "You're just going to start sweating again immediately afterward. What's the point? Anyway, I brought us beers." She reached into her giant bag and pulled them out. "And contraband cigarettes. I figured we should go out with a bang."

Mona and I had both quit smoking on my thirtieth birthday. Well, I had. She claimed to have as well but always seemed to have cigarettes on her person. On a different day—one when I wasn't about to move several hundred miles away—I would have given her shit for it. Not today.

Today a cold beer and a cigarette on the stoop with my best friend sounded perfect.

"Thanks," I said, lighting mine and taking a deep drag. I rubbed the beer bottle across my forehead. "I've always wanted to do that."

Mona gave me a sideways glance. "You're such a weirdo, Sar." We watched the Italian man across the street water his roses, a cigar hanging precariously from his lips.

"So, this is it, huh? You're moving to freaking Virginia?"

"Yeah, this is it." I took a swig. "Am I doing the right thing?"

"Sure you are. You've been over New York and your job for years now. It's time."

"I know, but what if I miss it? What if bitching is all I know how to do?"

"Sar, you certainly have other talents. Don't be dramatic."

"Like what?"

"Hmmm. Let's see . . . Oh, I know, you're very good at French-braiding."

"That is true. It is a coveted skill. I was very popular in middle school."

"Hey, remember our move from Union Square to Brooklyn?" Mona asked.

"I still have the scars to remind me."

"How did you manage to fall directly into that mirror?"

"What did you expect? We were loading the truck ourselves during rush hour on one of the busiest streets in Manhattan. I was a little stressed."

"How old were we?"

"Twenty-three, I think? Or maybe twenty-four?"

"Babies," said Mona.

"Shattering glass must be a thing for me. I dropped an entire box of framed photos down three flights of stairs earlier today."

"Yikes."

"I wonder what that reveals about me psychologically."

"What what reveals?"

"The broken-glass thing. Am I predestined for bad luck?"

"No, you're just a complete spaz."

"Yeah, I guess." I took another swig from my bottle, relishing its fizzy chill, and placed it beside me.

"What am I going to do without you?" asked Mona softly. "I'm going to be so bored."

"Nuh-uh. You have a million friends to keep you company."

"Facebook does not a friend make. It's not the same."

"I know. But we'll Skype and visit each other all the time. Flights are so cheap, Mona."

"Yeah, yeah." She lit another cigarette. I opened my mouth to protest. "Cigarettes don't count today. Listen, if you hate—what's this place called that you're moving to? Farmtown?"

"Farmwood."

"Right. If you hate Farmwood, you can always move back. It's a one-year contract, right?"

I sighed in response and looked up and down the block. Over there was where Josh had kissed me for the first time—a lingering peck that had turned into more and from which I had broken away, flustered and talking a mile a minute.

From the beginning, I had known that he was special, that he possessed a kindness and reliability that no one who had gone before possessed. What's more was that I still really liked him despite all that. Pre-Josh, I'd had a penchant for man-boys who couldn't even commit to a sandwich.

I put my arm around Mona. I disagreed with what she had said. It just wasn't true that we could move back here if Farmwood was a bust. Even if we did, New York would always know that we had strayed. She was the kind of city that was entitled to hold a grudge.

2

Josh emitted a deep burp that rattled the cab of our moving truck.

"You're not going to complain about the food we just ate for the rest of the night, are you? And blame me?" he asked.

"Maybe."

We had just inhaled an entire aisle of a Quick Mart. I groaned as I peeled my sweaty thighs from the vinyl seat.

"Oh look, there's a piece of Chex Mix in my bra." I reached into my left cup and pulled out a tiny pretzel O. "Are we there yet?"

"Almost."

I hung my arm out the window and undulated my wrist in the warm air. While Josh had been down to Farmwood a few weeks earlier to rent our house, I knew nothing about our new city, or the South for that matter. I'd never been below the Mason-Dixon Line before.

"Is it like *Steel Magnolias*?" I asked. "Lots of women in big-brimmed hats and tiny purses? Floral prints and in-home salons?"

"What's *Steel Magnolias*?"

"You've never seen *Steel Magnolias*?" He shook his head. "You're missing out." I stared out the window. "Josh, what if we hate it there?"

"If we hate it, it's one year, Sarah. One year. Do you know how quickly one year flies by?"

"Yeah, but then what?"

"It's a year for you to figure some things out, Sar. You hated your job, right? You hated New York. This is a chance for you to spend some time figuring out what it is that will fulfill you, you know? I'll be making decent money, and the cost of living is like, nothing. You can score a relatively relaxing day job and take it easy for a bit. We'll make a baby."

"Yeah, a baby." I forced a smile.

Whenever Josh brought up babies, a giant clock descended from the sky and hovered over my head like a UFO. It was go time, despite the fact that I had about a million reservations about my maternal aptitude—reservations that I had not breathed a word about to Josh. Our plan had always been to have kids. If I waffled now, I would be reneging on my part of the bargain and breaking my husband's heart in the process. I kept telling myself that I would get over it, that it was just stage fright, and as testament to that mantra, I had gone off of my birth control a month earlier. Still, every time we had sex, I uttered a silent prayer that my eggs were playing hard to get.

"As much as I hated my job, there was a sort of twisted comfort in it," I said, changing the subject.

"You took comfort in the complaining?"

"Well, that, and also, I was good at it. Granted, I may not have reaped any creative fulfillment from it, but I got the job done and then some. Plus, it's all I know. What if I can't do anything else?"

"Sarah, of course you can do something else. You just need the freedom to figure out what that something is."

"You're right. It's easier to marinate in the cesspool of your own displeasure than to actually do something about it. No, I'm glad we're moving, I really am. I needed a kick in the ass, obviously. I'm just scared."

"I am too. But I think this vulnerability will be good for us. I really do." He reached over and squeezed my thigh. "Look out, here's our exit!" He crossed one lane, and then two, and then we were officially off the highway and that much closer to our new home. A home that claimed more than one and a half rooms—that had a yard, even. I hadn't lived in a home with a yard in eighteen years.

Strip malls, fast-food joints, farm stands, screened porches, and sprinklers passed us by in the summer twilight. I took a deep breath in, relishing the smell of grass clippings, barbecue, and heat. In the city, summer smelled like burned asphalt, rotting trash, and body odor. This was nicer. Much nicer.

"I'll take you by the school tomorrow," said Josh. "It's such a gorgeous campus. Still bummed about the rents down there, but what could we do?" Homes closer to campus ran for a much steeper rent than those farther out, so Josh had picked accordingly.

I nodded absently as the strip malls disappeared and the scenery turned to grass and trees exclusively. A little country living would be good for me. Maybe I would start an organic baby food business from the garden I would create—like Diane Keaton in *Baby Boom* minus the planting, gardening, or pureeing. Okay, never mind.

"Just how far out from campus are we?" I asked.

"It's not so far. Once we have the car we won't even notice." He had purchased a used car from a fellow faculty member. He was so excited about it—finally, we wouldn't have to schlep our groceries, dry cleaning, and laundry—but whenever he spoke about it I felt like I was listening to Charlie Brown's teacher. *Wah wah wah wahhhh, transmission, wah wah wahhhh, gas mileage.*

The last time I had been behind the wheel, I was eighteen. I'd never had a car in high school, relying instead on the kindness (and sometimes resentment) of my friends, and when we went home now to visit my mother or Josh's parents, they drove everywhere. I used my license for identification purposes only. Driving was as foreign a concept to me as those people who claimed they "forgot" to eat. My brain could not compute.

Once Josh had signed on for the job and our move was imminent, I had told him repeatedly that I was apprehensive about driving, but he always brushed me off. *You're better than you think*, he would say. *You just need some practice.* I would nod absently in response, hoping he was right. I had never gotten over my first and last interstate experience, with my mother frozen in fear by my side. "YOU HAVE TO LOOOOK!!!!!!" she had screamed as a monstrous tractor trailer veered out of the way of my reckless merge.

As more greenery passed us by and Josh didn't appear to be slowing down in any way, shape, or form, my anxiety mounted. Walking to civilization and any type of gainful employment did not appear to be an option. And forget about grocery shopping. The wheels of our trusty granny cart—our old neighborhood's version of a Lamborghini—were not cut out for off-roading. Perhaps I could take up gardening after all. It could sustain us completely. Vegans in Virginia. Better yet, I would write a cookbook: *The Virginian Vegans*. I envisioned photo spread after photo spread of butter beans and lettuce wraps, Josh and I laughing uproariously over two jars of sweet tea on our front porch. Finally, Josh turned off the road.

"The house is fantastic," he said, "which makes up for the

fact that we're a little farther out than I'd like to be." *A little farther out?* "Sar, we have brand-new bathroom fixtures."

"No!"

"I waited to tell you." I had been dreaming about a bathroom that had been built post-1965 for what felt like my entire adult life. A faucet that didn't leak; floor tiles that did not wear the grime of fifty years of bare feet; an actual bathtub as opposed to a stall shower that could only be shaved in if the water was turned off—these were the things I pined for during my New York apartment-dwelling existence. Not to mention, a bathroom free of wildlife.

"Remember the pigeons?" I asked.

He laughed. "The image of you standing over me, white faced and shaking with a shampoo bottle in your hand, will stay with me forever."

Before moving in with Josh, I had lived in my own studio apartment in the East Village. Grimy and tiny, it had reeked of chicken and broccoli from the Chinese restaurant next door, but it had been mine. For that reason alone, I had done my best to turn a blind eye to its faults and probable health code violations, the worst of which was the presence of two pigeons in my shower one morning.

They had squeezed through the partially open window and were happily crapping down the side of the wall when my bleary-eyed self had discovered them. Not knowing what to do, I had grabbed the shampoo bottle and waved it in the air like a maniac, which had no effect on the birds, who regarded me with Zen-like stares. I had run to the bed, where Josh slept like a baby, and hovered over him, shaking, until he opened his eyes shortly thereafter. Ever my hero, he had cranked open the window and basically shoved them out as I cowered behind the commode.

"I still worry that I contracted something from those beasts," he admitted now. I reached over and massaged his neck.

"No pigeons in Farmwood, I bet."

"Nope."

At the end of a street of well-spaced-out homes with carefully manicured yards, there was our house. It was gray stucco with white shutters, and its airy front porch claimed a cozy wooden swing hanging from the rafters. The sweet smell of honeysuckle perfumed the pink air.

"I can't believe this is home," I whispered, taking Josh's hand. "It's so pretty."

"I know, right? It's a real house. Why are we whispering?"

"I don't know." I laughed as a firefly flitted by the windshield. "Let's go in."

3

When two vehicles meet on a steep road, the vehicle facing downhill must yield the right of way by backing up until the vehicle going uphill can pass.

Where is my Knicks T-shirt?" Josh yelled from the bedroom. That's what we had to do now—yell to each other from opposite ends of the house. There was a certain joy in not being five feet away from each other at all times, which had been the reality of our urban cohabitation.

"How do I know?" Since we'd begun the Herculean task of unpacking, he asked me at least twenty times a day where something of his was, as though he hadn't packed it all himself. As though I had some sort of magical sonar built into my uterus.

"I found it!"

"Good. Congratulations."

Stomp, stomp, stomp. Josh appeared in the doorway of our kitchen, where I was unpacking box after box of kitchen appliances that we had received from our wedding registry and that I very rarely used.

You'll want this ninety-pound mixer that costs four hundred dollars, my married friends had said knowingly when I'd asked them for advice about what to sign up for. I will? For what? *Get the red, the red is the best*, they would continue, ignoring my reluctance. And so I did. I struggled now to hoist it out of its box. I had never even so much as plugged it in.

"You need some help with that behemoth?" Josh bent down to grab it. He placed it on the counter. "What is this?"

"I'm not exactly sure, but I think it bakes cakes? Or something?"

"You're going to be baking cakes?"

"Maybe. On second thought, it could be bread that it makes." We both eyed it suspiciously.

"Let's drive into town and get some lunch," Josh suggested. "I read about this great fried chicken place near campus."

"Fried chicken? It's one hundred degrees out, Josh." He danced over to me and pulled me in for a musty hug. "Do they serve anything else?" I asked crankily. "Like a salad?" I already missed our Brooklyn sandwich joint—the same joint that had driven me nuts with its foodie-inspired specials and imported pickles that cost nine bucks a jar.

"C'mon. You can drive." We had picked up the car two days before and I had yet to sit behind the wheel.

"Maybe you can just pick me up something and bring it back," I said as he scampered off down the hall to fill up his requisite water bottle. Josh was the most hydrated man on the planet.

"No way!" he yelled over his shoulder. "You need to get out of here for a while—see town. You've been unpacking nonstop for two days."

I exhaled deeply and pondered a way to excuse myself from driving. I could say that I was too hungry to drive. *No, lame.* What was wrong with me? It wasn't like I had never driven before. How hard could it be?

"Let's roll, lady." Josh tossed me the keys as he walked out the door. I followed him begrudgingly, eyeing the car with a furrowed brow. If I stared at it hard enough, maybe it would turn into a bike. Approaching it, my palms were like tear ducts. My fear frustrated me beyond belief. I was a ball-busting former associate VP, for chrissake! What was it about driving that reduced me to such a heart-racing, stomach-roiling mess?

I took a deep breath and got in. Screw this; I was taking charge. I checked my rearview mirror carefully and pulled my seat up before buckling myself in, my heart beating like a drum all the while. It was hard to breathe.

"Jesus, you're practically sitting on the steering wheel," joked Josh. "You sure you don't want to scoot back an inch or two?"

"I'm sure." I shot him a look.

"Okay, I'll shut up. Sorry." I turned the key in the ignition, jumping a little as the car came to life. *Okay, good work. Car is on.*

"I have to back out of the driveway?" I asked meekly.

"Well, yeah. You okay with that?" He looked at me curiously.

"I'm not so good at backing out," I confessed.

"All right, well." He cleared his throat. "We'll go slow," he said reassuringly. I nodded gratefully and pressed my foot on the gas.

"Whoa, not so hard!" said Josh as we jumped back several feet.

"Sorry. Nervous foot." I gulped. The entire steering wheel was now coated with my sweat, like a glazed donut. I eased up and we began to move slowly.

"Okay, turn your wheel a little, you're a bit crooked," said Josh.

"Which way do I turn it?"

"What do you mean, which way?" He looked at me incredulously. Finally, he was getting it. I was cartarded.

"Well, if I turn the wheel to the right, the car goes to the left, right? I mean, correct?"

"Huh? It's front-wheel drive, Sarah."

"I know, but like, the back of the car tilts the opposite way from the way I turn the wheel, yes?"

"Sarah. What the hell are you talking about?"

"I don't know!" I shrieked. "I don't know! I don't know how to drive, okay? I'm an idiot!" I put the car in park, opened the door, and attempted to get out, just as I realized that my seat belt was still fastened.

"Shit," I grumbled as I undid the buckle and escaped. Josh looked out at me through the window, his mouth slightly agape. He turned the car off and opened his door. I stepped back, examining the grass.

"Hey," he said quietly, taking my hand. My lip trembled. "Hey, Sarah. Look at me." I shook my head as a tear rolled off the tip of my nose. "C'mere." He kissed the top of my head.

"I'm a moron," I sobbed. "I don't know how to drive."

"You're not a moron, Sar. You're just out of practice. It's okay. It really is."

"You didn't believe me when I told you I couldn't drive," I offered.

"I know. I just—well, I thought you were exaggerating."

"Yeah, no. Not so much."

"Mmmm-hmmm. Well, you'll practice with me."

"No, noooo. No way." I pulled out of his hug and wiped my nose.

"Why not?"

"I'm not going to do that to our marriage, nosir. Ten minutes on the road with me behind the wheel and one of us will be thinking about purchasing a firearm."

"It's very easy to do here, by the way. Buy a firearm, I mean."

I wiped my cheek with the back of my hand. "Maybe I can take driving lessons or something."

"Like a fifteen-year-old?"

"Yes, like a fifteen-year-old, Josh. Thanks for the support."

"No, of course. Of course I support you. It's very smart of you to go about it this way. Very responsible."

I leaned my torso against the passenger side of the car and folded my arms on its warm roof. "You're patronizing me," I announced.

"I'm not, I swear." He put his hand on my shoulder and squeezed it gently. "I know this must be hard for you." He moved in closer and kissed the side of my face. "And frustrating. It's like me and my fear of flying."

"Sort of. Although, you can get around flying and not be a total recluse."

"But I wouldn't if it wasn't for you. Remember our honeymoon?"

"I basically carried you onto the flight."

"How many glasses of scotch did I consume at that airport Chili's, anyway?"

"Enough. I think at one point our waitress just brought out the bottle."

He grimaced. "So I owe you, is what I'm saying. I honestly don't mean to patronize you at all. I understand. We'll get through it."

"Thanks, Josh." He rested his forehead against mine for a moment before opening the passenger-side door for me with a smile.

On the way into town, I texted Mona. *Is it weird for a 36 yr old woman to take driving lessons?* Nothing fazed Mona, except for the occasional uncommunicative suitor. She had not only a scuba certification but a skydiving one as well. She would have a field day with my driving phobia.

I hadn't spoken to her since we'd arrived, which wasn't entirely inexcusable—we'd only been here three days—but it was still bothersome. I'd left two messages. She'd probably already forgotten all about me. Out of sight, out of mind. *Call me, you jerk!* I added, and slipped my phone back into my bag.

"Here we are," announced Josh, pulling into a parking space in front of a small house that looked a lot like our own.

"They make chicken out of their house?" I asked.

"Yeah. Must be pretty convenient. Just roll out of bed and into the kitchen."

"Yeah, but what about the smell?" I asked as we got out of the car and made our way toward it.

"The sweet smell of crackling skin? Sounds delightful to me."

"Josh, right?"

I looked up. A very tall, very blond Uma Thurman lookalike floated toward us. My hands balled into fists reflexively.

"Yeah! Iris?"

"Yes, yes. Great memory. It's actually a miracle that I remembered your name at all, truth be told. My brain is like a sieve." She smiled, and her face lit up like a choir of angels singing. I both hated her and desperately wanted her to like me.

"This is my wife, Sarah," explained Josh. I reached out

my hand to shake hers, immediately wishing I hadn't. What was this, a job interview? Nerves had an alarming effect on me. Once, I had greeted an ex on the subway with a high five, much to my, and his, chagrin.

"Hi, Sarah. It's nice to meet you. I'm a professor at the college as well. Josh and I met at that painful faculty lunch on Wednesday."

I nodded, pretending to have known this already. "Oh, of course! It's so nice to meet you."

"How are you liking it here? Big change from New York, huh?"

"Yeah, it's def—"

"So, Josh, you ready for Monday?" she asked, cutting me off midanswer. So much for southern hospitality. I pretended to be fascinated by the strings of my cutoffs.

"Ready as I'll ever be, I suppose. I have a crazy course load this semester. Four classes with about a thousand kids."

"Good God," said Iris. "That's insane. Guess we have a lot of mathematicians in the making here."

"What do you teach?" I asked.

"Art history." Naturally. I bet she made pottery on a wheel in her backyard too, amid the wilds of the fresh herb garden that she had planted herself. And that she drove an antique pickup truck and baked her own bread as well, without the help of a ridiculous mixer that weighed a thousand pounds.

"Cool," I offered weakly. Impossibly, an Adonis approached us with a wry smile on his face.

"Hi," he said in a gravelly baritone, slipping one giant hand around Iris's waist and offering Josh the other.

"You must be Mac," he said, shaking his hand firmly. "I'm Josh."

"Great to meet you."

"And I'm Sarah," I added, my voice cracking under the visual pressure of beholding two of the most gorgeous humans I had ever seen.

"Hi, Sarah."

"Y'all here for Denise's chicken?" Iris asked. "It's out of this world."

"That's the word on the street," answered Josh. He smiled broadly, clearly dazzled as well.

"Well, enjoy. We're headed to the farmer's market." *Of course you are.* "They have the most amazing produce for nothing. Y'all should check it out. Sarah, it was great meeting you."

"You too." I smiled awkwardly.

Iris gave a graceful wave and they floated off, her white jeans impossibly white. I gave Josh a smirk.

"What?"

"Jesus, that gene pool is worth a million dollars, at least."

"No kidding. Wow. They seem nice, though. We should get dinner together or something." He glanced at me. "Why are you wrinkling your nose?"

"She's not really for me."

"How do you know? You met her for all of two minutes."

"I dunno. I just don't like her."

"Sarah, come on. You don't like her because she's pretty?"

"No!" I blushed. "Well, maybe. And also, a little too smug. I don't know, she doesn't seem like a girl's girl to me. Did you see the way she cut me off?"

"Sarah."

"Fine. Guilty as charged. But I swear, it's not just her looks that rub me the wrong way."

"A double date would be good for us. Maybe they can shed some light on the Farmwood scene after-hours." He wiggled his eyebrows.

"Oh God, there's a scary thought."

"Don't be such a snob, Sarah." He took my hand and led me to the front door.

"I can't help it." I sighed. "It's part of my DNA."

4

Before changing lanes, signal, look in all of your mirrors, and glance over your left or right shoulder to make sure the lane you want is clear.

"Call me if you forgot something, I'll pick it up on my way home," said Josh as he nestled the last bag onto the remaining sliver of counter space with one hand while patting his pant pockets with the other.

"They're in your shirt pocket," I said, peeking out from behind a paper bag filled with ears of corn.

"What are?"

"Your keys."

"Oh right, thanks." He grinned. "Okay, I gotta dash or I'm going to be late for class. Your mom gets in at five thirty, right? Delta?"

"Last time we spoke, yes."

"She's flying out of Newark?"

"Yep."

"Got it. Text me if anything changes."

"Will do. Go! You're going to be late."

"Thanks, Sar. Love you."

"Love you too."

The door closed behind him and I slowly spun around, surveying my bounty of both space and product. While cooking had held about as much appeal for me as driving stick shift in Brooklyn, here in Farmwood it was a different story. You could have fit six of my former kitchens in this magazine-ready one. It practically screamed for cutting boards and bubbling pots, wine decanters and bowls of gleaming fruit.

In the middle of it stood an island carved from some beautiful amber-and-mahogany-swirled wood whose name I couldn't begin to guess, and above it were hooks from which copper pots were supposed to hang. At the moment, our decidedly noncopper pots hung there instead, embarrassed by their own inadequacy. Granite counters and glass-paned cabinets hugged the walls, which were tiled in varying soothing shades of blue, as the appliances quietly hummed in all of their stainless-steel efficiency. Here, I would cook. Or, at the very least, try.

I began to unpack the bags, marveling at the picture-book perfection of each piece of produce. At my old grocery store in Brooklyn, you'd fight over the one tomato that didn't appear to have been mauled by cats and were lucky if your lettuce made it home without going limp. To even hope to eat a salad at home, I'd had to either trek to a produce stand a mile away with my trusty grandma cart in tow or fork over a sizable chunk of my paycheck at Whole Foods. Not the case in Farmwood, where the aisles were wide enough to lie down in and the vegetables misted at five-minute intervals without fail. Sure, I was friendless and borderline agoraphobic here thanks to my crippling driving fear, but on the plus side, I was getting all of my daily vitamins and minerals.

Tonight, my mom was stopping over on her way to Sarasota, which was technically her winter home but was becoming more like her late-summer, fall, and winter home as the years passed. She spent the rest of the time in South Orange, New Jersey, in the home where I had grown up. She and my father had divorced when I was three, and so, save for the occasional summer trip to Los Angeles to visit him, it had just been she and I, bless her poor, battle-scarred heart. I had not been an easy kid. Then again, she had not exactly been an easy mom either.

Nevertheless, our love ran deep, and it was my master plan to have a delicious meal in the oven when she walked in. I smiled, imagining her reaction. Her version of a home-cooked meal for me growing up was Kraft mac 'n' cheese with cut-up hot dogs riding its orange waves like tiny pink sailboats.

I pulled my just-purchased cookbook off the top of the

refrigerator and flipped to the recipes I had chosen to tackle for the occasion, losing confidence in my ability to pull them off as I looked through them. *What happened to all of this food after it was styled for these shoots?* I wondered. In New York, we had done a shoot with avocados for an organic line of moisturizers that we were touting, and by the end of the first hour, each one had turned an aggressive shade of brown. The brisket I was currently admiring seemed a lot less appetizing suddenly. I turned the page to reveal a glistening bowl of spaghetti and meatballs and thought of Mona immediately.

Mona was a good cook because of course she was. She claimed that it was part of her genetic makeup. When we lived together, she would trot to the farmer's market on a Sunday morning and by nightfall, voilà—the very type of meal that stared back at me now. My stomach growled.

It had been a tradition, our Sunday nights. She would cook, I would provide the wine and an always purchased, never home-baked dessert and we would curl up to watch whatever HBO program was de rigueur for the season. The *Six Feet Under* finale had us both clutching our respective couch arms, doubled over in tears; *Sex and the City* had us holding hands; and *The Sopranos* had us facing each other with mirror images of the same *WTF?* expression. Man, I missed her. Where was she? Why wasn't she returning my calls?

Okay, focus, Sarah. Never mind Mona right now. Roasted chicken, an Asian slaw, and corn on the cob. I eyed the clock.

It was two thirty. Too early for a glass of wine? I thought about my mother's impending arrival and the stress that invariably went with it. Just a little one.

I reread the chicken recipe carefully, gasping in horror upon realizing that I was supposed to cut the backbone out of the bird. Did that mean I had to crush bones to do so? With a pair of scissors, no less? Did we even own scissors designed for such strenuous activity? Hell, was I designed for such strenuous activity? A one-handed chop through actual bone?

I opened the giant drawer that held spoons, spatulas, and whatever else we had that fit somewhere on that utensil spectrum, and sure enough, there they were—a giant pair of very shiny and very sturdy scissors. I pulled them out and splayed the chicken on its stomach.

"Sorry, friend," I whispered as I attempted to devertebrae her.

Cutting through the bone, I wondered what it would be like to have my mom in this house. When I'd told her that I was leaving my job and that we were moving to Farmwood, she'd asked me if Josh was making me do it. When I informed her that it was a very mutual decision, that New York had lost its luster for me, she'd raised her eyebrow.

"Sarah, don't do something you don't want to do. The minute you lose your spine, they walk out the door, and you're left holding the bag."

She was, of course, referring to my father. In her words,

which I had heard a million times plus, she had been a promising assistant copyeditor at *Cosmopolitan* when they met and a bedraggled New Jersey housewife with a toddler when he left.

"I'm not you, Mom. This is not your life," I had replied angrily.

"I'm having a hard time believing that moving to Kentucky is your decision."

"Mom, it's Virginia. And yes, it is. Josh is taking on much of the financial burden so I can figure out what it is exactly that I want to do. It's the opposite of what happened with you and Dad, actually."

Although I knew she hadn't meant to, my mother had always expressed a prevailing sense of regret about what could have been if only she hadn't gotten married and had me. Now that same regret haunted my own baby-making predicament. Most of my reservations stemmed from not wanting to find myself in the same position she had been in and unknowingly making my child feel responsible for my sense of inadequacy as a result.

I nestled tiny potatoes around the splayed bird. Mothers and daughters. Always so complicated. Josh didn't have this problem with his mother, but then again, she was a high-powered divorce lawyer who loved her job. When my dad left, my mom had taken a job as an executive assistant at an insurance firm in Jersey City, which she had dutifully hated for thirty-two years, right up until the moment of her retirement. Apples and oranges.

I covered the chicken in aluminum foil and put it in the refrigerator, intending to pop it in the oven after I had made the coleslaw and before I shucked the corn. Feeling smugly capable about my time management skills, I poured myself more wine and opened the screen door to the back porch. Birds chirped loudly as I settled into a lawn chair. *Pretty, pretty, pretty*, they called, as a bunny stopped to graze at a particularly lush patch of green. I leaned back against the headrest and stretched out my legs, closing my eyes.

Sarah?"

"Josh?" I sat up abruptly, knocking the wineglass that had been perched on my armrest to the ground where it shattered on contact. "Shit."

"Sarah, what are you doing?" he asked, concerned. "Are you okay? The kitchen is a mess." He came closer. "And your face is covered in drool. Did you pass out back here?"

"I guess I did," I answered, surprised. "Wait, is my m—"

"Where's my hostess with the mostest?" she called from the kitchen. I wiped my mouth quickly, still disoriented and now, remembering all of the prep work that I was supposed to do and had not, quickly moving into panic mode. My mother appeared at the screen door, her shape pixilated.

"Hi, doll," she announced, opening the door. She gave me a wry smile. "So much for the grand welcome. Your kitchen looks like a tornado hit it." She looked me up and down. "As do you."

"Hi, Mom," I replied, standing up to hug her. She smelled

like she always did—of roses, spearmint gum, and hairspray.

"It's so good to see you, honey. You okay?" She released me, holding me at arm's length and taking me in.

"I swear, I just closed my eyes for a minute," I explained exasperatedly. "I had planned this grand welcome, with the chicken in the oven and the sides all ready to go." I peered over her shoulder at the vegetables and dirty dishes that cluttered the counters. "Alas."

"Not to worry, Sar. I appreciate the thought. We'll order in."

"No, Mom, we can't order in," I replied, annoyed by her naïveté. "This isn't New York. The chicken is prepped, I just have to put it in the oven. Could you help with the coleslaw and corn?"

"Sure, calm down. How hard can it be? I'm at your service."

"Me too," added Josh. "I'll get rid of the broken glass, and then, did you want to put the corn on the grill?" The three of us glanced over at the dusty, spiderweb-accessorized appliance shoved into the far corner of the porch.

"I guess I didn't think to clean it first," I replied dejectedly.

"Oh, you can just boil them," said my mom, saving the meal from further disaster.

I gave her a grateful smile. "You can do that?"

"I may not be a Michelin chef, but I know that. Boil 'em and slather 'em with butter, and we're all set." She clapped her manicured hands together. "Now, who wants some wine?"

Later, with the slaw prepared and the corn shucked, Josh

went for a quick run. My mother and I sat on the porch together as the chicken cooked.

"Well, one thing is certain, this place sure beats that shoebox you were living in in Brooklyn." She raised her glass and I clinked it accordingly.

"Yeah, there are some perks to southern living," I replied.

"Tell me about them."

"Well." I cleared my throat. "There's space, you know? Literally and figuratively."

"And what are you doing in this space?" In the lavender light, fireflies twinkled.

"I'm detoxing from New York; you know that. Trying to connect with what it is I want in a career." She nodded in response. "I know you think that this wasn't my decision—that this was all part of Josh's grand plan—but you're absolutely wrong."

She waved her free hand in the air, dismissing me. "I was wrong about that," she admitted, looking at me directly. "I apologize. Josh is not your father, and you are not me." I sat back, realizing that my anticipation of an argument with my mother had me practically hovering over the seat.

"Well, that's surprising. Thanks, Mom."

"What, it's so surprising for me to apologize?"

"For being self-centered, yes."

"Don't be fresh, Sarah. And fine, point taken. It's a very personal issue for me though, this whole leaving-your-career-for-your-husband thing."

"But I didn't leave my career for my husband! How many

times can I explain that to you? As a matter of fact, I left my career for me. I was the one that was desperate to leave New York and the grueling demands of a job that I found ridiculous, Mom. Not Josh."

"I know that now, but I didn't initially. Initially, I had a knee-jerk reaction like I always do. You're a different generation, you and Josh. What do I know about emotional support from a husband?" She patted my hand. "Not a whole hell of a lot, let me tell you."

"I thought I was going to have to defend my decision until I was blue in the face."

"Oh, well you're not in the clear just yet on that front. I still think that you rushed into this a little too rashly. I mean, maybe Josh would have been able to get a teaching job somewhere a little less . . . rural. You had a very good thing going in New York at Glow. I don't know what kind of career you plan on getting off of the ground here." She took her last sip. "Tupperware sales?"

"Very funny. You're a regular comedian. I'm not sure if you're aware, but there's this thing called the Internet, Mom. Everyone works remotely these days."

"Okay, wise guy, doing what? What is this passion-filled career you're seeking?"

"We haven't even been here a month; give me a break. I don't know yet."

"You're not going to throw away all of your marketing knowledge, are you? That's a lot of experience and a big commodity these days."

"I don't know. It all seems so silly."

"Well, it's not. Just look at all of these idiotic reality television stars! Without skillful marketing, what are they? Nobodies. Think about it."

"Yeah, but I'd like to contribute to the betterment of society, not help to destroy it."

"Oh, don't be so dramatic, Sarah. Besides, maybe on your own terms, you can make it better, if only in small ways. My job may not have been much, but eventually I convinced that fat son of a bitch to start funneling some of his enormous sums of money into charity. That was no small feat, I'll have you know."

"I never knew that."

"There are lots of things you never knew. You're my daughter, not my shrink."

"That's debatable."

"Who's the comedian now? Let's check on that chicken, shall we? I'm starving." She stood up and I followed her back inside, feeling more positive about our relationship than I had in months. An apology like the one she'd just given was unprecedented.

"Ten more minutes," I announced, checking the timer. "Should we boil the corn? Josh already shucked it."

"Sure, why not. Where's the biggest pot you own?" I pulled it out of a cabinet and presented it to her. "Great." She carried it over to the sink as I took a seat on a bar stool, resting my elbows on the island.

As she waited for the pot to fill, I watched her closely,

feeling nostalgic. I would know that narrow back, that hair the texture and color of a Frosted Mini-Wheat, that sound of clinking gold bangles as she turned the water off anywhere. My mom. She turned around and faced me.

"Good God, are you crying, Sarah?" She placed the pot on a burner and turned it on. "You're not pregnant, are you?"

"Do I have to be pregnant to be happy to see you? And no, I'm not."

"Okay." She refilled her glass. "Do you want to be?"

"I'm not sure," I replied carefully. The wine had loosened my tongue.

"You're scared, Sarah." She sat down next to me. "And I don't blame you. The concept of having a child is terrifying."

"Did you regret having me?" I blurted out.

"What? Sarah, are you kidding?"

"I—I don't know, Mom. Growing up, sometimes I felt like you resented me for inadvertently ending your career and then your marriage."

"I made you feel that way?"

"I don't think you meant to, of course, that's just how I interpreted it."

"That's unforgivable, that I should make you feel that way. You have always been the light of my life. What was it that made you feel that way? Was it the way I talked to you about your father?"

"Maybe. But maybe it was just the way I saw things, considering the sacrifices you had to make to raise me and the way you spoke so fondly of your pre-marriage and pre-me days."

"Me and my giant mouth. I should have had someone else to vent to when you were younger. You were all I had. I was too damn tired to make friends."

"I know. I'm not blaming you for anything, Mom. Please don't think that I am. I never for a moment doubted how much you loved me, I just—especially now, with babies on my brain—always wondered if that resentment was real or imagined."

"Oh, honey, the only resentment I had was toward your father. He was and is an asshole. You were the best thing I ever did, and I mean that sincerely—through all of our ups and downs. Even your teenage years."

"You never thought to yourself, oh, if Sarah wasn't around I could start my life over? Go back to Manhattan? Live the life?"

"Listen, I'd be lying if I said that once in a while, when things were at their darkest financially or emotionally, I didn't have a woe-is-me moment. I had many of those, as you well know. Hell, the first ten years of your life were one big woe-is-me moment. But that said, I never, not even for a second, wished you gone. You changed me in all of the right ways. You still do. That's what kids do for their parents, I think."

"I'm just at this point where I feel like in order to be a good parent, all of my own dreams have to be fulfilled first, so that I don't place any undue stress on their tiny little heads," I explained.

"That's part of the parent profile—placing undue stress on tiny little heads. It just happens, for God's sake, whether or not you're satisfied with your personal progress or not. That's an awful lot of pressure to put on yourself beforehand, Sarah. And by the way, stress comes in all shapes and forms. I know plenty of mothers who were doing what they loved in terms of their career and experienced massive amounts of guilt as a result."

"Why?"

"Because they felt like their kids would always feel second best. You're never free from the guilt as a parent, especially as a mother."

"Sounds wonderful."

"That's the thing. Somehow it is wonderful, despite everything."

"What's wonderful?" Josh appeared in the doorway, smiling and drenched in sweat.

"Nothing," I answered, nervous that he'd overheard our conversation. "Just girl talk. Period stuff."

"Sarah, really," said my mom, wrinkling her nose.

"On that note, I'm going to shower really quickly. I'll be back to help in ten minutes."

"Take your time," my mother replied as he turned to leave, his shirt already off. She looked at me. "He doesn't know that you're scared?"

"No, not really."

"But, honey, why?"

"Why burden him with it? They're just growing pains."

"Sarah, you're in this together, you and him. I'm sure telling him how you're feeling would help. Who knows, maybe he's scared too."

"He's not scared, trust me. I don't want to let him down."

"Let him down? It's your uterus. You have to tell him, Sar. Don't struggle with this by yourself when you have a partner who loves and adores you. It's unnecessary stress."

The water began to boil, the steam rising from the pot like fog.

5

Hey, Mona, it's Sarah. You know, Sarah? Your best friend? Where are you? How come you won't call me back? Do you have something against southerners? Call me, damn it."

I hung up the phone and gazed at the parking lot listlessly. My dress stuck to my thighs as my bottle of water, courtesy of my husband-slash-chauffeur, sweated profusely on the bench beside me. After spending another week online shopping instead of soul searching, I had had it. Maybe my mother had been right. I had been putting too much pressure on myself to find my dream career. My aha moment would come, but in the meantime I needed to get out of the damn house.

I took a sip of my water and stood up. I was smack-dab in the center of a strip mall, which, for a former New Yorker, seemed like the most depressing place on earth to be. Everything that New York was, a strip mall was not. No style; no individuality; no tiny, obscure clothing stores with unpronounceable names selling overpriced tank tops that I had to have but did not need. Just grocery and dollar stores and Starbucks as far as the eye could see. And fast-food restaurants. And gas stations. Or even fast-food restaurants attached to gas stations, of which I had now seen two.

Frustrated, I closed my eyes and took a deep breath. Josh had informed me that this strip mall was the "upscale" strip mall, and I supposed that was because the word "dollar" was nowhere in the vicinity. Instead, there was an accessories boutique, a kitchen goods store, an independent coffee shop, and what appeared to be a cozy, self-run bookstore. Through the process of elimination—I did not cook and the most complicated coffee maneuver I had ever executed began and ended with pouring milk into a mug—I intended to apply for work at the boutique and the bookstore, my reasons being that I enjoyed accessorizing and reading. The fact that I was a thirty-six-year-old woman basing my job search on the same principles as, say, that of a sixteen-year-old girl was not lost on me.

I adjusted my dress, which was now a wrinkled, damp

mess, and redid my bun, flipping my head over and piling it back on top before resecuring it with my clip. The bookstore was my first stop. *Here we go.*

Inside, it looked like a television-show set. Lots of honey-colored wood, a few display tables with note cards indicating staff members' recommendations, an overstuffed couch and chair in the corner, a tabby cat lounging lazily in a sunbeam. I was impressed. A man-boy who looked roughly fifteen years younger than me sipped coffee behind the counter, his eyes downcast.

"Hello," I said quietly, in my best bookstore voice. He looked up from his book, startled.

"Hello," he replied. "Can I help you with something?"

"Whatcha reading there?" I asked, immediately wishing I could take back the tone of my voice. For some reason I had ended up sounding like Elmer Fudd's distant cousin. Bored, he held up a graphic novel in response.

"Can I help you with something?" he repeated.

"Yes, actually. I was wondering if you guys were looking to hire anyone at the moment," I replied, willing my voice back to its normal register.

"Oh." He took a judgmental pause. "I don't know, actually, but I doubt it." We regarded each other coolly. I did not like this little punk's attitude. Not one bit.

"Well, can I speak to someone who does know? Is your boss around?"

"Yeah, she's in the back." He sighed and retrieved a cigarette from his breast pocket to hold his place. "I'll go get her."

"Thanks so much," I replied sarcastically. "Hope it's not too much of an effort to walk," I mumbled, rifling through a box of conversational buttons. Did people still wear these? I heard some sort of backless shoe clip-clopping toward me. I pulled my hand out of the bin and stood up straight.

"Hi there," a Judi Dench lookalike said, emerging from the bookcases with authority. New York authority. Could it be that she was one of my own? I practically wilted with excitement at the prospect.

She eyed me warily and extended her hand, which I shook as forcefully as I could without overdoing it. *I'm a grown woman from New York*, I wanted my handshake to say. *I could eat your current employees for lunch. Hire me. Be my friend.*

"I hear you're looking for a job."

"Yes, I was—"

"We're not hiring. Sorry. I'm up to my eyeballs in college help. Maybe over the holidays, though. Come back then." She turned abruptly.

"College help?" I blurted out, channeling my inner warrior. "That's all well and good, but wouldn't you like some adult help? Someone that you can trust completely?" My loneliness was palpable.

"Not really. Sorry. Now, if you'll excuse me."

"But I'm from New York!" I blurted out as she walked away.

"And I'm from Texas. So what?" she replied, her back to me as she disappeared into the stacks. I had misjudged her. Not a New Yorker at all. I guess you could be a no-

nonsense bitch anywhere. I briefly considered stealing an "And?" pin but thought better of it and exited quickly. Outside, the register boy smoked. He raised an eyebrow at me in greeting.

"You're better off, anyway," he said. "Carol is a real see-you-next-Tuesday, if you know what I mean."

"Yeah, I know what you mean, kid. Best of luck."

Kid? Now I was Humphrey Bogart? Jesus, it was hot. I made my way toward the boutique. As I came closer, I noticed its sign. BAUBLE HEAD. That was bad. Then again, what was in a name? "Book Snob" had impressed me and that turned out to be a holding pen for Attila the Hun. I peered into the window. It was clear that Farmwood and I did not share the same definition of "boutique." Nevertheless, I forced a smile and opened the door.

The color palette inside socked me in the gut. Fuchsia clutches, shiny lemon-yellow purses and aquamarine baubles encircled in rhinestones for the wrists, earlobes, and décolletage winked gaudily at me while gold, silver, and ceramic earrings as big as serving platters twinkled in the overhead lights. I was the kind of woman for whom gray was a statement. I couldn't apply to work here, I just couldn't. I turned to go, temporarily blinded by a faux-emerald choker.

"Well hey there, honey, how can I help you today?"

"Oh, um, I'm just looking," I replied, turning around.

If Judi Dench ran the bookstore, then a Paula Deen/later-years Liz Taylor hybrid held court here in Bauble Head.

Big black hair sprayed into a helmet with bangs framed a feline face shellacked with foundation, powder, rosy blush, and lavender eye shadow. Her mauve lips were outlined and glossed to within an inch of their lives. She glided toward me on bedazzled flip-flops, her toes boasting a pristine French manicure, with the exception of her left big toe, which was the canvas for a tiny, jewel-encrusted palm tree.

"Can you believe that they can fit an entire palm tree on one tiny toe?" she asked, catching me looking.

"It's really something," I replied. Her voice was melodic in its southern-ness, like syrup cascading down a stack of pancakes. I smiled down at her, as she only came up to my collarbone.

"You sure you're not lookin' for anythang special?" she asked. "A pretty girl like you could use a little spawrkle."

"A little what?"

"Spawrkle!" She fingered the faux emeralds.

"Oh, sparkle! Sorry."

"Oh no, I'm sorry. My accent is an acquired taste. My husband and I have been together for forty years, and even he needs a translator sometimes." My God, this woman was charming. It was like talking to a cupcake.

"You're not by any chance looking to hire, are you?" I asked quickly.

"Well, now I need the translator. What did you say, darlin'?"

"Sorry, it's my New York–ese."

"You're from New York? Get out!"

I nodded.

"I just love Elaine. She is a trip."

"Elaine?"

"From that show? *Seinfeld*? I just love her."

"Oh. Yes, she is funny. But I was wondering, are you hiring?"

"Oh my goodness. You know what? You are not gonna believe this. I need to sit down. Come on over here to the register so I can park myself." She perched delicately on a pink stool and took a sip from the straw of her pink plastic tumbler of iced tea. "Well, first of all, my name is Mitzi. What's yours, darlin'?"

"Sarah."

"Sarah, I swear to the big man that my associate just up and quit yesterday. I mean, talk about kismet. I didn't even have time to put a sign up and here you are! I just love it." She clapped her hands enthusiastically. "So, what's your résumé like? Have you worked retail before?"

"Yes, in college. I worked at a Gap."

She eyed me quizzically. "Not to be rude, but somethin' tells me that college was not exactly yesterday. Am I right?"

"You are right," I replied, blushing. "To be honest, it's been a while, but I'm a fast learner, and I actually, well, my former career in marketing is not so distant from retail work."

"What do you know about jewelry? And purses? And can you hawk spawrkle?" She looked me up and down.

"I can do sparkle."

"Do you really want to work here, or are you just desperate for a job?" She took another sip.

"Well, it's a little bit of both, to be honest. I'm at a crossroads of sorts, and new in town, and I—well, I need a reason to get out of the house."

"Tell me how you really feel! My goodness." She pursed her lips. "Sarah, you know what?"

"What?"

"I'm gonna hire you. Lord knows, I appreciate some honesty, even if it reads a li'l sad. Because life can be sad, you know? That's why we need spawrkle." She winked at me. "When can you start?"

"As soon as you need me, Mitzi." I extended my hand to shake the softest hand I had ever grasped in my life. It was like shaking the arm of a mink coat.

As we settled the terms and I filled out the requisite paperwork, my enthusiasm waned. Yes, Mitzi was entertaining, but how was I going to work here? I could not have been more out of place—like a cactus in the rain forest. All around me, baubles in every color of the rainbow garishly sparkled as Mitzi adjusted and then readjusted each display, leaving a trail of vanilla and almond in her wake.

"So, I'll see you tomorrow?" I asked Mitzi as I handed her my sheaf of papers.

"Yes, ma'am. You wouldn't happen to own any makeup, would you?"

"What?" I blushed, embarrassed by her bluntness. "Uh, yes, of course I do."

"Good. Wear it." She patted me on the hand. "Now, go enjoy your last day of freedom."

I waved and walked into the shimmering heat. Using makeup in these temps was like attempting to ice cake batter. What was the point if it was all just going to slide off of my face anyway? I meandered back toward the bench, wondering how exactly I was going to get to work if just the idea of getting behind the wheel gave me a panic attack.

As I dug in my bag for my phone to call Josh, what appeared to be a giant mouse mobile pulled into a parking space. Two huge, furry ears were strapped to its roof and a tail protruded almost obscenely from its bumper. I moved closer to get a better look. DON'T BE A MOUSE BEHIND THE WHEEL! CALL MINNIE! a chartreuse-and-black sign plastered across the driver's side yelled. Her number followed.

A giant man emerged from the car. At around six foot three and easily two hundred and eighty pounds, I wondered how he fit into it to begin with. His head was shaved and tattoos ran up his left arm in a dizzying maze of black squiggles. He lumbered toward the door of the coffee shop as I watched curiously.

Mitzi had said that kismet was responsible for my landing the Bauble Head gig, and now, here it was at work again, in the shape of a mouse mobile driven by a tattooed lumberjack. Who was I to deny kismet?

6

If a person has had more than one drink an hour, one hour of "sobering up" time should be allowed for each extra drink consumed before driving.

I eyed the clock. The lumberjack driving instructor's name was Ray, and he would be idling in my driveway momentarily. Already I was terrified. On cue, I heard a car and nervously peeked between the blind slats. The Mouse Mobile was here.

As Ray emerged, I released the blinds and hugged the wall with my back. "What are you doing, idiot?" I asked myself aloud. "Get ahold of yourself." Spending most of my days alone had me talking to myself quite a bit—a habit that did not alarm me like it probably should have. The doorbell rang and I opened the door.

"Ray?"

"That's me."

"I'm Sarah."

"Yeah, I figured."

"Sorry, I'm a little nervous."

"No worries, I get it."

"I'm from New York," I declared. *What? Why did I say that?* Ray looked at me blankly.

"Sorry, I don't even know why that matters. It's driving. Just the thought of it gives me Tourette's."

"Well, Sarah, hopefully I can help ease some of your stress. And my cousin has Tourette's, by the way, so please don't joke about it."

"Oh God, she does? Or he does? I'm an asshole. Please forgive me."

"Naw, I'm just playin'." He smiled wryly at me. "Just wanted to freak you out a little bit."

"Mission accomplished."

"You ready to go?" he asked.

"Really? Right now?"

"Yeah. Unless you made me lunch. Did you?"

"Oh no, sorry, I didn't. But I have some cold cuts in the fridge if you'd like tha—"

"Sarah, I'm playing! You're gullible, huh?"

"Oh God, sorry. I'm normally a very funny person, I promise."

"Sorry to prey on your anxiety. That's the last bad joke

you'll hear from me. Scout's honor. Now, you ready?" I nodded, locked up, and followed him to the car.

"Minnie's not much for subtlety, huh?" I asked as we stood in front of it.

"You're lookin' at Minnie."

"What?"

"Me. I'm Minnie." He smiled broadly. "Clever idea, huh?"

"Oh, so who's the lady I spoke to on the phone?"

"That's just my wife, Vanessa. She handles the appointments. You thought there was a real Minnie?"

"Yeah, I guess I did."

"That's funny. But I guess, why wouldn't you? Anyway, I just started this business about a year ago, so I'm still on a learning curve of sorts. Never had an accident, though. Don't worry."

"God, I hope I'm not your first."

"You won't be," he replied assuredly. "So, you like the concept? The Mouse Mobile? Pretty dope, right? My oldest son and I came up with it."

"Very dope," I answered, because saying otherwise would have been impossibly cruel. The lumberjack was a teddy bear.

"Cool. Thanks. Now go on, get in the driver's seat. I'll hop in beside you." Minutes later, we were creeping along the road—mirrors adjusted and seat belts strapped.

"We're just going to cruise around the neighborhood for a bit," said Ray. "See how you handle the basics."

I nodded in reply. My nerves were such that speaking without bursting into tears was not an option. My anxiety astounded me. Never had I been this riled up about anything.

"So what brings you to Farmwood?" asked Ray.

"Husband got a job," I replied through chattering teeth.

"Hey, you all right? Pull over. Right here, that's it. Now put the car in park." I did as he instructed, suddenly freezing in the air-conditioning and longing for a sweater.

"Sorry, Ray, I haven't been behind the wheel in almost twenty years."

"Hey, hey—don't apologize. I understand. It's a big deal to be drivin' again. It would be crazy if you weren't nervous."

"Yeah, you're right, it would." I exhaled. "Okay, I feel less like a lunatic. Let's try this again." I put the car in drive and started back up.

"You know, you're not even a bad driver," said Ray. "This woman I took out yesterday—she wouldn't stay in her lane."

"No way."

"Yeah, she just couldn't get it. Two of the longest hours of my life. Hey, make a right here. Nice. Very good." A wave of pride washed over me, followed by immediate embarrassment that a completed right-hand turn was the highlight of my day.

"Hey, Sarah, you have to make a complete stop at the stop signs. Don't get cocky on me, now."

"Oh, of course. Sorry. I can't even imagine how stressful this gig must be. You must have the patience of Mother Teresa."

"Yeah, it is what it is. Just happy to have some money coming in, you know? I got three kids to feed."

"You do? How old?"

"Eleven, seven, and three. All boys." He smiled triumphantly. "You think you know shit about life, have yourself some kids. They'll change the game."

I nodded absently.

"You got kids?"

"Not yet."

"You want 'em?"

"I'm not sure."

I had never said that aloud to anyone. Not even Mona. Where the hell was Mona, anyway? Had I done something to annoy her or was it merely an "out of sight, out of mind" scenario? It was hard to believe that that was the case. Our fourteen years of friendship was bigger than that. Or so I thought.

"Make a right here, onto the main road," said Ray, interrupting my inner monologue.

"The main road?" I asked, alarmed. I stopped the car. "Already?"

"You're doin' great, Sarah. We'll just get on it for a little bit. We can get right off if you need to." I gulped. "Okay?"

"Okay." I put my foot on the gas. "Wait, wait! Just one more time around the neighborhood. Then I'll be ready."

"You sure?"

I nodded.

So the driving lesson went well?" asked Josh as I applied my mascara dutifully in front of a mirror that magnified my face to obscene proportions. I was practicing for my first day of work tomorrow.

"Yeah. Ray is cool. I feel a little bit better about things." I smoothed out a sticky black blob with my thumb and forefinger.

"Good. I'm proud of you." He kissed the back of my neck. "How do you stand this thing?" He stared horrifyingly at his reflection. "No wonder you're so neurotic. I can see straight through to my cartilage, practically." I switched off its accompanying fluorescent light.

"So don't look. This is not a toy for the faint of heart."

"You look beautiful, Sar." He surveyed me appraisingly. I wasn't sure if I would ever get over the fact that he truly seemed to mean it when he told me I was beautiful—no irony, no sense of begrudged obligation. I blushed.

"Thanks, you too."

Josh had the uncanny ability to look cool without appearing to have tried too hard to do so. His jeans hung just so; his plaid button-down was just the right amount of crumpled; his shoes were perfectly scuffed and his hair ideally rumpled. An island of scalp was just beginning to make itself known at the back of his head, but somehow even that was okay.

I assumed that this talent had something to do with his

mathematically inclined brain—statistically, if each piece of his wardrobe was the slightest bit off, it would inevitably add up to perfection. That said, he was also a bit of a metrosexual—there were more than a few facial and hair products in his bathroom drawer—but that was not his fault. A man couldn't live in New York for fifteen years and emerge without a compulsion to moisturize and deep-condition.

"Thanks. You ready to go?"

"Yeah, I think so." I grabbed my bag and followed him down the hallway, switching lights off as I went. "What sort of bar is this again?"

We were headed to a faculty drinks night at a bar near campus. As far as ambience went, I did not have high expectations, but I was looking forward to some human interaction. I needed some friends to add to my paltry collection, which currently began and ended with Ray, whom I technically employed. I checked my phone. Still no Mona.

"Oh, you know, just a divey place. Think football and beer."

"Great."

"Sarah, don't be a snob. I heard they have a good jukebox. And wings!"

I wrinkled my nose. "Josh, you know how I feel about food that stains your fingernails."

"Hey, you want to drive?" He tossed me the keys with a smirk.

"No, jerk. Not yet." I tossed them back.

"Why am I a jerk?"

"I'll let you know when I'm ready, okay? There's no need to put the pressure on."

He held up his hands in surrender. "Fine, sorry."

"Are Iris and Mac going to be there tonight?" I asked once we were on the road.

"Yeah, I'm sure."

I bristled, despite myself. Iris made me feel like a catty cliché. I wanted to start over—to erase my initial perception and behavior. Women who resented other women for being good-looking and able to wear white jeans were lame on principle.

"Maybe you're right. Maybe we can be friends."

"Definitely," said Josh. "They could show us the ropes around here."

We pulled into the dirt parking lot of what appeared to be a large wooden outhouse. The front porch sagged under the weight of the beams holding up the roof, and Christmas lights were strung haphazardly around its perimeter. A few people, cloaked in a gray fog of nicotine, smoked outside.

"This is it?" I asked.

"Sarah," pleaded Josh.

"How is it staying upright? Chewing gum and staples?"

"Very funny. This place has been here forever, apparently. We're safe. And since when did you become Bob Vila?"

"Fine, I'll stop. Just point me toward the alcohol." I took Josh's hand and we made our way inside.

"Professor Simon?" At the entrance, a cherub-faced boy-man extinguished his cigarette quickly before removing his baseball cap. His plaid button-down strained slightly at its seams. "It's me, Randy, from your calculus class."

"Oh yes, of course, hi. How ya doing?" Josh gave him his best teacher salute and we continued inside.

"Did you have any idea who he was?"

"Not the slightest. But cut me a break. There are sixty people in that class and it's only the second week of school."

"Is it weird that we're drinking among your students?"

Josh led the way through the crowd, which congregated along the bar like honeybees. "No, not really. Hey, Bob!" Josh dropped my hand to wave at an older, round man whose bald head gleamed like a lightbulb.

"Hi there, Josh." The man lifted his glass of what appeared to be bourbon. "Cheers!"

"This is my wife, Sarah."

Josh nudged me forward slightly, a habit of his that I found incredibly irritating. Josh behaved like a pageant mom at his faculty events, watching my interactions with focused intensity. I was always surprised that he managed to refrain from mouthing the words he wanted me to utter.

"Hi, Bob, nice to meet you." We shook hands.

"I'm gonna get a drink at the bar," Josh said. "Sarah, the usual?"

"Actually no, I think I'll take a whiskey tonight." Josh raised his eyebrows in surprise but knew better than to challenge my beverage selection in front of Bob, who was sipping his own tawny liquid with a bemused expression on his face.

"Okay. Be right back."

"These things are a drag, huh?" he asked.

"Oh no, not at all, I just, well—being 'the wife of' instead of Sarah usually requires something stronger than white wine."

"Touché." He raised his eyebrows. "Notice my own wife is not here. Or still married to me, for that matter. I'm sure you two would have a lot to commiserate about." He took another sip as I fidgeted awkwardly. "What do you do, Sarah?"

"I'm sort of in the middle of a transition at the moment. I was in the marketing game in New York." I wasn't ready to admit to my Bauble Head–employee status yet. Not here, anyway. Bob nodded, looking bored.

Josh returned with my drink, and I took a giant slug before being whisked away. I spent the rest of the evening being passed like a platter of hors d'oeuvres at a wedding cocktail hour—from this professor to that one, nodding politely and trying my best to not appear too drunk, which I was one drink away from becoming. Only when Patrick Fitzpatrick, the chair of the sociology department, appeared to have two heads did I switch to water. Or rather, a water was seamlessly slipped into my hand by a wary Josh.

"Is it obvious?" I tried to whisper.

"You're swaying. Here, sit on this stool."

"Josh, if you squint, the whole room lights up like a Christmas tree," I informed him.

"Sar, you're wasted."

"I'm not, I'm really not. Okay, I am. Sorry." He lowered his forehead to mine and pressed up against it gently, his eyes just millimeters away from my own. "Can we go back to New York?" I asked.

"What?" He stood up abruptly.

"I don't want to sell rhinestone jewelry at a strip mall." All evening, as I was passed from Josh colleague to Josh colleague, my discontent had been simmering. I missed cool bars. I missed having friends. I missed me! Who was I here other than Josh's wife? The idea of the efforts I had forced myself to make—the job and the driving lessons—exhausted me suddenly. Why had I come here again? Just as I was about to say all this, a wine-colored fingernail suddenly tapped his right shoulder. He swiveled to respond.

"Go left, go left!" I mumbled. On cue, a head appeared there. And not just any head. Iris's perfectly formed and naturally blond head—each wave in her hair a seemingly effortless S of bounce and shine.

"Hey there," she purred. "How are ya?" She gave Josh a hug and reached down to squeeze my shoulder. I felt impossibly short and toadlike—perched, or rather slumped, over on the metal stool like an afterthought. I forced myself to sit up straight.

She and Josh launched into what appeared to be a passionate conversation, about what I could not say. I couldn't hear a thing over the noise of the bar, which was comprised of raucous football conversation and a jukebox devoted solely to country music.

I shouldn't have said that to Josh about New York, I thought to myself as I watched Iris entrance him. Wait, was she not wearing a bra? Really? I narrowed my eyes and focused. A hint of nipple; a slight curve that suggested the French countryside—nope, she wasn't. The nerve! I hated her. That was it. Immaculate white jeans and no bra? These were impossible friendship obstacles to overcome, lame or not. And where was Mac, by the way? Had he dodged Faculty Night? Lucky.

My purse vibrated. A phone call? For me? I hadn't had one of those in what felt like years. I plumbed its depths like a deranged sand crab.

"Mona!" I yelled, temporarily jolting Josh and Iris out of their conversation. "Mona!" I uprooted myself from my stool, landing on wobbly feet.

"Sarah! Where are you? The rodeo? I can't hear a thing."

"I know! It's so loud in here. Hold on a second." I pushed through the crowd with no apologies. "Let me just get outside."

"Sarah! I can't hear anything. I'm going to bed, anyway. Call me back tomorrow, okay?"

"No, no! Please. It'll be quiet in a second, I swear. Just give me one second." The line went dead. Outside at last, I desperately tried to dial her, but it went straight to voice mail.

"What the hell?" I whined. Why was she being such a hardass? I looked at the time. *Midnight. Okay, fine. Bedtime. But still! Doesn't she miss me like I miss her?*

I wove my way over to the bench and plopped down dejectedly. A girl who couldn't have been more than nineteen smoked a cigarette beside me and pouted.

"Want one?" she asked through the haze. I nodded hungrily and lit up.

7

To avoid last-minute moves, look down the road ten to fifteen seconds ahead of your vehicle so you can see hazards clearly.

I lay in bed like a dehydrated zombie, fascinated by the ceiling fan. *Get up*, I commanded myself for the eleventh time, to no avail. *Get out of bed and get into the shower.* Round and round it went.

Josh slept soundly beside me, his body radiating heat like a well-tended fireplace. I curled toward him lazily and traced the outline of his right shoulder blade with my finger. His skin was impossibly smooth. A wave of affection washed over me, quickly followed by annoyance. *Get up and get me a glass of water*, I willed him silently. Nothing. Not even a stir of acknowledgment. I sighed loudly.

Okay, here we go. One-two-three. I gingerly removed the sheet from my body and placed my feet on the floor. Already the room was spinning, and I was not yet vertical. *Brown alcohol is not your friend. It is the devil. Don't forget that again.* I tried to open my mouth, but its dryness acted as a preventative lock. I stood, finally, and the room swiveled slightly beneath my feet. I shuffled to the bathroom like an octogenarian en route to a subpar early-bird buffet.

In the shower, I reflected on the night's events. I didn't think I had done anything grossly inappropriate. I hadn't said anything catty to Iris, had I? I didn't think so. But had I had any weird conversations with Josh's colleagues? That was a distinct possibility. Or worse yet, his students? Had my cigarette bum turned into a conversation? This was ringing a faint bell and making me queasy in the process. I squirted a mound of soap onto my loofah and scrubbed myself absently. The bathroom door opened. *Clank* went the toilet seat. I peeked out from behind the curtain.

"Morning, sunshine," I croaked.

"Hello," he croaked back.

"Are you as hungover as I am?"

"Probably not." I noticed a distinct lack of affection in his voice. This worried me. I closed the curtain and replayed the night's events in my head. My memory seemed to end abruptly after I had bummed that cigarette.

The door closed as Josh left, and I turned off the water. Snapshots began to filter through the muddy waters of my brain as I squeezed the water from my hair. *Oh no.* I had been advising those poor girls on the harsh realities of the postcollege dating experience in my signature too-much-to-drink, *Let me tell you somethin', girllll* way. It was not exactly Josh's favorite persona of mine.

I wrapped myself in a towel and opened the door. Josh lay on his back on the rumpled bed, like an unmotivated, boxer-brief-wearing snow angel.

"Josh?"

He grunted in response.

"Josh, did I make an ass out of myself last night?"

"I'm afraid so," he mumbled. "If 'myself' means me as well."

"Oh no." I sat on the bed beside him. His eyes remained closed. "What happened?"

"All I know is that when I came looking for you, you were holding court on the front porch with a gaggle of nineteen-year-old girls surrounding you, hanging on your every word."

"Was I—?"

"Yes, you were definitely milking it."

I rubbed my temples. "It's coming back to me."

"What were you saying to them? They were transfixed."

"Oh, I think I was just answering some questions they had about New York." This was not entirely untrue. "None of them were your students, right?"

"No, at least I don't think so. But that doesn't mean that they're not friends with my students. Whatever you said to them could easily be passed on."

I cringed. "I don't think I did any real damage."

"Okay, let's hope not. Although, who knows, maybe this could lead to a new career for you." I stood up too quickly and immediately sat back down. "A 'Dear Abby' for the college set."

"Yeah, right. Speaking of, I have work in an hour. What a great impression I'm going to make. I haven't been this hungover since I was in college myself." I massaged my temples. "Which was around four thousand years ago. By the way, where was Mac?"

"He was on call."

"He's a doctor?" I asked incredulously.

"An orthopedic surgeon."

"Of course he is. They're like a human Ken and Barbie. How long have they been married, anyway?"

"Not sure. You can ask her yourself, though, on your coffee date today." He yawned.

"Say what?"

"You asked her to coffee last night, as we were leaving."

"Shut up."

"You shut up. You did."

"You're fucking with me."

"Sarah, why would I fuck with you about this? You made a big to-do about it, and she agreed to meet you. I was standing right there."

"Why would I do that?"

"Beats me. Although I think it's a good idea." I put my head in my hands and peeked through my fingers. I needed a pedicure desperately. Mitzi would have a heart attack if she knew these puppies lurked underneath my shoes.

"Okay, well, do you know where I'm meeting her? Or what time?"

"You typed it into your phone." He grabbed it from my bedside table and dropped it on the bed next to me. I picked it up and sure enough, there it was. *Coff w Ira aft work.*

"I can't think of anything I want to do less. Great."

"Are you driving yourself?" he asked hopefully.

"Josh, I'm not ready."

"Sarah, come on. It's Sunday in the South. The roads will be empty. Everyone is at church."

"I'm not ready. You're going to have to drive me."

"Fine." I lay back on the bed beside him. "Maybe Iris can drive you home, though."

Super. Not only did she reduce me to a thirteen-year-old in terms of physical insecurity, but now she would be coming here, to my home, and making me feel inferior about my interior-decorating skills as well. Me and my ridiculous driving phobia, not to mention my big mouth. Why in God's name had I asked her to coffee? Guilt because I hated her, probably.

"I hope she wears a bra today. I'm too hungover for nipples."

"She wasn't wearing a bra last night?"

"Give me a break, Josh." With his eyes still closed, he smiled slightly. I pushed him playfully, and he took my hand.

"How come you never see ceiling fans in Brooklyn?" he asked, opening his eyes to watch ours go round and round overhead.

"I've seen 'em before."

"At rich people's apartments?"

"Mmmm, not just."

"I don't believe you. The ceiling fan is Brooklyn's Loch Ness monster. An urban legend." He cleared his throat. "Speaking of Brooklyn, can we talk about what you said to me last night? About moving back to New York?"

"I said that?"

"Don't play dumb. I know you remember that." He was right. I did remember it.

"I'm just lonely, Josh. And that bar was depressing."

"I know. It was depressing." He held my hand. "What can I do to make this transition easier for you? I don't want to move back to New York, Sarah. I sort of like it here. The pace is so . . . what's the word I'm looking for?"

" 'Tranquilizing'?"

"I was going to say 'refreshing.' "

"No, it is. I agree. I'm just going through some growing pains. Ignore me." I hoped these were just growing pains and not permanent pangs of unhappiness. "If you get up and make coffee, I will give you a million dollars," I said, changing the subject. He slowly sat up.

"Okay. That sounds fair."

He got out of bed and I followed, heading to the bathroom

resignedly. I had a half hour to spackle my face and emotionally prepare for what lay ahead.

En route, I opened the blinds and gasped upon my discovery of a virtual ladybug superhighway. The insects traveled like teeny-tiny red, yellow, and orange cars—up, down and across the entire double-paned expanse. I looked around, unsure of what to do. There were so many. One by one, I picked ten off of the glass, crushing them mercilessly between my thumb and forefinger before continuing on my way.

What's with the scarf?" asked Josh, glancing at me in the passenger seat.

"What? It's ridiculous?"

"A little, yes. I mean, it's roughly ninety-five degrees out."

"Oh God, screw it!" I unraveled it from around my neck and threw it on the floor.

"Sar, are you okay?"

I covered my eyes with my hands dramatically. "No, I am not okay. I am hungover beyond belief. And, to add insult to injury, on my way to work at a place called Bauble Head." I rubbed my eyes. "Oh fuck, I'm wearing mascara. I forgot." I looked at him beseechingly. "Is it all over my face?" He glanced over again.

"No, you're good. I think you are, at least."

I pulled down the visor. "Great, no mirror. Anyway, remember I told you that Mitzi told me in no uncertain terms to jazz up my appearance? That's what the makeup and this stupid scarf are about."

"You know, when you came out of the house in it, I thought it was a bit weird. Especially considering how adamant you were in New York about the hipster summer-scarf trend being ridiculous."

"I know. I'm ashamed. I panicked."

"Sarah, you're beautiful. You don't need jazz."

"Thanks, Josh. Mitzi, however, disagrees with you."

"You don't have to do this," said Josh again as he pulled into a parking spot to drop me off.

"If you say that one more time, my head is going to explode and you will have to clean my brain fragments out of the air-conditioning vents. I accepted the job because hanging around the house all day is a bit too Little Edie for me. Even I'm tired of myself."

"Who's Little Edie?"

"Never mind. Okay, here we go. No more complaining. Time to hawk some rhinestones." I leaned over to give him a kiss. "Do I really have to ask Iris for a ride home tonight?"

"No, I'll come get you. Just text me when you're ready."

"Thanks." I stood up, feeling immensely relieved, and waved good-bye. The coffee date itself was bad enough without the thought of an awkward ride home and invitation inside haunting me.

In New York, you said to someone, *Oh, we should definitely get together for coffee*, and that someone nodded politely while replying, *Definitely!* and then you never made any plans. There was a mutual understanding of the social code wherein sure, you wanted to get together, but in all honesty, wasn't it just too much effort? Here, apparently, you said something like that and the person on the other end of it answered with, *Great, what about tomorrow?*

Bauble Head's front window glittered in front of me like a bedazzled pocket square. I forced a smile and opened the door, setting off its cacophony of bells as I did so.

"Hey there, ladylou!" Mitzi's head popped up from beneath the cash register. "Just organizin' this mess. The good news is that I found my stash of Peppermint Patties!" She held up the silver bag proudly.

"Yum," I replied. "I love those."

"Me too. Just don't tell Nancy."

"Who's Nancy?"

"She runs my Weight Watchers meetin's. Total stickler." She shoved the bag back underneath the register. "Let's just say that I'm not exactly one hundred percent honest about my points. You ever done Weight Watchers?" She looked me up and down. "Prolly not, you old skinny thang, you."

"Oh no, I have. Before my wedding."

"Oh right, the tried-and-true true skinny-bride maneuver. I pulled that card too! Except I survived on celery and Tab for three months." I raised my eyebrows in response. "It was the seventies, darlin'. I am tellin' you, me and Clyde look at those pitchers now, and it's like lookin' at someone else's photo album."

"Clyde is your husband?"

"Thirty-eight years and countin'. Anyway, welcome, welcome. Your first day!"

"I know, I'm excited." I clapped my hands like a seal in an attempt to distract from the monotone in which I had delivered my reply.

"Okay, first things first, let me show you the merchandise." She flip-flopped away from me toward the front of the store.

"Do you possibly have a notepad and a pen I can use? I should have brought my own, but things were a little hectic this morning—"

"This isn't Harvard, sweetie. All you have to do is watch and listen." I scrambled to join her, willing my brain to cooperate despite the fact that it was sloshing around in a fishbowl of whiskey.

For the next hour, Mitzi expounded on the differences between crystals, rhinestones, and cubic zirconia. She extolled the virtues of faux (*Never say fake!*) versus real (*You can buy more of it; you can wear it to the pool and if you lose it, you're not up shit creek*) and schooled me on the varied rainbow of hues (*This may look like it's just blue, but it's cerulean, honey, and that's what you tell the customer. Take it up a notch*). She tried on tiaras and brooches and earrings, urging me to do the same. (*You're the salesperson and the model. Show them purty and they'll want purty.*)

By the end of my tutorial, I was wearing giant, dangling, silver-plated (*Not silver, we don't want to lie, now*) earrings in the shape of sailboats, a strand of faux pearls and a pink-gemstone-and-cubic-zirconia ring that swallowed my knuckle. I felt like a Christmas tree.

"You got all that?" Mitzi perched on her stool and reached for her trusty tumbler. Today, she was a vision in emerald—not green, but *emerald.* Purple—*no, amethyst*—earrings grazed the upturned collar of her tunic.

"I think so." I tried to smile convincingly.

"Okay, then I'm gonna head out." She took a last, long sip from her straw, coating it with her fuchsia lipstick.

"Very funny."

"What?" She stood up and dusted herself off. "Oh wait, right. Let me give you yer keys and show you how to set the alarm."

"You're serious? You're leaving me here with eighty-five minutes' worth of experience?" My voice cracked.

"Sarah, you are a thirtysomethin'-year-old woman with a college degree and a decade-plus of New York livin' under yer belt. I think you can handle a slow Sunday at a jewelry store." She looped her handbag over her shoulder. "Quit lookin' at me with those puppy-dog eyes. Follow me."

"But where are you going?"

"Clyde and I have a lunch date at the Mongolian buffet up the street. There are few things in this world that I love more than a Chinese food buffet, let me tell you. If there was an award for eatin' egg rolls, I would win it, hands down."

She stopped in front of the alarm.

"The code is 'grits.' Just punch it in here"—she mimed doing so—"and run like hell." I looked at her in alarm. "I'm just kiddin', darlin'. So serious! But really, you should move quickly. My last associate was about as slow as a turtle. By the time he got out the door, a SWAT team was in the parking lot. Sarah! I'm kidding again! Well, sort of. Are you all right, honey?"

"Yes, I'm fine. Just a bit panicked about manning the ship all by myself. What if I screw up the register?"

"Listen. The odds of someone coming in here are about slim to none. Between you and me, business is slow these days."

"Oh."

"Yeah, I'm tryin' to figure out a way to get more bodies in here, but so far my focus is laughable at best. I'd rather be eatin' egg rolls, I guess. Soon, though, I'm chainin' myself to my stool until that lightbulb goes off."

"I could help you if you wanted," I offered.

"Aren't you sweet? Thanks, honey. Let's make sure you don't burn down the place first though, mmkay?" She glanced at the clock. "I gotta scoot. You be sweet, ya hear? Call me if you're in trouble. And relax, for goodness' sake! Your face is much prettier when it's smilin'." The door's resounding jingle mocked me as I watched her sashay to her car.

Great. This job was supposed to be, at the very least, a social life raft for me, and now it was becoming clear that not only did the store have no patrons, but its owner wasn't even interested enough to stick around. I wandered dejectedly back over to the register and looked at the clock. The time was 1:22. I had three hours and thirty-eight minutes to stare into space.

I put my head down on the counter and then immediately

sat back up and scanned the ceiling corners. The lenses of two video cameras blinked back at me. An image of Mitzi and Clyde—who I assumed looked exactly like Wilford Brimley for some reason—watching surveillance footage later that evening as they nursed their MSG hangovers flashed through my mind and I quickly stood up. I may not have liked this job, but I certainly didn't want to be fired from it.

My stomach growled. *So much for lunch.* I crouched down to locate the Peppermint Patties. As I unpeeled one from its silver wrapper and popped it into my mouth, I eyed a feather duster that was crammed into the back of the shelf. *Dust. I will dust.*

I pocketed a few more Patties and set out on my mission to dust everything within an inch of its life. The dusting turned into Windexing display cases turned into vacuuming turned into organizing receipts alphabetically, and suddenly it was 4:52. Eight minutes until closing. I had done it. Hallelujah.

Now I only had to survive my coffee date with Iris and I would be home free. I removed my earrings, necklace, and ring, pretending to be a Hollywood starlet post Golden Globes but not quite succeeding. I held my breath as I keyed in "g-r-i-t-s" on the alarm panel and hightailed it into the warm evening air. Success.

Not one customer today. That was a problem. My inner marketer went to work as I dragged my feet over to the coffee shop. How was Mitzi advertising? And why not skew her product line a little younger? This was a college town, not Fort Lauderdale. And Bauble Head? Why? Surely there was a more palatable, sophisticated store name she could be happy with.

As I opened the door to the coffee shop, I said a quick prayer that Iris would be late enough for me to wolf down some sort of sustenance. Though I had managed to plow through almost the entire bag of Patties, I was starving. I made a beeline for the pastry case.

"Sarah?" I turned too quickly and ended up checking Iris with my shoulder.

"Oh God, sorry! My balance is off today—along with everything else. Hi!"

She was dressed in workout wear that hugged her every perfectly proportioned curve and was literally glowing with sweat. It beaded on her forehead like a crown of diamonds.

"Hi!" We hugged awkwardly. "I biked here," she declared. "I just thought, oh, it's such a gorgeous evening, I can't let it go to waste."

Great. In addition to everything else that rubbed me the wrong way about Iris, she was an athletic bragger. I couldn't stand athletic braggers—always casually mentioning that they ran seven miles that morning before work or boxed with a trainer for ten hours every Wednesday or walked eighteen miles to your apartment just to get some fresh air. It was the fake nonchalance that killed me.

"I'm barely standing," I answered. "I'm impressed. And jealous. You must feel great."

"Oh no, I feel pretty normal. Mac and I bike quite a bit." She smiled at me condescendingly. I gave her a big, fake, dead-eyed smile in return. "Let's order, shall we?" Iris pointed to the giant chalkboard menu behind the register. "I'm thinking beer," she said, after a few moments of studied silence.

"They have beer?" I practically shouted with glee. *Thank you, lord. Thank you.*

"Yep, and wine too. See, over on the left-hand side of the menu, toward the bottom?"

"Oh, awesome. And a cheese plate!" I practically wept tears of joy. "Are you interested in that at all?"

"Oh no, trying to stay away from dairy these days." She grabbed at her nonexistent love handles. "But you go ahead."

"Okay, thanks. If you change your mind, by all means." We both placed our orders.

"Hair of the dog," Iris said as we sat down at a table by the window. The late-afternoon light played on the golden highlights in her hair. I self-consciously fiddled with my own mousy-brown ponytail in retaliation.

"Seriously. I drank like a fish last night. Who knows what got into me?" I replied.

"I'd say about a liter of whiskey." She laughed a little too uproariously for my taste. *That's it, no Camembert for her even if she does change her mind.* "I'm glad that you suggested this," she went on. "I've been meaning to ask you to drinks myself, but with the start of the school year and everything, I'm sort of all over the place."

"Oh yeah, I bet. Thanks for coming." We both nodded at each other awkwardly as the waitress slipped our drinks and my cheese plate onto the table in front of us. I tried my best to remain ladylike as I sliced off a piece of brie and popped it into my mouth. Heaven.

"So what do you think of Farmwood?" she asked.

"Oh, it's lovely here. The pace is so refreshing, you know?" I answered, parroting Josh's comment from earlier that morning.

"Is that the politically correct way of saying nonexistent?" She smiled at me.

"No! No, it's not." I took a sip of my wine. "I really do like it. I just haven't really extended myself yet."

"What are you working on?" She took a sip of her beer.

"Working on? Well, I was an associate marketing VP, but I'm hoping to transition into something a little more fulfilling here." Usually, I left out the "VP" part, but hanging out with Iris made me feel like I had to prove something.

"Marketing wasn't for you?"

"Actually, I'm not sure if it was marketing as a whole or that particular job. At any rate, I have the freedom here to hopefully figure it out. I'm actually working at that jewelry store for the moment." I pointed nowhere, hoping that she would just nod.

"Bauble Head?" She looked at me in disbelief.

"That's the one."

"That's . . . unexpected." She took another sip of her beer.

"Well, we're in the middle of a recession, you know." God, I hated her. "It's not like jobs are growing on trees."

"I know. Sorry. Forgive me."

"It's okay. You're right, it is unexpected, considering I'm about twenty years too young for Mitzi's demographic." I smiled wryly.

"Are you guys trying to have a baby?" she asked bluntly.

"Come again?"

"You and Josh. Sorry, was that too direct?"

"I'd say so. Geez." Her thinking about me and Josh's sex life made me uncomfortable.

"It's not my business," she said, reading my mind. "I just thought, oh, they left New York, she's in her midthirties, they've been married awhile—yadda yadda yadda. Mac and I are never having kids. Too much work, plus how could we travel?"

I put my wineglass down, envious of her unapologetic delivery. She regarded me with a small smile.

"I just wanted to put that out there. Get it out of the way. I know it's a controversial stance, believe me."

"No, no. To each his own, Iris. I like the fact that you own it. It's not easy to do that, I'm sure."

"Yeah, a lot of people look at us like we're the devil incarnate when we tell them. But you know, Mac and I were both very clear about the fact that we didn't want children pretty early into our relationship." Here, her voice wavered ever so slightly, causing me to wonder if there were tiny cracks in her bravado. "I take it that you and Josh do?"

"Want children?" My throat went dry. "Yes, we do. But we're not in a huge rush or anything. I'd like to be a little more settled before I hand my body and brain over to someone else."

"Sure, of course." She stared at me keenly, as though she knew I wasn't telling the entire truth. It seemed that we were both suspicious of each other.

"So you two travel a lot?" I asked, fidgeting under her gaze. She answered by going off on a familiar tangent—*Morocco . . . Brazil . . . and wow, this time of year in Paris is our favorite*—as I inhaled both my cheese plate and my wine. The only thing worse than an athletic bragger was a travel bragger. Turned out that she was both.

"So how long have you and Mac been together?" I asked her when she had finished.

"Twelve years." She smiled broadly. "I was one of his patients initially."

"Get out! That's so soap opera-y."

"I know, isn't it? Guess there was a plus to my wonky knee after all."

"Josh and I met at a—"

"Oh my God, I am so sorry to do this, but I really have to go. I've got to get these grades posted or else the dean will have my ass. Terrible planning on my part."

"Oh no, it's okay." I watched her stand up and brush invisible crumbs off her flat stomach.

"We have to do this again. Do you and Josh own bikes? The four of us could head up to the mountains one Saturday and ride some trails."

"Sure," I lied. "Sounds good." She gave me a double kiss good-bye—*of course*—and I sat back down as she left. A friendship match it was not, which, in a way, really sucked. She was the only woman my age I had met, or even seen for that matter, thus far. Plus, I sensed more to her stark anti-procreation declaration, which would have been fodder for a true bond if the rest of her wasn't so off-putting.

Maybe I wasn't giving her enough of a chance. Then again, the thought of enduring any more humble-bragging, assumed familiarity, and terrible listening skills was enough to make my head throb.

Whatever. I had made it through this day alive, which was no small accomplishment, my recent borderline agoraphobia and aversion to jewelry and Iris considered. Kudos to me.

8

He looks like Kate," I declared, staring at the computer screen.

"How can you say that?" asked Josh. "What about him looks like her?"

"His lips." I tilted my head. "And his face shape. Totally Kate."

"Why is everyone so obsessed with which parent the baby looks like? Franklin's essentially been inside a jug of water for nine months. He looks like a manatee with a hat on."

"Josh!"

"What are you thinking about?" he asked. Truthfully, I was eyeing Franklin's swaddled shoulders and wondering about the current state of Kate's vagina.

"Not much. Just in awe, I guess. I mean, he was inside of her less than twenty-four hours ago, and now he's not."

"Tell me about it." He grabbed the phone. "I'm gonna try to reach Ben again."

As he dialed, I wandered into the kitchen, reminding myself to breathe. Franklin's birth had sent my baby anxiety into overdrive. With every text from Ben, from *All systems go!* to *He's here!*, I'd felt myself holding my breath in the anticipation of Josh's revitalized vigor for a baby of our own. I could hear my mother's voice in my head—*Talk to him, Sarah*—but I just couldn't bring myself to do it, especially not now, in the midst of his fraternal excitement.

"No answer again." Josh came up behind me and massaged my shoulders. "Wow, Sarah, you're tense."

"Really? I don't feel tense," I lied.

"You sure?" He nuzzled my neck.

"Well, maybe a little." I dropped my shoulders, surrendering to his touch. "That feels good. More, please."

Beneath his hands, my neck felt like marble. As he prodded, I imagined the oxygen running through my veins as blue cartoon bubbles, like the ones in those bathroom-cleaner commercials.

"Let's make love," Josh whispered. I cringed. The phrase "make love" made me gag, but Josh was one of those rare people who literally meant the words. He refused to, as he said, *adapt his vernacular to suit my immaturity*, so here we were—me reacting like a fourth grader every time, without fail. His hands traveled down my arms, working them as though they were made of dough. It was mind-numbingly pleasurable.

"I don't have to be at work for a good forty-five minutes. Come on."

He spun me around slowly and began to kiss me. It felt good. Really good. I couldn't remember the last time we had had sex. He lifted me up onto the counter. As he unbuttoned my pants and slid them off of me, I tried my best to focus on the undeniable sexiness of the scenario and not the fact that in a short while his sperm would be sprinting toward an open goal. I was off birth control, true, but the odds of his impregnating my thirty-six-year-old self so quickly were slim to none. *Right? Right.*

"Are you okay?" asked Josh, pulling away briefly.

"Yes, yes," I replied, pulling him closer. "Come here."

And so, we did it, on the kitchen counter, in the middle of the afternoon. With his forehead pressed to my sweaty clavicle afterward, my head was quiet, finally—if just for a moment.

Hello, Mona. This is the eighth message I have left for you. Under normal circumstances I would panic that you were dead, but since I saw you on Gchat this morning, I know that is not the case. Do you hate me? Seriously. This is getting ridiculous. Oh Christ, here comes another ladybug. I'm killing it now, can you hear me squooshing it? Anyway, for the love of God, call me back! Please?"

I hung up and sighed heavily, from worry about both the state of my relationship with Mona and our home's apparent ladybug infestation. I was killing them by what felt like the hundreds, and still, there they were.

"Fuck it," I announced, removing myself from the bedroom and entering what we called the office but was really a storage space for the boxes of books we had yet to unpack, which now, at over a month and a half of living here, was officially unacceptable. I eyed the empty bookcase and grabbed a pair of scissors from the desk drawer, slicing through the biggest box's tape with gusto.

Out came my self-help library, Josh's math textbooks, dictionaries of various mono- and bilingual varieties, my thesaurus from high school with my maiden name scrawled in black marker along the pages' edges, and an old deck of tarot cards with their accompanying guide. I had spent hours with Mona in my early twenties releasing questions into the universe and assembling the cards in various formations that would reveal the answers. These questions almost always pertained to the guys we were dating, or more likely, sleeping with in the hopes of actually dating.

"Why can't I talk to Josh about my baby issues?" I asked aloud, fanning the cards facedown in front of me. I plucked one from the left-hand side and turned it over. A frazzled woman screaming with her head in her hands looked up at me. Nine of Swords. Or in layman's terms: fear, guilt, and doubt.

Bingo. When we had first talked about having kids, before we were married, it had been a no-brainer. *Of course we'll have them. At least two, maybe three.* As the clock ticked on and loomed larger in the process, I had become less enthusiastic, always claiming that work was too busy, that as soon as I got through the next makeup season's launch, I would go off my birth control.

Josh, remarkably, had never expressed impatience with me—probably because he was just as overwhelmed by the idea of raising said kids in our version of New York. But now that we were here, in Farmwood, with no excuses other than my as-yet-undeveloped need to "find myself," it was a different story. I didn't want to let him down, and so, despite the raging inferno of doubt within me, I had thrown out my trusty pack of pills. I just hoped, secretly, that my eggs were as shy as I was about the prospect of procreation.

I gathered the deck back together, re-bound the cards, and placed them reluctantly on the shelf. If I let myself, I could spend all afternoon asking questions I already knew the answers to.

I opened the next box and smiled, recognizing all of my photo albums. Pictures fluttered out of them like sparrows as I pulled them out and piled them on the floor. I opened one to a page of Mona and me on vacation in South Beach. Oh, how young we were! Our moon faces with their caterpillar eyebrows smiled up at me, and I touched Mona's wild, dark hair with my finger, remembering the trip.

We were twenty-three, no, maybe twenty-five—yes, twenty-five, because we had gotten our tattoos here, at a dirty shop off the main drag. I remembered it like it was yesterday.

We'd spent a day at the beach tanning in the way only twenty-five-year-olds can tan, angling our towels to follow the curve of the sun as the morning turned into afternoon; flipping from front to back at timed intervals; sharing cigarettes, gossip magazines, and outrageously expensive margaritas brought to us by dutiful cabana boys. All day, we'd flexed our manicured feet and considered the prospect of matching (tasteful, of course) navy stars between our big and second toes—mine on my right foot and hers on her left. Finally, after the nine thousandth time we presented the pros and cons of such a venture, Mona had had it.

"Enough already with this! It's a tattoo, not a mortgage."

"But both of them are forever," I had replied, watching her in disbelief as she began to gather her things.

"So what? Let's go, we're getting tattoos."

"We are?"

"Yes, first we're going to do a shot of tequila each, and then we're getting tattoos. I can't talk about it for another second."

"But what if we hate them?" I had whined, wobbling after her in my margarita-and-sun-induced stupor.

"We won't."

"But what if we think they're cheesy?"

"We might. But we also might not. We're talking about

tiny stars here, Sarah, not 'Thug Life' across our shoulder blades. Besides, it's a story."

"That is true." I paused to readjust my bathing suit. "When we're old and gray and living in Boca together, we can show them off to our grandkids."

"Exactly. And you might be old and gray, but I plan to be old and fabulous. Like Blanche Devereaux fabulous."

"Well duh, obviously."

And so, we had done it. Mona had gone first, lying to the tattoo artist about our alcohol intake with ease, and I had held her hand as she stoically received her permanent South Beach souvenir.

"Does it hurt?" I had asked nervously.

"Like a bitch," she had replied calmly. And just then, the Beatles' "With a Little Help from My Friends" had wafted from the shop's speakers.

"You hear that?" I had asked, my mouth agape.

"Yeah," she had replied with a grin.

"Fate," I had whispered. I could still hear her laughing at my drunken proclamation. I glanced at my foot now, with its small and faded navy star, and smiled. *Oh, Mona, I miss you.*

Outside, a car pulled into the driveway. *Shit. Ray is here.* Time for my driving lesson, of all things. I closed the album and ran to put on my shoes.

I thought we might try a little lane changing today," announced Ray as we cruised the neighborhood.

"Already?"

"Sure, why not?"

"But we just started," I whined. "Can't we just stick to rights and lefts for a little bit?"

"You serious?"

"Yes." I rolled up to a stop sign in front of the elementary school.

"Girl, ain't nothin' to be scared of. I'm right here with you. You see this brake?" He gestured to the foot pedal underneath his Nike. "I got your back."

"Ray, I hear you, but I have a lot on my mind today. My focus is off."

"You think that every time you get behind the wheel your mind is gon' be clear?" He shook his head. "You trippin'. My head may as well be Seattle for all of its cloudiness. That don't mean I can't check my rearview mirror and change a damn lane, Sarah. You're makin' this harder than it is."

"All due respect, Ray—duh. I know that I'm making driving harder than it is. That's why I'm here."

"You're testy today, huh? Go 'head and go around the neighborhood again if you really think you need more of a warm-up. I know better than to argue with a woman when she has that tone to her voice. There's a reason I've been married for twelve years."

"I don't have a tone," I halfheartedly argued. "Well, maybe a little bit of a tone. Like I said, I'm not a hundred percent today."

"You want to talk about it?" Ray asked.

I glanced over at him. "Ray, you're already putting your life on the line by getting into the car with me. I don't want to bore you to death as well."

"Suit yourself. But I doubt I'll find it boring. Don't let the brawn fool you. I'm a sensitive man. And like I said, I've been married for twelve years, so maybe I can offer some advice. Trust me, Vanessa and I have been through some shit."

"It's not a marriage issue. It's a friend issue."

"I got plenty of friends too. Make a left here, we're goin' on the main road."

"The other way? But we've never been that way."

"I think we're gonna be okay, Sarah, just make a left. I know where we're goin'."

"Right, okay. Left. Sorry."

"So, what's up with your friend?"

"My best friend. She won't call me back."

"That's it?"

"Yes, that's it. I've been here for nearly two months and haven't heard from her, despite the fact that I've called her a hundred times. I'm hurt."

"Maybe she's workin' through somethin'. Doesn't feel like talkin' much at the moment. Make a right here into this park." A few playground pods dotted a vast expanse of green.

"What are we doing here?" I asked.

"We're gonna practice parking. Regular and parallel."

"Parallel? No way."

"Man, you are stubborn. I'm in charge, okay, Sarah? Even

if you're terrible at it, ain't no one around for you to run over."

"Fine. Sorry." I drove past the three cars parked at the front of the lot. "And it's not like her to shut me out. We help each other work through things. We always have. What I think is that she's over me. Out of sight, out of mind."

"How long y'all been friends? Go ahead and make a right into that spot right there."

I turned the wheel abruptly, and glided diagonally in. "Shit," I grumbled. "And fourteen years, to answer your question."

"Back it up and straighten your wheels." I put the car in reverse and took a deep breath before attempting it again. "That's right. Take it slow and steady. We got an hour to get this right. Take your time." After wrestling the wheel like it was a pair of Spanx just out of the dryer, I managed to slide between the lines. "Good work, my friend."

"Do you mind if we take a little break? Just turn the engine off for a minute?" I asked.

"Sure, no problem," said Ray. "You wanna step out of the car for a second, get some air?"

"Yeah, that sounds good," I answered gratefully. We got out and I leaned against the hood, slowly circling my head to stretch my neck. Its tendons burst into virtual flames as I did so. Ray came around and stood beside me.

"Fourteen years, huh?" he asked. "That's a long time. Lots of changes to go through together."

"Exactly. And now, poof. Nada. I don't understand. For other friends—less important friends—to forget me, that's perfectly understandable. But this . . . this is different."

"Just be patient. She'll be back around."

"I guess. I just miss her so much. It's hard, being here all alone. I may not have liked my life much in New York, but at least I had one."

"Well, you ain't all alone. You got your husband."

"Yeah, I know. But that's different than having a best friend. Or even a friend, for that matter."

"I'm your friend."

"You are?"

"Sure. You think I shoot the shit like this with all of my clients? Nosir."

"Really?"

"Really. You're interesting, Sarah. A little self-involved, maybe, but interesting."

"Excuse you!" I laughed. "I'm self-involved?"

"Don't take it personally. Everyone without kids is, I've noticed. You ain't got anyone to worry about but yourself, so you lose sleep over the fact that your friend hasn't returned a phone call or two."

"That's not fair, Ray. I think I would still sweat something like this even if I did have kids. What, you're saying that kids turn everybody into Mother Teresa? Please."

"Naw, that's not what I'm saying. Not exactly, anyway. You'll see." Would I? That was the whole point, wasn't it?

That I wasn't done worrying about me and therefore didn't have what it took to worry about somebody else?

"So how do you get your clients anyway? Do you just drive around and hope people call?"

"Worked with you, didn't it?"

"True, but you could do a lot more with this whole Mouse Mobile angle."

"Like what?"

"You could cross-promote with a popular extermination company. Or what about that pet place by the grocery store?"

"That Pet Place?"

"Yeah, what's it called?"

"That Pet Place."

"I know, but what's the name?"

Ray laughed. "That is the name. It's called That Pet Place."

"Get out! What is the deal with store names in Farmwood? They are hopelessly awful."

"You know, that's not a bad idea, Sarah. How come you know so much about cross-promoting? That's what you called it, right?"

"I worked in marketing in New York."

"No shit, where?"

"Glow? The makeup company?"

"Glow! I know them. Vanessa loves their crap. You miss it?"

"Working for Glow?" I shook my head. "Not at all."

"Well, you're good at this marketing business. I'm gonna call up That Pet Place this afternoon. Thanks for the advice."

"My pleasure." And strangely, it was my pleasure. Brainstorming off the cuff like this was fun for me. What if the fulfilling career that eluded me was the one I'd had all along, minus the bureaucratic constraints? Finally, some sort of clarity. It was about time.

9

"What do you think about these? I just think they're darlin'." Mitzi pulled a pair of bedazzled red devil horns out of a box. "For Halloween!"

"Cute!" I replied as effusively as I could. I didn't know who she expected to buy these headbands, as the youngest clientele I had seen could not have been a day younger than sixty-eight.

"What are y'all gonna do for Halloween?" she asked.

"Oh gosh, I don't know. We don't really get into holidays all that much."

"You're kiddin'! Me and Clyde go all out for every last one. Our neighbors hate us."

"Who are you dressing up as?" I asked, steeling myself for an answer that would make me uncomfortable.

"Danny Zuko and Sandy Olsen. You know, from *Grease*? The movie?"

"Of course!" I forced a smile as I tried to shake the vision of Mitzi in a poodle skirt. "Cute."

"Thanks, doll." My phone rang in my pocket. "Go ahead, you can answer it. I'm gonna go unpack some more boxes in the back."

"Thanks, Mitzi." I pulled the phone out. "Mona!" My heart surged with happiness just anticipating the sound of her voice.

"Hey, Sarah. Sorry it's taken so long to call you back." She sounded hoarse. "Work has been a bear."

"I'm sure." I decided not to give her shit. Not now, at least. "I mean, I remember, sort of."

"How's life out of the rat race? You must be loving it. No subway, no commute. No midtown. Oh my God, what I would do for a life free of midtown."

"Yeah, I guess." Without warning, tears welled in my eyes. I blinked them away. "Anyway, tell me everything. What's been happening?"

She paused. "Well, some unexpected stuff, actually."

"You're in love!"

"No."

"You got a promotion?"

"Nope."

"You're moving to Virginia?"

"Not quite. Listen, uh—it's sort of serious."

"Mona? What is it? Wait." I lowered my voice to a whisper. "Are you pregnant?"

"No."

"What is it then? You're killing me."

"Man, this is harder than I thought it would be." Her sigh echoed in my ear like the crash of an ocean wave. "I have cancer."

"What? How? What are you talking about?" I fiddled nervously with a pair of hoop earrings.

She cleared her throat. "Remember a couple of months ago, when I had that weird spotting?"

"Yeah."

We had talked about it over sushi and a bottle of wine at our favorite spot, outside on the back patio. She had mentioned it as casually as she would a sample sale she was excited about, and I had responded in kind before refilling her glass. *It's nothing*, we had agreed. *But maybe get it checked out*, *just in case.*

"Well, I kept thinking it was going to go away, but it never did. I went to see my gyno about it and she was concerned, you know?"

"Okay."

"So they did a transvaginal ultrasound and found a pretty sizable cluster of benign fibroid tumors."

"Oh my God." I squeezed my eyes tight.

"Yeah. Then they did a colposcopy and found the cancer cells in my cervix. I've been diagnosed as early stage two." I could hear sirens in the background.

"Are you smoking on your fire escape?"

"Maybe."

"Jesus, Mona! What the hell? You're smoking?"

"This is my last pack. I only have four left."

"Fuck. I can't believe you're smoking with this!" I sat up quickly and shook my head at the phone.

"Yeah, well. This is it. I always said I would quit when I got pregnant, so now, I'll quit when my chances of ever getting pregnant are nonexistent."

"What do you mean?"

"I'm going to have a hysterectomy."

"No. Oh, Mona, they're taking everything?"

"No, not everything. I'll get to keep my ovaries as souvenirs."

"Do you have to do this? Have you gotten a second opinion?"

"I do, and yes, I have. Three opinions, actually. Because it's relatively early, and the cancer hasn't spread beyond my pelvic wall, this will hopefully"—she paused, and although I couldn't hear it, I knew that she was knocking on the brick façade of her brownstone—"get rid of it once and for all. And I won't have to undergo any chemo or radiation."

"But what about—"

"Babies?"

"Yeah."

"Oh well."

"How are you feeling? What's going through your mind right now?"

"Nothing, really. It's horrible. I'm depressed as hell. I'm just glad that they caught it early enough to hopefully get rid of it forever, you know? If I had to find the silver lining, I suppose that would be it."

"I'm coming up there."

"Oh my God, get a grip. For what?"

"To take care of you!"

"Sarah, I have plenty of help." Her window creaked open as she climbed back into her apartment.

"Does Roxanne know?" Roxanne was Mona's mom. She lived in Hawaii and was about as maternal as a wolf spider.

"She's next on the list to call. Although, I can't imagine how she would be of any real help."

"So what do you mean, you have help?"

"Sarah, believe it or not, I have other friends besides you."

"I know, I know. I just—I want to be there for you. I'm coming. When is your surgery?"

"Sar—"

"Mona, listen to me. I want to be there for you." I lowered my voice to a whisper. "To be honest, I'm not really doing much of anything here. I'm coming."

"The thing is, Sarah, I'm not sure that I need any help. Apparently it's a pretty simple procedure. They call it a laparoscopic hysterectomy, and it's actually performed by a robot in less than an hour. And you're out of the hospital in twenty-four hours, or less, even."

"Fine, but who is going to take you to and from the hospital? Who is going to take care of you while you heal? Cut the Superwoman act, already."

"Listen, can I call you later? I'm feeling really tired all of a sudden."

"Yes, of course, call me later. But listen, Mona, I want you to know—"

"Sarah. We'll talk later. I need a nap."

"Okay. I love you."

"Me too."

What would Ben and Kate say if they knew we were eating here?" Josh lowered the Chili's menu so that his eyes peeked over its glossy manila expanse.

"We can never tell anyone about this," he added quickly. "We take it to the grave. Deal?"

"Deal," I replied blandly, staring at the page but not reading anything.

"Want to split some fries?" he asked hopefully, too excited about the prospect to notice my puffy eyes.

He had picked me up from work and suggested stopping for dinner, and I, still shell-shocked and grateful not to have to pretend to want to cook, had complied. I hadn't told him yet about Mona. Mostly because once I said it out loud, then it would be irrefutably true.

"Sure, why not."

"Hey, are you okay?" he asked, closing the menu and laying it on the edge of our table. "We don't have to eat here, you know. I just thought it'd be fun, in a kitschy way."

"No, no, this place is fine. I mean, I can't believe we're here, but it's fine." I put my own menu down as well and stared at my empty plate.

"Mona has cancer," I declared.

"What?" Josh leaned forward, his mouth agape.

"Mona has cancer," I repeated.

"Oh my God." Josh got up and came over to my side of the fake-mahogany-paneled booth. "Scoot over." I did and he sat down, facing me. "Is she sure? What kind of cancer?"

"She's sure. Cervical cancer."

"Oh no." He pulled me into a hug and I limply reciprocated. "What's the treatment?"

"Hysterectomy," I numbly replied.

"Everything out?"

"Not everything. She gets to keep her ovaries."

"Wow." He sighed deeply. "No babies?"

"No babies."

"But will the cancer be gone, afterward?"

"That's the hope. I mean, I think so. I didn't really think it was the time to ask her technical questions, you know?"

"No, of course. Sorry. I'm just so shocked is all."

"I know. Me too. My poor Mona."

"Is she all alone?"

"She says she's not, but I don't believe her."

"This is unbelievable. She's what, thirty-six?"

"Yep. Just like me."

He took my hand in his.

"I just—I just can't even imagine what she's going through right now. I need to be there for her," I said.

The waitress approached and took our orders. At the last minute, I added a glass of their house chardonnay to mine, despite the fact that I was pretty sure it would taste like perfume. As she left, I faced Josh, who, despite the waitress's raised eyebrow and my own slight discomfort, was still snuggled in beside me.

"I want to go to New York to take care of her," I confessed. His eyes widened. "I feel like it's the right thing to do."

"What about her mom?"

"You know her mom is relatively useless. She hadn't even told her yet when we spoke."

"Honey, I don't mean to be an asshole, but she has other friends, you know. Friends who live in New York and don't have to uproot their entire lives to help her out."

"But see, that's the thing. If her friends live in New York already, chances are good that their lives are jam-packed. They're not going to have time to help her the way I'll have time to help her." Josh nodded reluctantly. "And I would only be gone for a week or two."

"That's a long time."

"Oh, come on, it's not that long. You're so busy with school that you won't even notice I'm gone."

He frowned at me, hurt. "That's not true, Sarah. Anyway, does Mona even want you to come up?"

"Yes! Very much so," I lied.

"You sure about that? She's so independent. I would think

she'd want to handle this herself, or at least appear to handle it herself."

"Josh, she's having her insides scooped out like a goddamn butternut squash. Independent is one thing, but insane is another. How's she going to get around? And why should she have to pay a nurse? She's my best friend and she's all alone. I can't just sit here doing nothing."

"I get it, Sar. I really do. I just—what about you starting your life here? What about your job? There's no way Mitzi is going to let you take off for two weeks."

"Oh, so what? Let's get real: losing my position at Bauble Head is not exactly a career setback."

"Well, yes, but it's more the principle of it that I'm talking about."

The waitress arrived with a beer mug the size of Josh's head and my goblet of golden liquid. As he got up and returned to his side of the table, I took a sip, wincing at the unfortunate accuracy of my prediction regarding its taste.

"Just the other day you were encouraging me to quit Bauble Head if it was making me so unhappy, and now you're talking about principles? What about the principle of letting my best friend suffer through the most physically and emotionally debilitating experience of her life all by herself? I think that principle trumps any bad blood over at Bauble Head, Josh."

"Okay, I'm just going to go ahead and say something that may make you think I'm an asshole."

"Fine. By all means, go ahead."

"I think that there may be a little bit more to this than you're acknowledging."

"How so?"

"I think that yes, you of course want to be there for Mona, but you also want to get the hell out of Farmwood."

"So you're saying that I'm using Mona's cancer as an excuse to get out of here?"

"Basically, yes. Which is not to say that she wouldn't be grateful for your help once you were there—I definitely think it would bolster her spirits tremendously—but I am saying that your decision to return to New York to nurse her was made at lightning speed." He took another sip. "The kind of speed that implies distinct dissatisfaction with your own life here. With me."

"Josh, are you really making Mona's cancer about you?" I hissed.

"No, actually, I'm saying that, indirectly at least, you're making it about yourself."

"You are talking nonsense." I unrolled my burgundy cloth napkin roughly, and its enclosed silverware clattered loudly on the table. "That's not what this is about. I am happy here. Sort of." I paused as the waitress deposited a mountain of French fries that rose up impressively between us.

I continued. "I've been trying my best to make Farmwood work for me. I'm conquering my driving fear, I got a job. I even had coffee with Iris, for chrissake. And I had an idea about the next phase of my career the other day."

"You did? That's terrific! What was it?"

"It's just a small granule of an idea. Tiny, really."

"A granule is something. Tell me."

"I was talking to Ray about how to better promote his business, and it occurred to me that, stripped bare, I really do like marketing, or the idea of it anyway. Brainstorming for him made me happy. I felt like me for the first time in a long time."

"Sar, that's great. You know, you could start up your own consulting business here."

"Yeah, maybe. Like I said, I've only just begun to consider it."

"Okay, you don't want to make a big deal about it yet. Got it. And I know you're trying here. I didn't mean to imply that you weren't. It's just, I know you. I know you're unhappy. I can hear it in the way you sigh when it's time to get up in the morning and I can see it in the way you pour yourself an extra gulp of wine when you think I'm not looking."

"I poured myself plenty of extra gulps in New York, thank you very much."

"You know what I mean."

"I do miss it, it's true. But I know in my heart that I don't really miss the true New York. I miss my idealized version of it."

"And what's happening with the baby thing?"

"What baby thing?" Heat rose to my face.

"Our baby," he said softly. "I thought that we were all-systems-go here."

"We are," I replied, avoiding his gaze.

"Are we? Are you? Because every time I mention it, you change the subject or get shifty, like you're doing right now."

"I'm not shifty!"

"Look at me, then. Are we still on the same page?" His puppy-dog eyes broke my heart.

"Of course we are," I lied. "Why are you bringing that up now?"

"Because everything else is on the table, I guess. I've been scared to ask you about all of this. You've got your invisible force field thing going on."

"I do?"

"Yeah."

I scooted over and patted the empty space beside me. "Come back here." When he did, I took his hand. "Sorry about the force field. I've been dealing with a lot of transitional stuff, I guess. Stuff I don't want to burden you with because I'm not sure if they're legitimate worries or just growing pains." There, that was the most honest I had been with Josh since we'd moved. God, it felt good.

"Sarah, your 'stuff,' as you call it, is never a burden to me. Is my stuff a burden to you?"

"No. But your stuff is neater. Less complicated."

"Is that an insult?"

"Not at all."

He raised his eyebrow as he plucked a French fry from the plate.

"Honestly, it's not. There are moments when the idea of a baby freaks me out, but I'm pretty sure that those are just moments."

"Pretty sure?"

"I mean, I'm off birth control. What more do you want?"

"What more do *I* want? Shouldn't it be 'we'? Shouldn't we both be rooting for it?"

"I am. I promise. Can we just keep winging it for a while and quietly hope that I get pregnant? Making a big fuss over the whys and wherefores of ovulation at this point seems unnecessary. It's only been, what, a month of trying?"

"Okay, fair enough. I just wanted to clear the air."

"And what does going to New York for a week or two have to do with our baby making? I'll have my period anyway."

"Maybe you won't."

"What do you mean?"

"The other day. In the kitchen? Who knows?" He smiled, and I summoned all of my strength to give him a convincing one in return.

"You're doing it."

"Doing what?"

"Surmising about the state of my uterus and shooting my blood pressure up in the process. Please, let's just play dumb for a little while longer?"

"Okay, you're right. Sorry." He squeezed my thigh.

"Josh, I know in my heart that Mona needs me now. I don't think I could ever forgive myself if I didn't use this time that I have to help her. I really don't. Even if she lived in Utah, I would want to go to her now."

"Utah? Really?"

"Well, maybe it would take me a bit longer to deliberate about it, but yes."

"Look, Sarah, I love you. Of course you have my blessing if you really want to go. Just come back, please."

"Of course I'm coming back." I hugged him. "I love you," I said, whispering into his ear.

10

U-turn: turning your vehicle around in the street to go back the way you came.

The straps of my backpack created sweat shadows down the front of my T-shirt as I marched determinedly down the main road to town. The ladybug infestation at home had driven me out. There were only so many tiny red-and-yellow bugs that I could pick off of blind slats before going certifiably insane. My mission was to make it to the coffee shop, drink a thousand gallons of water and ingest a sandwich, call Mona to tell her that I was coming whether she liked it or not, and then walk over to Bauble Head and promptly resign.

I rehearsed my resignation speech in my head as gnats dive-bombed me from all sides. A pickup truck wailed at me as it whizzed past and I gave it the finger. *So, Mitzi, I'm so sorry to have to do this to you on such short notice, but since asking for two weeks of vacation at this stage of my employment qualifies as the highest level of douchery, I'm afraid I have to resign.* I wondered how Mitzi would react to the word "douchery." It was probably not my best choice of words. *Highest level of inappropriateness?* Better.

Finally, the strip mall appeared like a shimmering mirage on the horizon. Inside the coffee shop at last, I gulped in the air-conditioning as though it were oxygen and collapsed dramatically at a small table in the corner. As I removed my backpack, I took in the other patrons. All of them looked like college students, the boys in ratty fraternity T-shirts and cargo shorts and the girls in some derivative of workout gear with their hair and makeup deliberately straightened and applied, respectively. Mitzi really had to change her tune, or she was never going to make a profit. Even if some of these girls were into bedazzled devil horns at Halloween, they wouldn't be caught dead at a place called Bauble Head. Unfortunately, I would never be able to tell her as much, unless of course I wanted to salt the wound of my resignation even further.

At the counter, I pulled a bottle of water from the cooler and guzzled it unapologetically as I read the chalkboard menu.

"Thirsty?" asked the woman at the register. I took the bottle from my mouth, embarrassed, and smiled.

"Sorry. I'm not used to this kind of heat in October."

She laughed and cocked her head. “You’re Mitzi’s new girl. From New York?”

I blushed, feeling conspicuous. “That’s me.”

“I’m Bonnie.” She extended her hand to shake mine. “Welcome to Farmwood.”

“Thanks.”

I ordered and returned to my seat. In New York, you could go years without ever so much as meeting your neighbor, but here, even as the employee of a friend, you were acknowledged heartily. It was nice. Well, nice until you screwed over said friend by quitting almost immediately after being hired. Something told me that Bonnie wasn’t going to be quite as cordial the next time I needed a caffeine fix. I dug my phone out of my bag and dialed Mona.

“Hi,” she croaked.

“You sleeping?”

“Not anymore.”

“It’s Monday.”

“And?”

“You took the day off from work?” My heart fluttered with worry. “Are you feeling okay?”

“Well, my surgery is next week. I’m just tying up some loose ends now and will take off for three weeks on Thursday. I just went in for an hour or two this morning.”

“Oh, got it. That must have been something—telling them about your diagnosis.”

“Yeah, well, it wasn’t a picnic. It is cancer, you know. Not like a pregnancy or anything, where everyone has to act all happy for you even if they're disgusted by the concept." Mona's boss was not a child enthusiast.

"What did Suzanne say?"

"She cried, actually. I was a bit taken aback." Mona coughed. "I mean, I realize that I have cancer, but in my mind I can't quite grasp the reality of what that means to other people when they hear me say it, you know? It's almost like I'm telling them about someone else who has cancer, not me. An acquaintance of ours or something."

"How are you doing with everything? Emotionally, I mean?"

"I'm a mess. A certifiable mess."

"Oh, Mona. I feel like an asshole."

"Why, because you don't have cancer?"

"Maybe. And because I'm not there."

"You know, I've been wracking my brain, trying to pinpoint any specific moment when the cancer would have taken hold, you know? I mean, it's all so fucking mysterious."

"Mona, I'm coming up to take care of you while you recover," I blurted out. "Please don't argue with me."

"I've been reconsidering your offer, actually. Maybe it's not such a bad idea," she said, surprising me. "I need to accept the fact that I am going to need help for a bit. Maybe two weeks or so."

"Good! Oh, I'm so glad to hear you say that. I was prepared for a battle."

"The question is, though, are you coming up here for me or are you coming up here to escape?"

"I want to help you, Mona, I really do. What am I doing here? Selling costume jewelry and feeling sorry for myself most days, to be honest. I can't think of a better purpose than helping my best friend. And I have the time, so why not?"

"What about figuring out what you want to do next? What you and Josh want to do? How does he feel about all of this?"

"He gets it. He loves you, Mona. And he knows how important you are to me."

"Still, he can't be thrilled about the fact that you're leaving him."

"In the grand scheme of things, two weeks is nothing. He'll survive."

"Okay, good." She sighed heavily. "Good."

"When is your surgery?"

"Next Wednesday."

"Oh wow, soon."

"Yeah, they're anxious to get in there. Sarah, I'm scared," she said, lowering her voice significantly. "I really am."

"I know, honey. I am too. But I'm not going to let anything bad happen to you. I promise. I am going to watch you like a hawk. Whatever you need—I don't care if it's tandoori chicken from Little India at two in the morning—I will make it happen."

"You will?"

"I will."

"What about if I crap myself and you have to change me?"

"Could that happen?"

"Probably not. But it might. You never know."

"I will change you."

"I love you, Sarah."

"I love you too, Mona. I'll try to book a flight for Friday, and I'll send you the confirmation."

"Okay."

"Okay. Go back to sleep."

"Okay. Bye."

Bonnie deposited my wrap in front of me. I thanked her and picked at it delicately, as though it might be alive. It was happening. I was returning to New York to take care of my best friend while she recuperated from a hysterectomy because she had cervical cancer. Cervical cancer.

Here I was, obsessing about the receptive state of my own uterus and having panic attacks about merging onto the highway, while my best friend was dealing with the fact that she was going to lose her reproductive system to cancer. Alone, no less. What an ungrateful asshole I was. I unwound my wrap and poked around its insides with indifference. My appetite was gone.

Well hey, darlin', what are you doin' here? I swear this is your day off. Or am I really losin' the few marbles I have left?" Mitzi was perched behind the register on her pink polka-dotted stool, daintily eating a Caesar salad, a crouton speared on the tip of her fork like the point of an exclamation mark.

"Oh no, it is my day off, I just, well, I was just in the neighborhood," I explained nervously.

"You miss me or somethin', Miss New York?" She eyed me coyly. "I know better than that. What's up?" She put her salad down and gasped, bringing her hands together in the prayer position. "Are you pregnant, honey?" she whispered excitedly.

"Nope, not pregnant." It occurred to me that I did not know that to be fact, which was a very strange realization indeed. Then again, I felt completely normal, all things considered. *Move it along, Sarah.* "It's something else entirely, actually."

"Uh-oh, this sounds serious."

"My best friend in New York, she—she just found out that she has cervical cancer."

"Oh my," replied Mitzi. "That is just terrible. Is she your age?" My eyes welled and I nodded. "Well that's just awful, honey. I'm so sorry."

"Thanks. The thing is, she's all alone. Single. I need to go up there to help her recover from her hysterectomy." I paused to take in a gulp of air. "Unfortunately, she's having it next week. And the recovery time is two weeks. So." I placed my sweaty hands on the glass counter and peered into the sparkling mass of gems below, immediately regretting the Windexing that Mitzi would have to do in my wake. "I realize that the timing of this is shitty, especially since I've barely begun to work here, but I'm afraid I have to resign." I looked up, finally, meeting her eyes.

"Why do you have to resign, Sarah?"

"Well, I just figured that that would be the best thing for me to do. Taking a two-week break from a job I've just been hired for is not exactly employee-of-the-month material."

"Lucky for you, we don't have employees of the month here at Bauble Head," replied Mitzi. "You don't have to up and quit, honey. Don't be silly." She pulled out the matching stool beside her and patted it with a French-manicured hand. "C'mere. Have a seat." Rendered speechless by her reaction, I complied silently.

"You know what?" she asked. I shook my head. "There are times in life when things make sense in unexpected ways. I call them my whaddayaknow moments."

"Your whaddayaknow moments?"

"Mmm-hmm." She smacked her forehead gently in mock surprise. "Whaddayaknow? Like that." She patted my hand. "About fifteen years ago I was diagnosed with breast cancer. It was the worst day of my life. I was shocked and, of course, terrified, as was Clyde. My doctor prescribed a double mastectomy along with aggressive chemo and radiation, and so of course, we hopped right to it."

"Oh, Mitzi, I'm so sorry."

"Thanks, darlin'. I was too, believe me. Now, I love Clyde with all of my heart, and he is nothing short of my ideal partner, but let me tell you, in terms of the sympathy and care that only another woman can bestow in that situation, he was crap. Utter crap. Bless his heart, he tried his best, but it just wasn't doin' the trick. So you know what I did?"

I shook my head. "I called up my best friend, Regina, who was livin' in Idaho at the time; cried my eyes out to her; and asked her to come down."

"You did?"

"I did. And you know what? She put her whole life on hold and did just that. She came down here to Farmwood to be my support system for a few months and saved my life. Not literally saved my life, the treatment did that, but emotionally, she saved my life. True story."

"That's incredible. What are the odds that you would have gone through the very same thing?"

"Zero to none, darlin'. That's why it's a whaddayaknow moment. Now, all of this is to say that I have no problem with you takin' off to take care of your friend for two weeks. I won't be payin' you, of course, but your position will be waiting for you when you return. If you want it."

"I want it," I replied, grateful and moved by her kindness.

Mitzi was a good person. I realized I could learn something from her, and maybe, if I came up with a new business strategy for her store as part of my consulting work, she could learn something from me in return. This realization didn't make the idea of selling costume jewelry any more enticing, but it did brighten my horizon a little bit.

Can I just pull over here?" I asked Ray as we drove around my neighborhood.

"Well, yeah, but actually pull over, you know? To the side of the road. You just parked right in the middle of it."

"Oh, okay, sorry." I eased onto the shoulder in front of the elementary school playground. A Cadillac passed me, its driver's face contorted into a scowl of extreme impatience.

"Oh, excuse me!" I shouted after him. "Sorry to make you late to bingo, asshole."

Ray laughed. "You havin' a bad day?"

"Well, I was. It took an unexpected turn, though."

"A good one?"

"I think so. I mean, in terms of being the recipient of genuine, uncalculated human kindness and understanding, it did."

"Imagine that."

"I know." On the playground in front of us, three little girls held hands and performed a slow Ring Around the Rosie. "You know my best friend? The one I was telling you about?"

"The one that wasn't calling you back?"

"Yes, that's the one. Well, you were right. She did have her own stuff going on."

"Big stuff?"

"Yeah, she has cancer." My eyes welled with tears. "It doesn't make any sense."

"It never makes any sense," said Ray. "I lost my mother to it."

"You did?" I felt nauseous. Did everyone either have cancer or know someone who did?

"Yes. Terrible, disgusting disease. Wouldn't wish it on my worst enemy."

"I'm so sorry, Ray."

"Thanks, Sarah. I appreciate it." He cleared his throat and turned to me. "Now, are we going to do some lane changes or what?" he asked.

"Uh, yeah, I guess we could do a couple," I answered, surprised by his abrupt changing of the subject.

"Okay, make a right here. We're going to the grocery store."

"We are?"

"Yes, ma'am. Get into the far right lane."

"This one? Right here?" My teeth began to chatter. "Anyway, I'm going up to New York to take care of her so I won't be around for driving lessons for a few weeks."

"Okay, that's cool. I'll take you off the schedule." We drove in silence for a moment before Ray spoke again.

"What kind of cancer does your friend have?"

"Cervical."

"That's terrible. Did they find it early?"

"They did." I dropped my shoulders, which were hovering near the tops of my ears.

"Well that's good. My mom wasn't that lucky."

"I'm so sorry. What did she have?"

"Stage-three lung cancer. Never smoked a day in her life, either."

"God, how awful. And unfair."

"It was. She was diagnosed and then gone, less than a year later. Move over to your left, into the other lane."

"Really? Now?"

"Check your mirror first." I checked. A pickup truck rumbled far behind me.

"Now, just turn your head slightly to check your blind spot." I turned my head and looked over my shoulder, taking the car with me. A horn wailed as the Volvo I had been seconds from knocking off the road swerved out of my way.

"Oh my God, oh my God, oh my God," I chanted, my heart thumping wildly.

"It's okay, everything is okay, Sarah," said Ray shakily, which panicked me further.

"Ray, I have to get off the road. You have to get me off the road."

"All right, let's just take this right into a neighborhood. Very good. Now just pull up on the side of the road. Put it in park. Turn off the car. Very good." I pushed my seat back and closed my eyes, willing my heart to slow down and my muscles to unclench.

"Listen, this sort of thing happens all the time, Sarah. That's why they call it the blind spot. The important thing to remember is to keep the wheel steady while you check it. It comes with practice."

"Ray, I'm really sorry. I don't want to do this anymore."

"Sarah, come on now. You can't just quit because you made a mistake. That's what learning is."

"I know, I just—I hate driving."

" 'Hate' is a big word."

"I know."

"I don't think you hate it, really. I just think you're intimidated by it. Anything new is scary."

"Yeah, but this isn't like new-lipstick-shade new. This is like one-false-move-and-I-could-kill-someone-else-or-myself new."

"Let's look at it from a slightly less hysterical perspective, Sarah. Take what just happened, for example. You checked your blind spot and accidentally took the car with you, right?" I nodded, feeling ashamed. "And what happened?"

"I realized another car was there and veered back."

"Right, and that driver also veered out of the way when he realized you were coming for him."

"So?"

"So, no one was hurt or killed. Your car is okay, his car is okay, it was just a mistake. And the more you practice driving, the less mistakes like that you'll make. You've got to think of the road as more of a community and less like the Wild West. Nobody wants to get into an accident. Everyone—well, everyone who's driving with half a brain—wants to help each other arrive at their destination safely."

"I guess I never thought about it like that. I always just assumed that everyone was out for blood."

"Don't get me twisted, there are reckless drivers out there, and you have to look out for them, but for the most part, everyone's cool."

"Okay, but even so, I hate not being good at things. I hate that I'm bad at driving."

"You're not bad at it, Sarah, you're just new."

I smiled at him gratefully. "Thanks."

"What? It's true."

"You must have had a wonderful mom if you can spontaneously dispense advice like that."

"Yeah, she was the best."

"How long ago did you lose her?"

"Three years ago. And thanks. Each year it gets a little easier to accept, I guess, but I still have moments when I think, *Oh, Mom is going to get a kick out of this*, you know? And then I remember that she's not here anymore. It's a lonely feeling."

"I don't know what I would do without Mona."

"Sounds like she's gonna be in good shape, though. Early is good. She have to do chemo or radiation?"

"No. But she's having a hysterectomy."

"Aw, that's too bad. She like kids?" I nodded. "That sucks." My stomach growled loudly.

"You hungry?" asked Ray.

"I am, actually."

"You want to hit a drive-through or somethin'?"

"A drive-through?"

"Yeah. Don't tell me you're not familiar with the concept."

"No, of course I am. I just—okay, I'll drive. How far away is it?"

"There's a McDonald's up the street."

"Any lane changes involved?"

"There doesn't have to be."

I considered the offer.

"French fries?" Ray prodded. "A chocolate milkshake, maybe?"

"Vanilla."

11

I'm headed to Brooklyn. Fort Greene," I said as the beleaguered cabbie hoisted my suitcase into his trunk and grunted in response.

I slammed my door and we were off, another yellow fish swimming upstream. As I rolled my window down, I breathed in the warm, dirty, thick-with-exhaust air happily. I was home. *How could we have left this?* I wondered, even as my excitement quickly turned to nausea. My driver was weaving in and out of traffic like the needle of a lie detector test. A bus roared past, blasting its horn and cloaking my face in soot. *Window, up.* I called Josh.

"Hey, New York," he answered. "You get in all right?"

"Oh yeah, fine. Flight was a piece of cake. Now of course I'm in traffic."

"Of course. You feeling carsick?"

"Yeah. How's Farmwood?"

"Same as you left it. I have class in a minute."

"Nice. You miss me yet?"

"Of course I miss you. Are you in love with New York again?"

"No. Not yet, at least."

"Good. Listen, call me later. I have to go."

I hung up and gazed out the window at the Manhattan skyline, which was just beginning to come into view. Building upon building, one on top of the other, the next one more imposing than the last. Energy radiated from the island in shimmering waves and my pulse quickened as I remembered the city's constant hum. Was I in love with it again? Maybe. I felt more alive than I had in months. Then again, I was watching it all go by from the inside of a cab. Out in the wild—that was a different story.

As we drove through Brooklyn, my heart swelled. People of all colors and shapes walking along the grimy sidewalks; corner bodegas selling everything under the sun; coffee shops and designer clothing boutiques nestled in between barbershops and tiny Caribbean food outposts; street construction and jackhammers at every other intersection. *Home.*

We pulled up to Mona's brownstone and suddenly, there

I was, alone on the sidewalk with a giant suitcase, a fistful of cash and a best friend on the other side of the door who had cancer. "Best friend" and "cancer" should never coexist in the same sentence, but here, they did. A window creaked open and Mona peered down at me.

"I know you're not expecting me to help you with your bags." A broad smile lit up her face, but even from this distance I could see how tired her brown eyes were. *Do not cry*, I reminded myself.

"Please, I got this."

I struggled up the stairs, scraping a significant amount of skin off my denim-coated left shin in the process. At the top finally, I dropped my bags and wiped the flop sweat from my brow.

"I take it you're not working out in Farmwood?" asked Mona, opening the door to my disheveled self.

"Oh, look who's the wise guy." I met her gaze and, of course, began to cry. "Oh God, I'm s-s-s-sorryyy," I blubbered. "Ignore me."

"It's okay, Sar." Mona hugged me. "I cry all the time too. Let's not pretend this doesn't suck, okay? That would just make everything worse."

"Okay. Okay." I sniffled. "I'm pulling it together."

"Don't even think about wiping your nose on my shirt."

"How did you know?"

"When you're friends with somebody for this long, you just know." She wiggled out of my embrace and held me at arm's length. "You look the same."

"So do you. I can't believe it."

"I know, right? The one chance I have in my life to be legitimately skinny, and nothing. It fucking figures."

"Mona, you don't have to be a comedian with me, you know."

"I know that, dummy. But I am seriously pissed about the weight-loss thing. People expect collarbones and hip divots when you tell them you have cancer, and here I am, looking healthy as a goddamn horse."

"You look beautiful."

"Thanks."

"How do you feel?"

"Let's talk about it inside. I'll pour you a glass of rosé."

"That works."

So, how are you feeling?" I asked, sitting cross-legged beside Mona on the couch, wine in hand.

"I feel okay, I guess. Tired, though. It's so strange. It's like I know the cancer is there, eating away at my uterus or whatever the hell it's doing, but since I don't feel anything, there are moments when I just forget."

"Like when?"

"You know, just everyday moments. Like waiting forever for the subway and cursing out the transit authority in my head like I did every day of my life before I found out I had cancer. Or ordering in sushi. You know, that moment when the buzzer rings and you get so excited that you don't know what to do with yourself?"

"Of course, the *Where's my purse, where's my wallet, do I have enough for a tip?* dance. I invented that."

"Remember that time the Thai delivery guy urinated on my welcome mat because we gave him a crappy tip?" Mona asked.

"Oh my God, I do. Wait, did he really do that or were we just really stoned?"

"We were really stoned, but yes, he did do that. One cannot conjure up the smell of urine."

"That's true." I took a sip of my wine. "So sometimes you forget?"

"Yes, but only for a moment or two. Then I remember again, and it makes me really sad. I know I'm supposed to feel lucky that they caught the cancer early enough to stop it in its tracks, but it's hard to. I'm losing my chance to have kids."

"But you can adopt?"

"If one more person tells me that I can adopt in an attempt to make me feel better I think I'll scream."

"Sorry. I just, I'm not sure I know what to say about any of this, Mona. All I want to do is make this better for you, make this not be happening."

"I know, Sarah. But it is happening, you know? And you're here to help me deal in the aftermath. That's huge. Just treat me like you always have treated me, please."

"Really?" I raised my eyebrow.

"Well, maybe a little bit nicer." She paused to take her own sip. "Okay, a lot nicer."

"Mona, what was it like finding out?"

"That I had cancer?"

"Yeah."

"It was the scariest moment of my life. All of it was the scariest moment of my life—the spotting, the colposcopy, the phone call asking me to come in."

"I can't imagine what it felt like to answer that phone call."

"I hope you never have to."

"You never want to hear 'Please come in' from your doctor," I added. "Mona, were you all by yourself? Through all of this?"

"For the most part, yeah. My friend Angela picked me up from the doctor's office and off the floor on a couple of occasions."

"Angela." I rolled my eyes. "I can't believe I haven't been here for you, Mona."

"Sarah, come on. Enough already. You're here now. Want some chips or something? I'm ravenous." She got up from the couch and headed into the kitchen.

"I'll never say no to chips."

I stretched out my legs on the couch, digging my feet into the warm cushion she had left behind. Mona's phone rang and I closed my eyes as she spoke softly in the next room. *Mona.* Talking to her felt so comfortable, like slipping your favorite T-shirt over your head after a day bound in work wear. If I lost her, I didn't know what I would do. A lump grew in my throat.

"Here we go," she announced, walking in with a tray of

refreshments. Bending over, she plunged a chip into some hummus before sitting down.

"So, something has come up." She chewed vigorously as her eyes danced.

"What do you mean?" I leaned over the cutting board to slice a piece from a gooey slab of cheese, but its odor made me gag involuntarily. I sat back, surprised. I hoped I wasn't getting sick. What kind of nurse would that make me? I swallowed, composing myself.

"I'm going to be having sex tonight," Mona said, "and I would like it to be here."

"Get out!" I replied, the shock of her statement trumping my intestinal anxiety.

"You get out."

"Wait, is that safe?"

"Sarah, cancer is not a sexually transmitted disease."

"I know that, but energy-wise—you're okay?"

"Who am I, Sting? We're talking fifteen minutes, tops. I'm okay."

"Who's the lucky guy?"

"Do you remember Nate?"

I cocked my head quizzically as I grabbed a chip, cataloging her conquests in my mind "Nate . . ."

"We called him 'Where's Waldo' because he always wore that stupid striped sweater?"

"Yes! Of course! Where's Waldo! Wait, where is Waldo? He's back?"

"I ran into him about a month and a half ago on the subway, and he gave me a call shortly thereafter."

"Just as you were getting diagnosed?"

"Yeah. Perfect timing, right?"

"Was it?"

"Yes, because I was so out of sorts. Normal me would have hemmed and hawed about whether or not to return his phone call, you know?" I nodded. "Cancer me was like, screw it. Carpe diem, sweater or no sweater. After all, who knows if sex will be the same after the hysterectomy? Emotionally, it certainly won't be, that's for sure."

"So it's a sex thing with Nate?"

"For the most part."

"Does he know about your cancer?"

"Sarah, whispering the word 'cancer' does not make it not exist."

"Sorry." I had morphed into my great-aunt Estelle. She couldn't *not* whisper the words "cancer" or "black."

"I'm not fooling myself into thinking that he's going to stick around after the fact. I mean, who would? We're just sleeping together."

"Any guy would, Mona, if it was you."

"You're sweet, Sarah, but let's get real. It's not going to be pretty after Wednesday."

"That's why I'm here. So what does he say about it? Was it awkward to bring up?"

"Ugh, I don't want to talk about this now. I'm trying to set the mood, not kill it." She stood up, avoiding my gaze.

"And I love you, but seriously, I need you to take a hike tonight."

"For real? Like for the entire night?"

"For real. Think of my uterus, Sarah. It's her last hurrah."

"Fine. But where am I supposed to go?"

"What about Kate and Ben's place?"

"Shit, I was supposed to call them from the airport this morning. I knew I forgot something."

"The baby is here now, right?"

"Yeah, he's a little over a month old, I think. Franklin."

"Franklin?"

"Yeah, I like it. What, you don't?"

"I bet they're super-adamant that no one calls him Frank, too. How are they doing?"

"Okay, I guess. Exhausted." I felt uncomfortable talking about babies with Mona. I could tell she did too. "Anyway, I'm sure it will be fine to stay with them. Maybe they could use an extra hand."

"I'm sure." She took a big sip of her wine. "So, are you going to call them?"

"Wow, you really want me out of here."

"It's an unusual situation."

"I'll say. I wouldn't do this for anyone else's uterus but yours. Pour me a glass of water, please, and I'll make the call."

"You got it."

Wow, he is so small."

I knelt in front of Franklin, who was sleeping in what appeared to be an infant chaise lounge in the living room. He was the tiniest human I had ever seen. "How old is he now?"

"Five weeks," answered Kate, who was sprawled on the couch.

"Five weeks," I repeated. "Does it feel like five years?"

"It feels like thirty-five years and five minutes at the same time, somehow." She sat up. "What time is it?"

I looked at my watch. "Seven."

"Yes! Time for Mommy's Percocet."

"Are you still in pain?"

"No. Well yeah, but that's not what the Percocet is for. It's my happy pill." She got up. "And don't ask me if it's okay for Franklin. The doctor prescribed it to me."

"I wasn't going to ask you that, Kate, I swear. Whatever gets you through the day. Or night, rather."

"Thanks. Sorry to be so defensive," she called over her shoulder as she jogged down the hall to her bedroom. A drawer opened and shut and then she made her way back. "Ben is such a pain in the ass about it. He gives me these judgmental eyes whenever I take one. You have no idea how annoying it is."

"I can imagine. Josh gives me those same eyes when I eat Oreos for breakfast." I stood up. "You mind if I grab a beer?"

"Not at all. Sorry I'm such a terrible hostess, Sar."

"Kate, please. We're family. I'm so sorry for my last-minute invasion. I want to help in any way I can, so just say the word. Diapers, bottles, whatever."

As I offered my services, I uttered a silent prayer that Kate did not, in fact, need help with any of those things. I hadn't a clue. I opened my bottle and faced her. She was sprawled out again, this time with her eyes closed and a bemused expression on her face.

"Hey, Kate, you okay?"

She opened one eye. "So good. Just waiting for the happy bubbles to begin frothing." She closed it again. "Please don't sweat the guest thing. It's nice to see another adult here. Makes me feel almost normal again. Almost. Let me tell you something. I love that little baby more than anything in the world, but this is the hardest job I have ever had."

Kate ran a catering company that she had built from scratch and now served what seemed to be every hipster wedding in the tristate area. She knew about hard work. I looked at Franklin again, who continued to doze peacefully, his tiny, sneaker-sock-clad feet crossed at the ankles.

"And apparently, this is the easy part. At least that's what all of my friends say."

"Wow. That's a sobering thought."

"Sarah, do I look like shit?"

"No way! You look great," I replied.

I had just told a lie. She did look pretty banged up. Beyond the general mushiness—after all, where did that extra skin go?—it was the circles under her eyes and the layer of gray film that appeared to enshroud her that were the most jarring. Bottom line, her appearance was certainly not doing anything to push me into the pro-having-a-baby camp.

"Really? I don't look like the grim reaper?"

"Not at all."

"Thanks. That makes me feel better. By the way, are you guys trying?"

"To have a baby?"

"No, to look like shit. Yes, to have a baby."

"Sort of." In his seat, Franklin began to move his limbs slowly, as though trapped in a Jell-O mold.

"Looks like the little man is waking up," said Kate. She sat up slowly and took a deep breath. "What do you mean, sort of? You're off birth control but not peeing on sticks yet or anything?"

"Yeah, exactly."

"Hi, baby," she whispered, kneeling to unbuckle Franklin from his chair. He opened his eyes and stared at her coolly. "Hello," she repeated, bringing him into her chest. I couldn't get over how impossibly small he looked. Like a deflated football. "Do you mind if I breast-feed him now?"

"Are you kidding? This is your house."

"Yeah, I know, but I feel like I have to ask. Less and less as time goes by, though. Can you hold him for a second while I get situated?" She handed him to me and I froze, holding him by his armpits like a wet puppy. I looked around for help, but Kate was busy arranging a plethora of pillows around her. Slowly, I brought him into me.

"Do I hold him like this?" I asked. "Is this okay?"

"Is he breathing?" Kate did not look up from settling herself into the nest she had amassed.

"Yes."

"Then he's fine."

I looked down into his face. Murky eyes with no discernible color, tiny eyebrows, a nose that turned up slightly and the pinkest lips I had ever seen. In my arms he felt like one of those baby dolls with a plastic head, hands, and feet and nothing but stuffed cotton everywhere in between.

"Hello," I whispered.

"How do you like his receding hairline?" asked Kate, finally situated.

"I guess we know what he'll look like at forty," I answered. I handed him gingerly to her, realizing that both of her enormous breasts were exposed, her nipples like mauve dinner plates. I tried to avert my eyes.

"Yeah, he has Ben's bald spot and everything. I guess that's hereditary." I watched her breast practically swallow Franklin's head whole and had to check that my mouth wasn't hanging open in disbelief. He latched on and sucked hungrily.

"Crazy, right?" She looked at me and then back down again. I nodded. "Getting this to work was almost as painful as the birth. And I went natural."

"Really?"

"Truly. They don't tell you that breast-feeding can be difficult at first in your birthing class. Or anywhere, for that matter. They make it seem like a goddamn Summer's Eve ad or something—all Vaseline-smeared lenses and rose-colored twilight—but let me tell you, getting the hang of this is hell on wheels."

"It is?"

"Yes. But worth it, eventually. At least that's what my mom friends say. I'm almost out of the woods, but it's still not a walk in the park."

"Huh." Part of me was intrigued and part of me would rather have been anywhere else.

"So, how is Mona?" she asked as she shifted Franklin to her left breast.

"Okay, I guess. She seems eerily rational, considering."

"Yeah, if you consider kicking your best friend who's traveled hundreds of miles to take care of you out of your apartment so that you can have sex with some random guy rational."

"Come on, Kate. She has cervical cancer. Her uterus is going to be removed in a matter of days. Honestly, I don't blame her."

"True."

"Besides, think about it. How does she know what sex will feel like with no plumbing? The odds of it being as enjoyable, at least for a long while, are pretty slim."

"Emotionally, yes. You're right. I'm a bitch."

"You are sort of a bitch."

"Mommy's a bitch, Franklin," she cooed at him as he continued to suck. "Does she feel well? What's her energy level like?"

"She says she feels fine—that sometimes she even forgets that she has it."

"What stage is her cancer?"

"Stage two-A."

"Is that early? It hasn't spread beyond her . . . well, what would it need to spread beyond?"

"Her pelvic wall. I have been a googling maniac since she told me, believe me."

"As has she, I'm sure. Although that will drive you to drink real quick. The number of message boards out there designed to terrify you is stunning." She shifted Franklin to her left breast.

"I know. But as I was saying, it's spread a bit beyond the cervix but not beyond the pelvic wall. This hysterectomy should hopefully take care of it entirely. Plus, she gets to keep her ovaries, so she won't have to deal with early menopause."

"No radiation or chemo either?"

"No."

"Well, that's good." She shook her head. "Poor Mona. I really am a bitch. Please forget I ever said that thing I said before."

"What thing?"

"Thanks. I have just been on such a roller coaster since Franklin was born. Up, down, side to side. I cry like it's my job now."

"You?"

"Yeah. And the night sweats! Unbelievable. I wake up to

feed him and it's like I just swam." I grimaced. "But—and this is a big but—it is all worth it." She cradled his tiny head in the nook of her arm. "Well, mostly. The vaginal tearing I could live without." Was there anything that Kate was not going to tell me? "Anyway, I'm crazy in love with this little worm. And for Mona now never to be able to have one of her own? It's awful."

"It is awful," I agreed. "And she was always so into kids." I was suddenly seized by the need for fresh air. "Hey, do you need anything?" I asked. "I need to stretch my legs."

"Ben will be home in about ten minutes with dinner." She cocked her head and stared into space for a minute. Below, on her lap, little Franklin did the same. "Ooh, if you got us some chocolate chip cookies from Bodega, I would love you forever."

"Done." I stood up.

"Sar, this is the first time I've felt like myself in weeks. Thank you."

"For what?"

"I don't know. Existing?"

12

I stared at the ceiling and listened to Kate attempt to soothe Franklin in the next room. It was 5:43 A.M., and I had just returned from the bathroom, tampon in hand, only to be rendered useless by the pristine appearance of my underwear. There was not even the faintest hint of anything red, pink, or brown anywhere in the vicinity, despite the fact that I was now two days late. The thing was, I was never late.

I clenched my fists under the down comforter as I talked myself off the ledge of uncertainty. Yes, technically I could be pregnant, but my body could also just be adjusting to its newfound freedom. It was only the start of my second month off birth control, and I had been on that since what felt like the dawn of time.

Sunlight slowly began to filter through the blinds. I unclenched my fists and took a deep breath. I was definitely not necessarily pregnant. A few more days of a no-show and then I would worry.

I thought about Mona. I hoped she was sleeping the sleep of a sexually satiated someone. As for Nate, I had tried to conjure up his face but could come up with nothing but that ridiculous sweater. Ben shuffled into the kitchen with Franklin nuzzled into his bare chest. *Okay, that's cute.* Even my noncommittal uterus agreed.

"Hey, Ben," I said softly. He turned around, surprised to see me swaddled on the couch. Only my eyes peeked out.

"Wow, Sar, I am so out of it that I literally forgot that you were staying with us."

I pulled the comforter below my chin. "I'm not sure how I'm supposed to respond to that."

"Don't bother responding. Exhaustion gives me no filter." He stood there silently for a second. "I forgot why I came out here."

"To make coffee?" I suggested.

"I don't think that was it, but that is an excellent reason." He seemed confused by the fact that both of his hands were occupied by his son.

"I've got it, don't worry. Take a load off."

I threw off the comforter and padded to the coffeemaker

on bare feet, only slightly self-conscious about my lack of bra. Last night, over Thai food and two bottles of wine, Kate and Ben had told me their birth story. Apparently Ben had been front and center. He could handle this, certainly. I located the coffee and scooped it into the machine.

"Is Kate drinking coffee?" I asked.

"She lives on it these days, even though she probably shouldn't."

"Why?"

"I don't think caffeine is so great for the baby." He shrugged. "But I'm not saying anything to her about it. I learned around day two of Franklin's life not to question her about anything she puts in her body. She practically knifed my mother when she was here."

I grinned. "What did she do?"

"Kate says she looked at her glass of wine funny."

"Cardinal sin. I can definitely see Sylvia pulling something like that, though."

"Oh, no doubt." He yawned. "Anyway, Franklin is a thriving little dude. I'm staying out of it."

"Good man." I leaned against the counter as the coffee machine percolated behind me. "How are you doing with all of this?"

"All of what? All of this dad stuff?" I nodded. "I don't sleep that much, and I'm stressed about money of course, but really I can't complain. Kate does all the work. Things will change when she goes back to her job of course, but right now I'm pretty damn happy."

"You like being a dad?"

"Love it." Franklin shifted slightly in his arms. "It was time for us, you know? Is it time for you guys?"

"Sure, I guess so." I fought the urge to turn away from him and rifle through their cabinets.

"That doesn't sound very convincing."

"No, it is." I didn't feel like getting into it with Ben. "Milk and sugar?" I asked.

"Both, please." I turned to make his cup, dropping my spoon in the process. It clattered loudly, and Franklin mewed in alarm.

"Sorry!" I said apologetically, practically knocking the mug off the counter as well.

"Every morning is another opportunity to feel as though I've been run over by a Mack truck," announced Kate as she joined us. Her eyes were slits behind her thick-framed glasses. She stopped to drape her arm over Ben's shoulder and gazed lovingly down at her son.

"Hey, Kate, you have a giant clump of baby puke in your hair," said Ben.

"I know," she replied with a sigh. "Every time it brushes my cheek I get an intoxicating whiff of spoiled milk."

"You've never been more beautiful," replied Ben with conviction.

As I stirred milk into my mug, I took in their new-family glow. Kate seemed happy. Exhausted, but happy. And her honesty about the trials of new motherhood was, although a bit over-the-top at times, refreshing. What's more, she didn't come from perfect parents—being a bridesmaid at her wedding had shown me that. Her mother was a perfectionist in the worst sense of the word—at one point she practically had the florist in a headlock over some slightly wilted chrysanthemums—a personality trait that I was sure had done a number on Kate.

Kate was working it out anyway—learning as she went. Why shouldn't I be able to do the same when the time came? I looked down, surprised to find my free hand resting on my stomach.

Later that morning, we set out to stroll the neighborhood. And what a production strolling with an infant was. The stroller, the baby bag, the packing of said baby bag, the baby, dressing the baby, getting out of the door without smacking him with it, only to hear the distinct rumbling of his tiny bowels. Back in the door, onto the changing table, out of the outfit, into another diaper, snap-snap-snap into another outfit, and once again out the door we went—forty-five minutes after our original starting time, at which point Kate started to obsess about where she would breastfeed him.

As we descended in the elevator, I wondered how people living in five-story walk-ups did this. On the bright side, there was no need for a gym membership. On the other side: everything else. On the street at last, Franklin blessedly passed out. On cue, the rest of us exhaled a deep sigh of relief.

"Jesus," I said.

"Tell me about it," Kate replied. She eyed my leather wristlet longingly. "Are you carrying everything you need in that tiny bag?"

"I am."

"Good for you. Savor it. You don't know what you've got till it's gone."

"Oh, come on, Kate. It's not that bad, is it?" asked Ben as he pushed the stroller.

"No, but getting out of the house alive is a miracle these days."

"It will get better," I said, as though I knew anything. "You're in the weeds now because you're only five weeks in, but soon you'll be a pro."

"At least you have a car in Farmwood," said Kate. "That is a game changer in terms of kids. You can just stash all of your supplies in there."

"Who says I can drive?"

"What, you don't drive?" asked Ben.

"I'm working on it."

"No kidding. Huh," said Ben.

"What?" I snapped.

"Nothing, nothing! I'm just surprised, that's all. You're such an independent person."

"Ben, independent people in New York City have no need to drive," said Kate. "Sarah lived here for an eternity. It's not such a big deal."

"Thanks, Kate," I said. "I'm embarrassed about it, I guess.

It's sort of become this Achilles' heel for me. I'm actually taking driving lessons."

"Well, that's smart." Ben leaned down to adjust the shade on Franklin's stroller. "You'll get it in no time." I wondered where Ray was at this moment. I hoped not careening into oncoming traffic courtesy of his latest student.

We continued our walk in relative silence. I studied Brooklyn as though I would be taking a test on it later. Such character this place had. Every brownstone was like a person to me—cracked and weathered from years of wear and tear, baking warily in the morning sun like a retiree in Florida. Kate's voice rose beside me, shaking me out of my daydream.

"Ben, when you talk to me like I am a crazy person, it makes me want to choke you," she yelled. "Don't make me feel crazy for worrying about when and where Franklin is going to eat. These are my breasts and my milk and this is my job. A job that you don't have the first clue about, and a job that you were adamant about me taking on, I might add."

"This whole blaming me for your decision to breast-feed is getting really old," replied Ben.

"I will blame you for whatever I want to blame you for!"

"Can I help at all?" I volunteered weakly.

"No," they barked in unison.

"Well, I just want to point out that there are some shaded benches around the perimeter of the park up ahead. Maybe you could feed him there?" I suggested. They looked at Franklin, who was just waking up, and then back at me.

"Okay. Good idea." Ben pulled ahead to wheel the stroller at a faster clip and Kate put her hand on my arm.

"Sorry, Sar."

"Please don't apologize! It's okay."

Hearing them argue about the whys and wherefores of baby care had reduced my libido to the size of a wasabi pea. *See, I'm not pregnant. In the movies, pregnant women are wildly sexual and everyone knows that movies are always true to life. Great, it's settled.*

I reached into my wristlet and eyed my phone. No word from Mona yet, and it was practically lunchtime. Well, lunchtime for geriatrics and new parents that had been awake since six A.M., but still. She and Nate were probably lingering over eggs Benedict somewhere with the rest of bed-headed, unmarried Brooklyn.

You didn't grab brunch with someone you were just using for sex. There was probably more to this Where's Waldo, Part Two, scenario than Mona was admitting to, but that was not a surprise. She'd always had a habit of playing down whatever it was that she was involved with.

Her official job title was editorial director, but whenever anyone asked her what she did for a living, she just said that she worked in publishing. Her father had been a famous art collector before he passed away, but she always just told people that he had liked art whenever they praised some of the work on her apartment walls. Stuff like that. It occurred to me that perhaps she was playing down her diagnosis as well, and my stomach dropped.

On the bench, Kate put what appeared to be a patterned sheet with a hole cut out of it over her head while Ben held a squirming and screaming Franklin beside her.

"One minute," she huffed as she fiddled with her bra underneath the sheet.

"What the hell is that thing?" I asked, baffled.

"They call it a hooter hider."

"You're kidding."

"I am not." She looked up and blew her hair out of her face in exasperation. "And I paid forty dollars for it."

"Isn't it uncomfortable?"

"It's horrible, okay? But how the hell else am I supposed to feed him without the whole world seeing my spare tire?"

"Your spare tire?"

"Yeah. I could give a shit about my breasts. It's the stomach that nobody needs to see."

"She's ridiculous," said Ben. Kate shot him a look that could have iced the bench she sat on. "Sorry. You ready for him?"

He passed Franklin, who began screaming even louder, and Kate wrestled him under the hooter hider apologetically. We watched the outline of his tiny body writhe underneath it as Kate attempted to get him to latch. Two endless minutes later, the hider was around Kate's neck, her breasts and stomach exposed to the world.

"Fuck it," she said. "I surrender. World, meet spare tire. Spare tire, meet world." The tiny slice of Franklin's mouth that was not involved in his lunch turned up.

"He's smiling!" announced Ben.

"Totally," I agreed. I leaned back against the bench and pulled my own shirt up. "All for one." Kate smiled at me appreciatively.

"I gotta get a picture of this," said Ben.

"Do it and die," I replied calmly.

Mona opened her door before I could knock.

"He's here," she whispered.

"Waldo?"

"Nate, his name is Nate. Don't forget that."

"But, Mona, I thought it was just you and me going to dinner," I whisper-whined.

"I know, I know, but he really wanted to meet you."

"For the record, this is definitely not someone you're just sleeping with, Mona, and you're kidding yourself if you think otherwise." We stared at each other, me angrily and her hopefully.

"All of this whispering makes me nervous," announced a deep voice. Nate emerged from the depths of Mona's apartment and joined us by the door.

As soon as I saw him I remembered that I had met him before, at a party on the Upper West Side a million years ago when he and Mona were doing whatever it was that they were doing. We'd had a pretty entertaining discussion while Mona pretended not to care that he had shown up when in fact, it was a very big deal to her that he had shown up—a classic Mona move.

"Hey, wait, I *have* met you before!" he exclaimed, reading my mind. He was cute in a tall and gangly way, with teeth that were slightly too big for his mouth and sandy brown hair that was cropped a little too close to his head. He smiled and reached out to shake my hand.

"I remember," I replied. "It's all coming back to me."

"Hey, let me get your bag." He reached to grab it. "Sorry, I should have met you downstairs to do this. Seems almost cruel to offer to take it now." He handed it back to me. "Here, you relish the finish." I set it down dramatically and smiled.

"Sarah, do you mind if Nate joins us for dinner?" asked Mona. "Ocean is his favorite sushi spot too."

"I understand if you'd rather have alone time," said Nate. "Just thought I'd ask."

"Sure, of course," I half-lied. Dinner would be fine with him. Not the same, but fine. He made Mona happy, and that was the important part. I needed to remember that.

Over dinner, I realized what it was about Nate that annoyed me. He was a comedian. Not a full-time comedian, but a part-time comedian who made a quasi-living as a paralegal during the day. There was something about a struggling comedian at thirty-eight that begged judgment.

"So, Virginia, huh? Is it exclusively for lovers?" he asked as he freed three edamame beans from their shell and popped them into his mouth.

"What? Oh, you're talking about the slogan." That was another thing. He just wasn't that funny. "No, haters live there too."

"Mona told me that you were having some trouble with the driving thing."

"Oh she did, huh?" I glared at Mona.

"Sarah, it's nothing to be embarrassed about. Lots of people can't drive," Mona said.

"It's not that I can't drive, Mona, it's that it makes me very anxious. There's a difference."

"I know, Sarah. Sorry."

"I mean, to say that I can't drive implies that I've never been behind the wheel or am, I don't know, retarded."

"Retarded! Sarah! I think you're a wee bit sensitive about this. I'm sorry I brought it up."

"Actually, you didn't bring it up, Monie, I did," interjected Nate. "It's my bad. Forgive me."

Monie?

"If it makes you feel any better, Sarah, I can't swim. Never learned how." He took a sip of his beer. "The ocean terrifies me."

"Eh, that doesn't really make me feel better, but thanks for trying."

"I'm gonna use the restroom," he announced. "BRB." I gave Mona the evil eye as he walked away.

"What?" she asked.

"Why did you lie to me?"

"About what? Him coming tonight? I swear it wasn't planned! I just felt bad for him. He loves this place."

"It's not about tonight at all! I don't care about that. Okay, maybe a little, but honestly, that's not what I'm pissed about. I'm pissed because you told me it was just a sex thing with him, when it's clearly much more."

"It's not that much more. But okay, mea culpa."

"Why make it less than it is?"

"You know me, it's my thing. I just, well, maybe I didn't want to jinx it."

"Do you even need me up here? Doesn't Nate want to help out?"

"Of course I need you here, Sarah! You're the one person that I want here for what's about to happen." Something clicked in my brain, like a gumball dropping into its chamber after the quarter was deposited.

"Oh no, Mona." She fiddled with her napkin guiltily. "Mona, look at me." She looked up hesitantly. "Holy shit, he doesn't know." She shook her head. "But why? And why lie to me about that too?"

"Sarah, come on. Cancer is not exactly an aphrodisiac. And as far as telling you that he doesn't know, what was the point?"

"Didn't you worry that I would bring it up and call your bluff unintentionally?"

"I guess I just assumed that you wouldn't. Who wants to talk about cancer?"

"And what about during your recovery? Didn't you think that I would find it strange that he wasn't around?"

"I didn't think it through that well. I happen to have a few other things on my mind besides whether or not you would ask me where Nate was."

"Well of course, but still. The fact that you feel that you have to lie to me at all is disconcerting. You're my best friend, for chrissake. Mona, I have to ask you something, and if you don't tell me the absolute truth I will never forgive you."

"Okay."

"Is your cancer really stage two-A and will this hysterectomy wipe it out, or is there something much worse going on?"

She looked me in the eye. "What I've told you about that is the absolute truth. One hundred percent."

"You swear?"

"I swear on my father's grave."

"Okay. Good." I reached over to grab her hand just as Nate approached.

"Hey, ladies, where's the funeral?" he asked, collapsing into his chair as though his urination had depleted him of all energy.

How could she not tell him? Every doctor appointment, every heartbreak, every woken-up-from-anxiousness moment in the middle of the night—she just swallowed them when he was around? To me, repression seemed like the very definition of cancer, something eating away at you on the inside despite your best efforts to ignore it.

"You guys are making me miss Josh. I'm going to step outside for a sec to call him."

"Go ahead," said Mona. "We won't eat your sashimi, I promise."

Outside, I pulled my sleeve over my free hand and shivered. The first nip of fall was in the air, and it felt amazing. There was only so much of summer someone could take before yearning for sleeves again. What would fall be like in Farmwood? I wondered.

"Hello, wifey," Josh answered.

"Hello, husband." Hearing his voice made me smile.

"I miss you. Can you come back already?"

"I'm starting to second-guess my decision to come here," I told him. A fortysomething woman in pigtails stomped past me. What was the deal with women over a certain age and pigtails? Why?

"Really? How come?"

"Well, that's not true. I think that Mona does really need me, maybe more than I even thought initially. She's got some serious head stuff going on."

"Like what?"

"Like she's pretty seriously dating this guy, but she has not told and has no plans to tell him about the cancer."

He whistled. "That's a doozy. Why? She doesn't want to scare him off?"

"I guess. Although, if I was him, finding out that my girlfriend had cancer and didn't mention it to me would scare me off way faster."

"But, Sarah, you're talking a lot for someone who thankfully has never had to have that conversation with anybody. How do you know what this feels like for Mona?"

"I know. I just, I want her to own herself with these guys she dates. What is she afraid of?"

"I guess you need to ask her that." In the background, I could hear the doorbell ring.

"Who's that?"

"I invited some people from school over for taco night," he answered.

"Taco night?"

"Sure. I make a pretty mean taco, you know that."

"When was the last time you made tacos?"

"Sarah, I'm bored here without you, okay? Don't be bitchy."

"I'm sorry, you're right. Good for you for reaching out. I would just stew around in my misery if I was there."

"I know. That's why we work together."

"Are Iris and Mac coming?"

"Yeah—them, Bob, this guy Raj, and one of my teaching assistants, Curtis."

"Cool. Well, go ahead, have fun. I can see that my sushi is ready anyhow." Through the window, a waitress descended upon the table with three boats of rainbow-hued fish.

"You too. And talk to Mona. Don't yell at her. She's in a really scary place, you know? I'd be shocked if any of her behavior made sense."

"You're right. I love you. Say hi to everyone for me."

"Will do." I swung open the door and put on my best game face. Mona clearly needed me, maybe now more than ever, and if that meant hanging up my judgmental shoes about her Nate situation, that's what I would do. For now, anyway.

13

Use your horn only when necessary to avoid collisions.

How are you feeling?" I asked. Mona and I were back in her apartment, just the two of us. I nestled a pint of ice cream between my knees.

"Fine, just super tired. I go and go and go and then when I finally sit, it's like—ahhhhhh."

"Is that good for you?"

"How can it be good for anybody?"

"No, I know, but you're particularly vulnerable. Why do it to yourself?"

"Because who knows what life will be like after Wednesday?"

"After the operation?"

She nodded. "I should make the most of my mobility now."

"Mobility as in the ability to put your legs over your head?" I asked, referring to Nate.

"Very funny. And I'm thirty-six, not seventeen. There are no legs over anybody's head. Although I will say that Nate is very flexible."

"Is he?"

"Yeah, he's into yoga and all of that holistic stuff."

"A yogi comedian paralegal?"

"Yeah, who knew that was a thing, right?"

I plunged my spoon back into the ice cream. "Are we going to talk about the fact that Nate has no idea that you have cancer?"

"If we have to, I guess."

"I'm just curious, is all, and also, saddened by it."

"What's to be sad about, Sarah? Cancer is a buzzkill. I like Nate, but I'm not, like, crazy head-over-heels about him."

"You sure? You seemed pretty into him at dinner."

"He's a yogi comedian paralegal who unfortunately is not that funny, Sarah. Not exactly marriage material."

"Well, yes, there's that, but beyond that, he seems like a nice guy. And really into you, I might add."

"He does?" Her eyes lit up, thereby betraying her feigned indifference.

"Yep." I handed her the pint, but she waved it away.

"I've thought about telling him, but every time I come

close, it just seems too absurd. Like a bad movie or something."

"So how do you handle your doctor appointments and stuff? How have you been handling not feeling well?"

"It's very easy. The doctor appointments are during the day, so what's the difference, and the tiredness I can easily mask with fake plans. He thinks I'm the most popular woman in the universe, which of course makes him more into me."

"So that rumor is true, huh? I don't think I ever played hard to get in my entire dating career. I was more of the *Plans tonight? Let me check—yep, I'm free* variety."

"Me too! Now I'm not, and let me tell you—those ridiculous dating books weren't complete bullshit. He can't get enough of me." She reached for the carton, peering inside when I handed it to her. "Geez, you've been busy."

"What? You refused it earlier! I'm stress eating."

"Why are you stressed out?"

"Because I just want more for you, is all. I want you to know how incredible you are, warts and all, and make no apologies for them, not tiptoe around some guy and lie to save his feelings of awkwardness. You deserve someone that you can really talk to, that you can trust will be there for you."

"Sarah, this is a really great pep talk, but you're speaking from the mountain of commitment and I'm living in the valley of dating death. It doesn't work like that. You ask the guy you're dating if he wants to go to a stupid wedding with you as your plus one two weeks in advance, and he stops returning your texts. That's the world I'm living in."

"Did that happen to you?"

"It did."

"What bullshit. Listen, I know you're right, and the last thing I want to do is come off as self-righteous. I just needed to say that. You knew I was thinking it. And just so you know, not all is peaches and cream atop the mountain. There are issues there too."

"What? You and Josh are in trouble?"

"No, we're fine. I'm just saying that all relationships take work and communication. And we're all guilty of fooling ourselves into thinking that that's not the case because in the short term, it's easier to avoid stuff."

"You sure you guys are okay?" she asked again.

"Positive. Just making a point." It seemed incredibly selfish, not to mention thoughtless, to bother Mona with my baby baggage now. "Let's get back to you."

"I guess I have this sort of weird, twisted belief that the more people I don't tell about my cancer and hysterectomy, the less real either of them are," she confessed. "Telling Nate about it would be the mother lode."

"Are you scared, Mona?"

"It's all so incredibly overwhelming," she answered. I squeezed her hand. "So if I need to make some ridiculous decisions regarding what I will and won't say to the guy I'm sleeping with, just bear with me, okay?"

"Okay. I will." I rocked her for a moment. "So, where does Nate think you're going for two weeks as you recover?"

"Paris for work. I told him that I have to go edit a manuscript alongside a famously difficult author."

"Which author?"

"That's what's great about dating a yogi comedian paralegal. They don't ask."

"C'est bien."

"*Oui*," she replied, touching my cheek with a sad smile.

The next day, while Mona was taking a nap, I wandered Brooklyn aimlessly, trying to not think about my missing period but instead to relish the fact that I had nowhere to be and nothing pressing to do. In three days, I was going into full-on nurse mode, even though I had no idea what exactly that would entail. The most care I had ever bestowed upon someone was when Josh had the stomach flu. My patience had worn out around hour fourteen, which did not bode well for Mona.

"Sarah?" I turned from the overpriced clothing storefront I had been admiring.

"Emily?"

Emily was a former coworker, and although I knew that she meant well, she had a terrible habit of asking a question and then answering it herself. Plus, she was the most offensive masticator I had ever been forced to share space with. What she did to potato chips should be illegal.

“I thought you moved!” She extended her arms for a hug and I reciprocated.

“I did, I’m ju—”

“Back here visiting? I bet visiting New York is a helluva lot better than actually enduring the daily grind, huh?”

“I guess.”

“What, you’re unhappy?” Her navy eyes bored holes into my skull.

“No, no.” I waved her off. “Just, I don’t know.” She continued to observe me keenly. “I’m sort of out of it this afternoon, you know?”

“Hungover?”

“Not real—”

“I’m hungover today too. You know what the best cure is? Spinning.”

“Spinning records?”

“Ha, you are so funny, Sarah. No, silly, spinning as in cycling. I sweated out about six liters of vodka this morning.” Athletic bragging, another one of Emily’s downfalls. She and Iris would have gotten along swimmingly.

“Good for you.”

“Have you ever spun?”

“Once, I—”

“I just picked it up over the summer, and oh my God, what a game changer. I’ve lost, like, four and a half pounds.”

“I can totally tell.” That was a lie, but one I knew I was expected to dispense.

“You can?” She jumped up and down in delight, her

brown bun bobbing on the top of her head like a wine cork in water. "Have you spoken to Meghan since you left?" she asked, composing herself. Meghan was my former boss.

"No."

"Bad blood?"

"Maybe a little. I do think that my resignation came as a shock."

"Yeah, we were all shocked, actually. You were just so good at what you did. Everyone assumed you were leaving to go somewhere else, but the move out of the business was surprising, not to mention the fact that you were leaving New York!"

"Yeah." I shrugged my shoulders, feeling uncomfortable. New Yorkers. They couldn't wrap their heads around the fact that people actually resided in the forty-nine other states.

"Although, good for you. I fantasize about getting out all of the time."

"You do?"

She nodded as she reached into her bag and brought out a pack of gum. "Sure, I just have no idea what the hell I would do. Want a piece?"

"No thanks."

She shrugged and unwrapped a piece before popping it into her mouth. I visibly winced, but it was to no avail. She was clueless about the offense she committed every time she inserted something into her mouth. "They still haven't filled your position, you know."

"They haven't?" My heartbeat unexpectedly quickened a little.

"Nope."

"Why?"

"I guess you're irreplaceable. You should call Meghan. Not that you want to, because you're happy with your move and all, but if you weren't, you know, I would call her." What was Emily insinuating?

"Thanks, Emily."

"Hey, you need a ride? I'm headed into the city." She pointed to her Zipcar. "I love these things. You ever rent one?" Emily the overtalker and overmasticator could drive, but I could not? That was unacceptable. It seemed like everyone on the road was dumber than me. *And yet . . .*

"No thanks, I'm just—"

"Oh, you're staying in the neighborhood? Okay, well, awesome to see you like this. Random, but awesome."

"You too."

"Stay in touch!" She bounded off, her shiny black leather boots practically crackling with each step. *Meghan hasn't hired anyone, huh?* That wasn't entirely surprising, considering how picky she was. She wasn't the easiest person to get along with either, which could explain the lack of in-house interest. A man walking an iguana on a leash passed by me. My phone rang. Josh.

"Hey!" I answered.

"Hey. How goes it?" he asked through a yawn.

"Did taco night go until the wee hours?" I teased.

"You know what? It actually did run pretty late."

"Was it fun?"

"It was. What can I say, I throw a nice party. And the tacos were delicious."

"Nice."

"I pulled our old Trivial Pursuit off the shelf and we played for hours. Curtis and I schooled everybody."

"Mazel tov."

"Iris was asking about you."

"Oh yeah?"

"She really wants to see you again."

"I bet."

"Sarah, don't be a jerk. She's cool, really. Not Mona cool by any means, but cool enough."

"Yeah, I guess so. There's still something about her that rubs me the wrong way. I can't put my finger on it. Actually, I can put my finger on it."

"What, she has the audacity to talk about her fondness for exercise and travel?"

"Talking is one thing. Bragging is quite another. Anyway, I'll give her another shot, just let me get around to it, okay? Don't force the idea down my throat." Josh's behaving as my Farmwood social chair really annoyed me.

"Sheesh, you are a crank today. Forget I said anything. Where are you, by the way?" Josh asked.

"Just taking a little walk."

"I wish I was walking with you."

"Even though I'm a crank?"

"Even though."

"Me too."

"How's Mona? Did you get to the bottom of her decision to keep this guy in the dark?"

"Yeah. It's pretty much everything you suspected. I'm hoping she'll change her mind and clue him in."

"The operation is Wednesday? And what's today?"

"Sunday."

"That's not much time to drop a bomb of that size on a guy you're casually dating."

"I know. Although, it looks like I'm out on the street again tonight."

"What? No way!"

"Way." I stopped in front of a deli. I was craving a black-and-white cookie, the kind that came wrapped in plastic and was mass-produced somewhere in Long Island. "It's not a biggie. I'm going to babysit for Kate and Ben."

"You are?"

"Don't sound so surprised. I'm not completely useless. I babysat all the time in high school. Of course, I raided the parents' liquor cabinets and rummaged through their bedside tables once the kids were asleep, but things are different now. I can drink openly, for example." *Not that I will, because there's a very slight chance that I could be pregnant.* I didn't want to mention it yet. There was no need for both of us to become overwhelmed by what-ifs, especially at such a distance, until I either got my period or, gulp, got a positive test.

"I think you should probably not drink, actually."

"Thanks, Dad. I was kidding, anyway. The truth is that I am a little nervous. Okay, a lot," I admitted. "But c'mon, it's the least I can do. This will be the second of who knows how many times I'm crashing with them with zero notice. I have to do something."

"Ben says they're loving having you around."

"Oh, you talked to him?" I walked to the register and nodded hello to the Indian gentleman behind the counter while depositing my cookie in front of him.

"Yeah, yesterday I think?"

My mouth dropped as what I had assumed to be a large cat lying on the windowsill behind him sat up and stared at me with sleepy eyes. It was not a cat at all, but instead a very petite toddler. I paid and waved away the change.

"Hello?"

"Oh, sorry," I replied, back on the street. "Something very strange just happened." I explained the circumstances and settled down on Mona's stoop to unwrap my cookie.

"Good ole Brooklyn," said Josh when I had finished. "I guess that's another thing I miss. You just don't see oddities like that in Farmwood."

"I literally thought she was a cat." I took a dainty bite of the cookie's white half. "Listen, I better go. You hosting another elegant dinner party tonight, Martha, or will you be around?"

"I'm around. Hey, maybe we can Skype with Franklin."

"Maybe. I'll call you."

"Hey, Sarah?"

"Yeah?"

"I love you."

"I love you too." I hung up and laid my phone on the stoop, just in time for a ladybug to land on its face. "And, Josh? My period is late," I whispered to no one.

I took another bite, this time much bigger, and watched the clouds float across the azure sky.

Call us if you need anything." Kate stood in front of me wringing her hands and biting the inside of her cheek. "We're just down the street." She looked at Ben beseechingly. "Ben, can you believe how nervous I am?"

"Yes, I can believe it. You've been attached, literally, to him for almost a year now."

"A year?"

"Yeah, if you include the pregnancy."

"You're right!" She fell to her knees in front of Franklin, who sucked his pacifier calmly. "Franklin, do you even know who I am?" she pleaded. He continued sucking, nonplussed by his mother's desperation.

"Of course he knows who you are," I said. "You're the milk lady."

Kate stood up. "Okay. Ben, let's go before I change my mind."

"Kate, you look very pretty," I said.

"Thank you. I actually put on mascara and realized that yes, I do have eyes." She smiled proudly.

"You look like a million bucks, honey," added Ben. "Now, for the love of God, let's go." I waved good-bye from the couch.

The door shut and I turned to Franklin, who continued to suck contentedly while strapped into his baby armchair. He had just eaten, and Kate had assured me that there was nothing else to do until he let me know otherwise. If I was lucky, that was.

"Hey, buddy. How was your day? Did ya get some good naps in?" He stopped sucking and the pacifier fell lazily from his mouth as I held my breath, waiting for him to erupt into tears. He seemed unfazed. I regarded the straps that held him in place. *Do I dare try to hold him? What if that sets him off? I won't.*

"Your mom and dad gave me specific instructions not to turn the television on if you were awake." He yawned. "I know, right? How dull are they?" I eyed the clock. They had been gone seven minutes and already I was bored. Not a good sign in terms of my mothering potential.

He began to mew softly. I reached for the pacifier and gently nudged it back into his mouth, but he spat it back out. His arms began to flail.

"All right, I'm going in," I announced. My hands trembled as I undid his straps. "Okay, here we go." I lifted him out and held him in the air in front of me, where he froze, whether in fear or amusement at my ineptitude I could not discern. I cradled him against me awkwardly.

"Could I have one of you around all of the time?" I asked him. He shifted slightly and I imagined what it would be like to feel that shift from the inside. Did it hurt?

I looked around the room—a room that used to frighten me with its cleanliness. Now it looked like a low-level tornado had struck, depositing patterned baby blankets, tiny socks, a variety of nipple creams and at least ten half-empty water glasses throughout. This was what new parenthood looked like. My phone rang.

"Wanna Skype?" Josh asked.

"I guess so."

"Don't sound so excited."

"No, it's not that. I'm just afraid that I won't be able to do two things at once."

"You mean, watch an immobile infant and talk to a computer screen?"

"I guess you have a point. Here, let me get Ben's laptop." I reached over to the far corner of the couch, opened it up and placed it on the coffee table. "Okay, I'm on Ben's computer. Call us." I slid as gracefully as I could to the floor, holding Franklin up a bit so that his head was level with the camera.

"You okay, little guy?" I asked, awkwardly peering around his shoulder to gauge his expression just as Josh's face appeared on the screen before us.

"Look at that," he said. "You with a baby." He smiled goofily, as though high from the visual.

"Josh, you're embarrassing me. Quit it." I smiled back at him. It was good to see his face. He looked so handsome. *That's my husband*, I thought to myself, feeling proud and shy all at once.

"You look so pretty," he said, mirroring my thoughts.

"Get out of here." I settled Franklin against my chest, careful to keep his wobbly head cradled. "You look pretty good yourself."

"Thanks. I showered for you guys. Wow, Sar, he is so tiny. Hi, Franklin. Hi, little guy." I moved the baby's hand to mimic a wave back in response. "What a cutie. I take back the manatee remark."

"I know, right? You should see him in person. He's pretty damn charming."

"I think he looks like Ben."

"You do? I see Kate."

"How's he doing?"

"Okay, I think. Still alive under my care, which speaks well about his survival skills."

"Indeed. Although I'm sure you're great with him. Sorry I was so negative earlier."

"It's okay. Believe me, I was worried too, but so far I'm not a total moron. That said, I haven't had to do anything yet other than hold him. What are you up to?"

"Not much. Just grading some papers on the couch."

"Grading papers or napping?"

"Little bit of both." He yawned. "How long are you on Franklin duty?"

"Just long enough for them to grab some dinner, although they'll probably skip appetizers and dessert if Kate is calling the shots."

"She had a hard time leaving?"

"Yeah. This is the first time she's been separated from him."

"Wow. What a different world, huh? Being a parent?"

"Night and day. Forget about 'me time' anymore."

"Yeah, at first. I think it gets easier to carve out small pockets as they get a little older. Hey, he just smiled at me!"

"No offense, but it's probably gas."

"Since when did you become Dr. Spock? He smiled at his uncle, thank you very much. Hey, buddy," he cooed. "It's me, your uncle J."

"You know, hanging out with Franklin has made me a little less ambivalent about the baby thing," I said.

Josh sat back. "Oh yeah?"

"Yeah. I mean, seeing a couple that we know deal with it in real time has made it slightly less terrifying. Just slightly."

"You know I'm trying my damnedest not to overreact to your proclamation, right? I don't want to scare you back into the hole."

"What am I, a groundhog?" I smiled and Josh laughed. He knew me well.

"Sort of. Punxsutawney Sarah."

"I appreciate it."

"Sure. The last thing I want to do is bully you into feeling a way that you don't authentically feel. I love you too much to put that kind of pressure on you. And by the way, I love you for you. I don't love you because of your childbearing ability."

"I know that. I've been thinking a lot about why I haven't been able to express myself to you. I think it's because my ambivalence makes me feel like a bad person."

"What do you mean?"

"What kind of person doesn't want to have kids? Cat people don't want to have kids. People who get really excited about different kinds of chutney. How could I be one of those people?"

"Sarah, you're not a bad person. It sounds to me like you're scared. And what woman wouldn't be scared?"

"I really hope that's all it is. Rationally, that makes sense. Is there any part of you that's scared?"

"Of course. I worry that my mathematically inclined brain isn't a good match for fatherhood. I get great joy from the neatness of equation solving. A baby isn't an equation."

"Well, that's not entirely true. Figuring out your baby is like solving an equation. What works, what doesn't . . ."

"That's true. Huh. I never thought of it that way. Great, so actually no, I'm not scared at all. I'll be the perfect dad. No worries here." I didn't reply. "You know I'm kidding, right?"

"Yeah, I know. It's good for me to hear that you're nervous too. I don't know why I assumed that you weren't. I guess because you never said as much."

"I suppose I thought that was implied, but that was unfair of me."

"Don't you worry that you'll inadvertently pass on your own neuroses?"

"I suppose that's a valid fear. Although, I think that I'm familiar with and wary of them. Maybe I'm naïve, but I think if I caught myself doing that, I'd retract fairly quickly. I don't want my children to be scared of flying or blamers."

"Blamers?"

"Sure, you know how I am. Instead of taking myself to task for a mistake, I tend to place the blame elsewhere. It's not an attractive trait."

"Right. Why was I thinking that you were perfect?"

"Beats me. Maybe because you've been putting so much pressure on yourself to be this perfect mom-in-training. You're human, you know? To not be scared of something as big as having kids is inhuman in my opinion."

"I'm scared that I won't figure out this career thing and will pass on my sense of inadequacy in the same way my mom passed on her sense of resentment to me. Kids are really perceptive, you know?"

"That's true, but I'm going back to what I said before. Your mom probably wasn't even aware that that's what she was doing. Your sensitivity will provide you with antennae, so to speak. Because you're more in tune with your neuroses, you'll actually be less inclined to pass them on."

Franklin stirred against my chest. I had practically forgotten that he was there. "You think?"

"Yeah, I do." I considered sharing the news about my missing period. Just as I opened my mouth, a distinct rumble erupted from Franklin's diaper.

"Hey, I heard that!" exclaimed Josh. "That was loud!"

"It really was." I laughed. "I think he just pooped." I would take it as a sign to stay mum until I was sure. Even with the progress we had made on the topic, I still felt vulnerable.

"Do you know how to change a diaper?"

"Well, no, but how hard can it be? I watched Kate change one the other night." Franklin started to flail. "Listen, I better go."

"Sarah, this was a great conversation, yeah?"

"It was fantastic." I paused. "I don't know why I was shutting you out on all of this."

"It was the force field, melting your brain."

"I guess it was. I'm sorry."

"Don't be sorry. That's who you are. I love who you are."

"And I love who you are. Very much."

"Okay, give him a kiss for me. Good luck with the diaper."

"Thanks, Uncle J."

I closed out, feeling better than I had in months.

14

Do not allow anyone to ride in the trunk of your vehicle.

I waited impatiently for the F train with the other Brooklynites. Despite knowing better, and despite the fact that arriving late to my destination was no big deal whatsoever, I peered down the tracks and tapped my foot like a cartoon character.

It had been a long night. Each time I heard Kate wake up, swing out of bed, and pad patiently to feed Franklin, humming soothingly all the while, I marveled at her devotion. That was love. When I told her so before I left, she had blushed slightly and shrugged her shoulders.

"You'll see when you have one, Sarah," she had said. "It's just what you do. Part of the program." Again that morning: no period. Soon I was going to have to bite the bullet and buy a test. Soon, but not today.

The train finally approached, and the entire platform exhaled. On board, grasping the top bar and on high alert for any open seats, I observed my fellow passengers. Tired and good-looking, most of them possessing that effortless sort of chic that I always strove to achieve but never quite did. I wondered if my Virginia-ness now clung to me like a cloak or if I could still pass as one of them.

A woman below me pulled out her makeup case, and I practically trembled with excitement. Network execs needed to take note of this phenomenon. Where else could you get an immediate glimpse of someone's ego and taste in less than twenty minutes, and better yet, right up close? It was reality television at its best.

A seat opened up at the next stop, and I collapsed gratefully into it, careful not to spill my coffee as the woman pulled out a tube of foundation without averting her gaze from the smudged mirror of her powder compact. She balanced the compact on the top of her purse and squirted a pea-sized beige dollop into her left hand before rubbing it gently into the palm of her right, the whole time staring straight ahead as if in a trance. Next, she raised her hands to her face and massaged its surface, giving special focus to the curvature of her nose, forehead, and chin. On the other side of her, gangster rap blared out of a young Asian man's headphones, but she did not lose focus. She retrieved her compact to gaze at what she had accomplished and began to set her mask with a liberal dusting of powder before proceeding to her eyeliner. I held my breath as she attempted and perfected a cat eye around the top lid of each eye and had to hold myself back from congratulating her outright. That was talent.

Before Josh, when I would find myself in the bed of someone else in the morning, I would inevitably wake up before them and sneak into the bathroom for a quick face wash, a gargle of mouthwash if it was available—if not, toothpaste on my finger would suffice—and a swipe of ChapStick. Then I would crawl back into bed and play possum. *Who, me? Yes, this is what I look like when I wake up. Tee-hee!* It seemed like a harmless white lie at the time, but in retrospect it was a metaphor for the way I had handled all of my relationships. I never wanted to let them see the real me, was terrified of it, in fact, because if I didn't it wouldn't hurt as much when whatever it was that we were doing fizzled out.

With Josh, things had been different from the very beginning. He had always encouraged the very realest version of me, despite my best efforts to present my trusty façade. For starters, he was the earliest riser I had ever known—up before the dawn to grade papers or go for a run, making me scrambled eggs and presenting me with a hot cup of fresh coffee as I stumbled by him on my way to the bathroom.

My feeling the need to keep my baby ambivalence from him for so long made more sense if I thought of it in the same terms as driving. It was fear. And I was fearful because it was new, this whole making-and-taking-care-of-a-human-being thing. I wanted to be good at it but didn't know if I would be because I had never done it before. But conception wasn't the Wild West, to quote Ray. It was a team effort, and the other half of my team was and always had been incredibly supportive, warts and all.

Hey, Sarah," Nate said, greeting me cheerily.

"Hey, Nate. Nice scarf."

He smiled, completely missing my sarcasm. "Thanks! Mona bought it for me. I feel like a jackass wearing it, but she's assured me that it ups my coolness level considerably."

"Doesn't he look European?" she asked excitedly.

"Sure. Hey, speaking of Europe, are you excited about your trip, Mona?" I gazed at her coolly, relishing her unease. Something about their devil-may-care happiness despite the reality of Mona's predicament had released my inner bitch.

"Uh, yeah, of course. What's not to be excited about?" Her eyes threw daggers.

"Can you believe she has the audacity to leave us behind?" asked Nate. "Who wants to go to stupid Paris anyway?" He put his arm around her and she laughed stiffly.

"So what do you guys want to do today?" I asked, immediately feeling guilty about being such a jerk. Poor Nate had no idea why I was here. As far as he knew, I was just on a fun trip to see my girlfriend. Maybe part of the reason I disliked him was because he was so clueless, and really, that wasn't even his fault, it was Mona's, and Mona was very sick and confused and scared. I vowed to be nicer to both of them.

"I thought we'd all go check out my acupuncturist," replied Nate. He pointed south. "He has an office in Chinatown."

I wrinkled my brow. "Do what?" I looked at Mona. She hadn't mentioned anything about acupuncture on the phone. She looked puzzled as well.

"Yeah, Nate, do what?"

"Mona, you're always so cynical about alternative medicine. I wanted you to see what it was all about, and I thought maybe having Sarah here to experience it with you might take down some of your guard." The sun peeked out from behind the clouds and he loosened his scarf.

"Nate, what do I need acupuncture for?" She faced him with her hands on her hips. I took a sip of my now-cold coffee.

"For your fatigue! I thought it would be a great way to rejuvenate yourself. I know that it helps me quite a bit, so I figured why not. You've just been so tired lately, you know? Unless, of course, you're not tired at all and just making excuses not to hang out." He waited for her to smile, and when she did not, he laughed awkwardly.

"Hey, Mona, why not?" I stepped up and took her arm in mine. "It might be fun." I did not in any way, shape, or form think that it would be fun, but as far as Mona's health went, who knew? It certainly couldn't hurt.

"Jesus, why are you looking at me like that?" She tugged on my arm playfully. "Fine, two against one. Why not. But it better not hurt, Nate."

"Just a little prick, I promise."

I'm just very tired all the time," Mona explained, squirming a bit under the acupuncturist's gaze.

"You work hard?" he asked, tilting his head and taking her in.

"Not any harder than any other New Yorker. Hustle, hustle, hustle!"

His stoic gaze did not waver. "You drink too much?"

"No." Pause. "Yes."

"Okay, you come with me."

Nate and I watched her shuffle off and I worried about my upcoming turn. Should I tell him that I *might be pregnant*? The idea of uttering those words out loud was more than mildly terrifying.

I snuck a sideways glance at Nate. What if he was in love with Mona and wanted her to have his kids? True, there wasn't a biological clock ticktocking ominously over his head, but what if he was one of those rare men who actually had a timeline? On second thought, he was a thirty-eight-year-old part-time comedian. I wasn't sure he knew what a timeline was.

"So, you come here a lot?" I asked him as we waited for our turns.

"Not a lot, really. More like once every three months. I try out all of my new material on this guy."

"Isn't the language thing kind of a barrier?"

"Sarah, I'm kidding! Sheesh."

"Sorry, I'm a bit slow today." I looked around, taking in the giant fish tank that glowed green, the scratched linoleum floor and wood-paneled walls.

"I know it's not exactly the Ritz, but this guy has really helped me through a lot."

"Really? Is your back a wreck or something?"

"Not exactly. I have a lot of anxiety issues, actually. The yoga helps, but not entirely. I tried antidepressants for a while, but I hated how they made me feel like a zombie. Plus, my penis was as limp as an udon noodle." I looked at him with alarm. "Sorry, TMI. My bad. There's no need for you to know about that. That's some new material, actually."

"It's part of your act?"

"I was thinking it could be. What, it's too much?"

"Well, maybe not. I guess in context it could be funny for a bunch of strangers. For your girlfriend's best friend, maybe not so much."

"Right. Thanks for the feedback, Sarah. At any rate, a buddy of mine recommended this place, and sure enough, it works like a charm for me. Who knows if it's psychosomatic or what, but it works. That's all I care about."

"I think it's really great that you've found such solace through something so—so organic."

"Thanks. I'm pretty proud of myself too. Never met a drug I didn't like back in the day, let me tell you. I also never would have thought I'd turn out to be this yoga-cum-homeopathic enthusiast or a thirty-eight-year-old struggling comedian paralegal either, but here I am." He laughed nervously. "Just so you know, I'm working on that angle." I made a *Who, me?* expression. "Come on, Sarah, cut the crap. Something would be wrong with you if you didn't think I needed to get my shit together."

"Listen, I'm a lost soul myself. I work at a costume-jewelry store in a town called Farmwood, for crying out loud. I have no right to judge."

"Yeah, but you have a career to fall back on and a solid marriage."

"Well, yeah, but I don't exactly live on Planet Care Bear or anything."

"Planet Care Bear?" Nate threw his head back and laughed. "Oh shit, I better keep it down. That's rich though, Planet Care Bear. Anyway, I really care about Mona, and she's somebody who does have her shit together. No question about it. I don't want to lose her, but I also know that she deserves someone that's her equal. I'm working on that."

"That's great, Nate."

"And I'm not just saying that, either. It's looking like I'm going to go back to school to get my master's in education.

I'll have loans to pay off forever of course, but I'm feeling good about it."

"Nate, I'm impressed."

"Thanks, Sarah. That means a lot, coming from Monie's best friend." The couch creaked beneath him as he shifted. "Speaking of, do me a favor and don't tell Mona about this. I want to surprise her with my letter of acceptance. I mean, I don't want to get ahead of myself, but I think my chances of getting in somewhere local are pretty good. I sent in my applications a week or so ago."

"No problem." I smiled at him. *So they both have secrets.*

The acupuncturist shuffled out in his plastic slippers and motioned to me to come.

"Well, see ya later, Nate."

"See ya."

Inspired by Nate, I explained to the acupuncturist that I was suffering from anxiety, which wasn't entirely untrue. He nodded sagely and inserted the needles into my skin, their penetration was barely detectable. As he hovered over my midsection, I waved him away, just to be safe.

"You okay? Hurt?" the acupuncturist asked, a needle poised over my sternum.

"Oh, I'm fine. Sorry." He nodded, and in moments, I drifted off, my body desperate for rest.

"Okay, turn and I be back," the acupuncturist said loudly, pulling me out of my shallow sleep. I opened my eyes but he wasn't in my room. He was just a voice.

Was he talking to me? I sat up a bit and took stock of the porcupine quills traveling up and down my most of me. *Really?* I asked myself. *He wants me to turn over onto these? Is this the dark side of acupuncture that no one talks about?* I looked around nervously. *Okay, one, two, three, Sarah.* I leaned awkwardly on my forearm and swung onto my stomach with the grace of a sea lion.

Ow, ow, ow, I whispered as a few of the needles began to plunge in. *This can't be right, can it? Will this hurt the baby if there is, in fact, a baby in there?* I did my best to channel Zen thoughts as I examined the ribbed pattern of the gauzy white curtain separating my cot from that of the patient next door. A shadow passed behind it and his voice returned.

"Okay, look good. Ten more minute."

Oh my God, what an asshole you are, I said to myself as I made the connection. He had been speaking to another patient. I wasn't the one who was supposed to turn, she was. Hoping to avoid the further mortification of allowing him to witness my idiocy, I flipped back over, working up a sweat in the process.

Moments later, my own curtains parted and he strode in purposefully. I closed my eyes and pretended to be deep in a meditative trance.

"What you do here?" he asked.

"Excuse me?"

"What you do here? You roll over? You bleeding."

"Oh no, I didn't roll over," I lied. "I'm bleeding?"

He looked at me curiously. I shrugged my shoulders, grazing my chin with a few of the needles in the process. He sighed loudly and mumbled something in Chinese under his breath as he began extracting them. When he was finished, he hovered over my face.

"Thank you," I said. He nodded and left the room. I sat up and gathered my things as quickly as possible. *Only me.* Outside, I rejoined Mona, who was sitting in the center of the couch and staring into the depths of the giant fish tank.

"Remember when fish tanks were the thing?" she asked. I sat down next to her.

"Yeah, like in elementary school?"

"The eighties, man."

"Seriously." We watched a small school of angelfish dart into a plastic castle. "How was your session?" I asked.

"He knew," she replied quietly.

"He knew what?"

"About the cancer. He knew." She continued to stare into the tank.

"He did?" I put my hand over hers. "What did he say?"

"He said, 'You sick. In uterus, you sick.' "

I gasped. "Shut up."

"You shut up."

"What did you say?"

"I cried, of course."

"Was he sympathetic?"

"He patted my shoulder and then jabbed my pelvis

with about thirty thousand needles." She wiped her cheek. "Maybe he cured me."

"He could have."

She turned to face me and rolled her eyes. "Sarah, I think I'll continue with the surgery. You know, just in case."

"I turned over like an asshole," I said. He hadn't said anything to me about being pregnant. I was surprised to feel deflated.

"What do you mean?" Mona asked.

"I rolled over onto my needles."

"Oh my God, why would you do that?"

"I thought he was telling me to turn over, but it turned out he was talking to a client on the other side of the curtain."

Mona put her hand to her mouth. "Poor Sarah. Did it hurt?"

"Hell yes, it hurt. Thankfully, I realized that he had not, in fact, been addressing me, about ten seconds in."

"Did he know? When he came back?"

"Yes. He asked me if I had turned over, so I lied and told him no. I was mortified. He was kind enough not to press the issue, but I think I heard him murmur 'What an idiot' under his breath in Chinese."

"You know Chinese?"

"No, but what else would he be saying? 'This girl should be in Mensa'?"

Mona giggled. "Pretty classic move, Sar."

"Tell me about it. Remind me again why you won't tell Nate about what's happening?"

"Why does he need to know?"

"Mona, come on. He's crazy about you. He's going to be really upset, and rightfully so, when he finds out that you didn't tell him about something as major as this."

"I didn't realize that you were so concerned about Nate's best interest," she replied drily.

"I'm looking out for your best interest!" My voice rose.

"Shhhh," Mona warned. "You can hear a pin drop in here."

"No pun intended."

"Hardy har har, Sarah." She smiled before continuing. "Like I told you, I don't want anyone giving me a pity party, and I don't want advice. I just want to go in and get it over with. Maybe I'll tell him afterward."

"Have you talked about kids or anything?"

"Oh God, no. We've only been hanging out for what, two months? I haven't even pooped with him in the vicinity."

"Josh likes to leave the door open when he poops," I replied. "It's awful."

"That is awful. Why?"

" 'Why not?' is what he would say. 'What's the big deal?' "

"Ugh, so much about that is a big deal."

"I miss him."

"What's he doing down there without you?"

"Not too much. Pining for me twenty-four/seven."

"Naturally. And taking open-door craps with abandon."

"And watching porn."

"Pining, Porn, and Poops: The Josh Simon Story."

"Are men really that simple?" I asked.

Just then, Nate emerged from the back. As soon as he noticed Mona on the couch, he smiled broadly. My breath caught a little watching it happen. I snuck a glance at Mona, whose cheeks were now rosy with delight, and smiled.

"Yes, but thank goodness," she whispered back.

15

If your accelerator becomes stuck, you should shift back to neutral, apply the brakes, and look for an alternate route.

Today is Mona day," I announced, strolling into her bedroom with the bagel I had just procured for her on a tray. Her favorite, pumpernickel with veggie cream cheese and tomato, lay open-faced on a white plate, a mug of coffee steaming beside it.

"Ergh," she moaned from underneath her gray-and-white-striped comforter.

"Breakfast in bed, my friend."

She sat up, her mass of dark hair falling like curtains on both sides of her face. "Well, well, well. You don't see this every day."

"No you do not." I set the tray down in front of her proudly.

"My favorite!" she exclaimed, clapping her hands and beaming up at me gratefully. "But where's yours?"

"In the kitchen. I didn't want to crowd the tray."

"Look at you, Little Miss Homemaker!"

"Let me go grab my bagel and we can eat together." I dashed into the kitchen.

"So what do you want to do today?" I asked, returning with my mouth half full. Mona finished chewing.

"On this, my last day with my uterus?" She looked down. "Uterus, what would you like to do today? What's that?" She cocked her head and held her ear as close to her lower abdomen as she could. "Uterus would like to go to Barneys, please."

"Done," I replied. As far as my own uterus went, I had just bought a pregnancy test on my way back from the bagel shop. With trembling hands, I had placed it on the drugstore counter, along with a Twix and a box of Tic Tacs as a hopeful means of distraction. Now it burned a hole in my purse, which I had carefully placed upright in the corner of the living room, as though tilting it would affect the test's eventual accuracy. Mona took a sip of her coffee.

"And oh, I want to go to Jane's and read the paper." Jane's was our favorite coffee shop. Quaint and homey, it smelled of books and cinnamon.

"Okay. I'll bring my laptop. Do some soul searching." *And not think about the pregnancy test.*

"Career-wise, you mean?"

"Yeah."

"How's that coming?"

I shrugged. "I'm making some headway."

"That's terrific! Want to tell me about it?"

"Not yet. Besides, I don't want to bore your uterus on her special day."

"She wouldn't be bored, but I understand. And this is the last I'll speak about it until you're ready to unveil your plan, but I was thinking that you're completely dismissing your own arsenal of talent by jumping out of the marketing game altogether. You were in that business for what, ten years?"

"Great minds think alike."

"Oh yeah?" She smiled broadly. "Cool."

"Did I tell you that I ran into Emily on the street the other day?"

"Emily?"

"The chip chewer?"

"Oh God, her?" Mona made a face. "What did she have to say for herself? Or rather, what did she ask you and then answer herself?"

"She told me that Meghan still hasn't hired anyone to replace me."

"Get out."

"It's true. Weird, right?"

"Not really. I always told you that Meghan liked you more than you thought she did."

"That you did. Maybe I'll e-mail her. Ask her to lunch or something."

"Good idea. You can pick her brain."

"As long as you're okay, though. My nursing duties come first."

"Right. Now, let's get back to my uterus, shall we?" asked Mona. "She says that she would like to buy me an overpriced cashmere cardigan as her parting gift."

I swung my legs like a little kid as I perched on a stool overlooking the Brooklyn street. A Tuesday in Brooklyn, and you would never know it. The percentage of freelancers-cum-writers-cum-sculptors-cum-whatevers in this borough was incredibly high, and they were all loping lackadaisically somewhere, looking more important than they were.

My laptop glowed beside me as I judged everyone who strolled past. Mona was curled up in an armchair toward the back of the shop, reading her paper with a look of utter contentment on her bespectacled face. The longer I stayed in New York, the less I missed it, which was a good thing. A *Been here, done this* feeling overrode most of my experience here now. I pulled my phone out of my purse and texted Josh just that.

I swiveled to face my laptop and checked my e-mail. *Ray!* I immediately panicked, thinking that I had forgotten to pay him.

Hey Sarah,

How's it going in the big city? Miss you on the road here. Done any driving up there? Remember to check those blind spots.

Listen, the promotional ideas you had were awesome. Looks like me and That Pet Place are a match. I'd love more advice. Can you help me, oh marketing guru?

Of course I would pay you for your time. Not New York money, but not Farmwood money either. Just a good rate. Did that make sense? I was trying to be funny, but Vanessa says that whenever I do that I end up being not funny.

Anyway, let me know what you think.

Best,
Ray

I smiled. Sweet Ray. "*Best*."

I took a sip of my now-lukewarm coffee. The timing here was uncanny. Of course I would help Ray. I e-mailed him back, asking for specifics. With each question, my confidence grew. Maybe this consulting thing did have legs.

I would e-mail Meghan about lunch. Worst-case scenario, she'd never respond, and best case, she'd dispense some helpful advice. I painstakingly composed what I hoped was the perfect paragraph. As I was reading it over for the twelfth time, Mona approached.

"You're mouthing the words you're reading," she informed me.

"Well, I'm concentrating really hard. '*Thank you so much for your time, and I look forward to hearing from you, Sincerely,*

Sarah,' " I said aloud as I read over my closing. I nodded to Mona and pressed send. "What's up, Mo?"

"I'm ready to go," she replied. "Part two of Mona day is now complete."

"Two?"

"Yes, part one was that delicious bagel you brought me."

I smiled as I twisted imaginary dimples into my cheeks with my forefingers. "Hey, so does Nate think you're actually in Paris now?" I asked, standing up.

"He thinks I'm leaving tomorrow."

"Ah." I turned my computer off. "Oh wait, so does this mean I have to make myself scarce tonight?"

"Indeed." I pouted. "Please?"

"Of course, no problem. I get it. It's her last hurrah."

"Literally."

"I'll call Kate. Maybe she and Ben will want another date night or something." I zipped my bag, slipped it over my shoulder, and followed Mona out of the shop while dialing my phone.

"Sarah!" yelled Kate. Franklin howled in the background.

"Hey, Kate, how's it going?"

"I'm losing my mind. No, I'm not losing my mind, he's a good baby, but well, yeah, I am losing my mind just a little. How are you? Did Mona have her surgery yet?"

"Tomorrow, actually." I glanced at her walking beside me. Tomorrow a robot was going to remove the majority of her reproductive system and today we were going to

Barneys. Was it okay to be so blasé about all this? Was Mona's joke-cracking just following my lead, or was it her preferred method of dealing with the situation? She stared straight ahead, seemingly unfazed by the fact that Kate and I were obviously talking about her. I continued. "I was wondering if you might be in the mood for a houseguest tonight."

"Oh my God, I would love it. Wait! You know what?" The howling abated. "By the way, I'm breast-feeding as we speak. In public, no less. Is that multitasking or what?"

"The ultimate. What?"

"I want us to go out, just me and you and a giant bottle of wine. Maybe some food, too. What do you think?" *I think I may be pregnant, Kate, so on second thought, let's get burgers and shakes.*

"I'd love to do that," I replied instead.

"Good. I'll tell Ben now."

"Okay. I'll be by in the early evening, all right?"

"Sure, sounds good."

I hung up. "Mission accomplished."

"Thanks, Sarah. I know it's been a pain in the ass for you to schlep your stuff around like a nomad."

"It hasn't been so bad, really. I swear. It's been nice to get to know Kate outside of Josh." We scampered halfway down the subway stairs together before Mona stopped abruptly.

"Fuck this. My uterus wants to take a cab into the city," she declared.

"Are you serious? That's, like, what rich people do."

"Well, anywhere but New York I'd probably be almost rich. We're doing it." She trotted back up the stairs.

"No arguments here."

In the cab, Mona continued the conversation. "So Kate is cool?"

"She is. I like her. Motherhood has made her more human, somehow." As soon as the words were out of my mouth, I wanted to gather them like Easter eggs and stuff them back inside. "I'm sorry."

"What, because you mentioned motherhood? Sarah, we can't tiptoe around the concept for the rest of our lives."

"I know, but it seems awfully insensitive to bring it up now."

Mona looked out her window as she spoke. "Well, it sucks, you know? No arguments here. But it's not the end of the world, and all things considered, I'm pretty lucky." She turned around to face me. "Even if I don't feel so lucky. Sometimes I think if I say it enough times, I will actually feel that way."

"Mona, is it okay that we're joking around so much about all of this? This whole uterus-day thing? The last thing I want to do is undermine the gravity of what's happening here."

"No, Sarah, it's good. It's good to have you here and be joking around. It's exactly what I need, I promise. It might not be what other people in my position would want, but it's definitely what I want."

"Okay."

"And the motherhood thing. You have to be okay with saying that word in front of me, you know? Because you're going to have kids, and—" She paused. "Wait, why are you making that face?"

"What face?"

"That face you make when you're uncomfortable."

"And what face is that?" I could see the red awnings of Barneys in the near distance. I had only been to this store twice in my life, both times with Mona.

"Your constipated face."

"Well, I happen to be constipated, so that's not a surprise."

"No, you did. You made the face."

"Near or far corner?" asked the cabbie from the front seat.

"Far," answered Mona. "Sarah, what's the story?" She swiped her card through the credit card machine on the seat back and we got out.

"Really, Mona, is this something you want to talk about now?"

"Shut up. You're pregnant?" I didn't reply. "Sarah! Holy shit!"

"I don't know, Mona! I mean, I'm not sure. I may be, but I'm not sure."

"Oh my God." Behind her smile I could see her sadness, like thunderclouds in the distance on a summer afternoon.

"Mona, my timing here is terrible. Let's not talk about it until there's even something to talk about. If there's even anything to talk about. Forget I said anything."

"Yeah, right! Hello, are you nuts?" shrieked Mona as I held the door to Barneys open for her. The sweet perfume of wealth—sun-toasted cashmere, champagne, and tuberose—poured out into the street.

"I agree that your timing is shit, but it's not like you have anything to apologize for, Sarah. You're thirty-six years old and married. If you weren't trying to get pregnant, you would be, like, one in a zillion. How late are you?"

"Five days," I whispered as we made our way to the escalator.

"Five days!" She hopped on in front of me and I followed. I looked up at her guiltily. "And you haven't taken a test yet? Hasn't the suspense been killing you?"

"Not really. I'm just ambivalent about the whole thing, really. Or maybe just scared. At least I thought I was until it became a very real possibility that I might be."

"So now that you may very well be pregnant, you're more into the idea?" We disembarked and she led the way to a rack of sleek black.

"Yeah. At least I think so. Also, hanging with Franklin has sort of tipped the scale a bit. He's a cool kid."

"Well, that's an interesting development. And very good news if indeed you are with child." She held what looked like a pair of opaque panty hose on a hanger against her chest.

"What is that?" I asked.

"A shirt."

"Seems a little insubstantial, no?"

"Sarah, that's the look."

"Fine, whatever." I approached a black-and-white-patterned dress and sighed in appreciation. "Mona, this conversation is making me very uncomfortable. I hate talking to you about this when you're in the position you're in."

"Why, because I don't have the choice to be indifferent about kids?"

"Yes." I rubbed a pair of black leather pants with my thumb and forefinger.

"Well, obviously I think you're nuts not to want to have kids."

I opened my mouth to protest. "Sorry, not to not want to have kids, but to be ambivalent about the whole idea. Pretty soon, if this time turns out to be a false alarm, you're going to have to shit or get off the pot, as my grandmother used to say."

"What a lovely euphemism."

"Isn't it though? Hold this." She handed me her jacket and purse and slipped into the cardigan equivalent of a cloud. "Your age is a nonnegotiable, you know."

"I know." I watched her watch herself in the mirror. She tilted her head and squinted. "That's really pretty on you, Mo."

"It is, right? I feel like this is what a convalescing actress would wear in a movie. Penélope Cruz, maybe."

"Totally. You look sort of like her, you know," I said, knowing full well that she did.

"Do I?" Her eyes danced. "Okay, I don't care what this costs, I'm buying it."

"I'm only thirty-six, by the way. I don't know why everyone has to dangle the stopwatch every time the word 'kid' comes up," I said. I took the cardigan from her and handed her back her things.

"Because, Sarah, it could take some time. You could feasibly be thirty-eight or older by the time your delivery date rolled around." She made her way toward the register. "And now my uterus is getting depressed, talking about your uterus on her day."

"No problem. I'm happy to not talk about it anymore."

"Oh no, now we have to talk about it! What does Josh think?" She handed the sweater and her credit card to the impossibly put-together salesperson and looked at me closely.

"I haven't told him."

"What!" She retrieved her card without missing a beat and slipped it back into her wallet. "Why not?"

"You know me, I don't like a big fuss before I've got a handle on things."

"But, Sarah, this is more than just a thing, wouldn't you say?"

"Yeah, but still. I just want to be sure first. If I'm not, I'll tell him after the fact when I'm home."

"And if you are?"

"Then I guess shit will hit the fan."

"So when are you going to take a test already?"

"I have one in my purse," I confessed.

"You're just carrying it around with you like a lip gloss or something?"

"Yeah."

"For God's sake, let's take it already! What are you waiting for?"

"But maybe it's too early?"

"Who cares? And it's not too early, anyway. Let's go." She marched toward the elevators.

"Here?"

"There's a bathroom in the basement that nobody uses."

"How do you know that?" I asked, following her.

"Sometimes I get a nervous stomach here after I spend too much money on something. Move it or lose it."

Do I just leave it here? On the back of the commode?" I asked from inside the stall. "The directions say that you're supposed to leave it alone while it works."

"Yes. Leave it there. We'll wait in the lounge," Mona replied through the door.

"But what if someone comes in this one?"

"We'll tell them not to. They can't actually enter the bathroom without going past us first."

"Right." I flushed and left, refusing to look at the test until the maximum seven minutes were up.

"God, I'm so nervous," I said through chattering teeth as I washed my hands. "This reminds me of my first driving lesson. My t-t-t-teeth. They ch-ch-chattered like this. So weird."

"Of course you're nervous." Mona took my arm and led me toward the couches in the lounge.

"Wait, do you mind if we sit right here?" I asked. "I know it's not the most sanitary thing, but I'm nervous to leave the test."

"You're kidding."

I shook my head.

"Fine. How dirty could it be? It's Barneys." We sat down and pressed our backs against the wall. "I hope no one I know comes in here," said Mona. "This would be a hard one to explain."

"Mona, you're amazing. I can't believe you're being so supportive with all that you're going through."

"I'm glad you told me. What were you going to do, wait until the baby came and be like, 'Oh, by the way, I had a baby'?" She shook her head. "I'm scared about tomorrow, Sarah," she added.

"I know." I snuggled closer to her.

"What if I come out and I don't feel like me anymore? What if all of this"—she glanced down at her abdomen—"is responsible for all of my Mona-isms?"

"I don't think that's biologically possible, Mo, but I certainly understand the worry."

"Why? Why isn't it possible? Hormones and estrogen are all I am on most days."

"Fair enough, but you'll still have your ovaries, right? Those regulate all of that stuff as far as I know."

"Yes, that's true. But still. Who knows?"

"Right."

"What's it called when someone loses a limb, but they can still feel it as though it's there?"

"Phantom limb?"

"Phantom uterus syndrome. PUS for short. What if I develop that? How apropos."

"But a limb is more obviously utilized, you know? When do you think about your uterus? Are you saying that you'll have phantom periods?" I asked.

"God, I hope not." She smiled slightly.

"Whatever you need, I'm here for you, Mona. There's nothing you can't ask me for."

"Okay."

"Is it strange to not have Nate know about any of this? Wouldn't it be nice to have his arms to fall into afterward?"

"Not really. Well, maybe. It's too complicated, though. If we were farther along in our relationship, sure. But we're not, so . . . Anyway, look at you, Little Miss Hypocrite! Your husband doesn't even know that you might be pregnant."

"Fair enough." I looked at my watch. "Mona, it's time."

Just then, a woman walked into the restroom, doing a double take as she noticed us camped out on the floor like tweens in line for Justin Bieber tickets. I stood up quickly and pulled Mona to her feet.

"Okay, I'm g-g-going in," I announced.

"Okay," Mona said. "Go on. Now or never."

I nodded and pushed the door open, my heart beating wildly. I closed and locked it before turning around to face the most powerful piece of plastic ever created.

I couldn't figure out exactly what I wanted it to tell me. "Not pregnant" would be both a relief and a letdown somehow, as though all of this worry and stress was for naught. "Pregnant" was an entirely different scenario altogether—the emotional dimensions of which I couldn't really imagine. Classical music wafted through the bathroom's speakers as I willed my feet to move.

Pregnant. I put my hand over my mouth, too shocked by the verdict to even pick it up. Without warning, tears streamed from my eyes. I was beyond overwhelmed with joy and fright, disbelief and wonder.

"Sarah?" whispered Mona on the other side of the parallel universe that this stall had become. A universe in which I was grown-up enough to be pregnant and excited about it. How could it be that I was delivering this news to someone who was about to lose her chance at ever seeing this word staring up at her? The scenario seemed so cruel, and yet, there was nothing that could be done. I opened the door slowly and Mona peered in, her face a mask of concern.

"What is it, Sar?" I held out the test, and she looked down, grabbing my forearm as she did so. "Oh my God," she whispered, her own tears beginning to fall. "Congratulations." We embraced fiercely, both sobbing.

"I'm so happy for you," Mona said through her tears.

"Mo, you don't have to be, it's okay," I sobbed back. "It's okay. I understand."

"Okay, okay. I'm not so happy." She pulled back and we regarded each other, her eyes puffy and mascara smudged. "It's not fair."

"It's not," I replied. "I hate that this is happening now."

"I know." She sniffled loudly. "Me too. But you'll be a good mom, Sar."

"I hope so. And so will you, Mo. I know you hate hearing the word 'adoption' right now, but I want you to pursue it when the time is right." She nodded halfheartedly. As we embraced again, the woman emerged from her stall apologetically and washed her hands at lightning speed, opting to dry her hands on her pants in an attempt to exit as quickly as possible.

"I forgot about her." I laughed.

"Man, does she have a story to tell at lunch." She wiped her eyes. "Speaking of, let's celebrate with a decadent lunch. My uterus is a little crestfallen about having to share her day, but some French fries should help."

"You got it." I held the test up. "What do I do with this?"

"Put it back in your purse."

"But it's covered in pee." I made a face.

"Sarah, God willing, in nine months' time, everything you own will be covered in pee. And poop, for that matter. Think of it as a head start on the inevitable."

I placed it in my bag's inside zipper compartment gingerly and washed my hands as Mona attempted to refresh her rumpled face.

"Life is crazy," she mumbled, wiping under her eyes with a Kleenex.

"No shit," I agreed.

Free at last, free at last!" sang Kate as we exited her building. She skipped a few steps in front of me. "This elation will last approximately two and a half minutes, and then I will plunge into a deep well of guilt and loneliness," she then informed me.

"About Franklin?"

"Yes, little man Franklin. The love of my life. That said, it does feel good to be out on my own again, without worrying about feeding or soothing anyone but myself."

I listened to her Mommy woes with considerably elevated interest. I hadn't told a soul but Mona about my newest development, although I had left a message for Josh to call me back. Not a "Call me back, I have news" message, but just a regular one.

"Do you even feel like you anymore? Or is it this new version of you?"

"You mean Mom me?" She stopped in her tracks. "Mom Me. M-O-M capital-M-E. I need to write that down. Hold on a sec." She tapped it into her phone. "Okay, genius moment captured. Anyway, where were we?"

"Do you feel like you anymore?"

"I have these very small moments, you know? Like when

I'm putting on makeup—which happens never, by the way, but I did tonight—my mind drifts and it's just me again, thinking about the benefits of mascara or whether or not I've shaved recently. You know?" I nodded. "And in those moments I suppose it feels like the old me. But so much of my brain is consumed by Franklin now, it's just—well, I guess there is a distinct divide between old me and mom me. Not that I mind. I mean, mascara and shaving are topics I am happy to shelve. My work though, that's something I still have to figure out. Hey, you want to eat here? I love this place."

She stopped in front of Ralph's, which specialized in small plates of appetizer fare, carafes of fairly priced wine and excellent lighting. How I was going to opt out of wine consumption inconspicuously was a mystery to me, but I would give it my best shot.

"Sounds good to me." We walked in, gave our name to the Winona Ryder–lookalike hostess, and settled ourselves at the bar.

"*Salut*," I said, and lifted my glass to toast Kate. "I say that when I want to feel cool."

"Do you feel cool tonight?" She clinked my glass and took a sip. I pretended to as well.

"I think I do, actually." I surveyed the room and found myself feeling not at all homesick for the scene that was Brooklyn. That was the second time today. "So, Kate, what did you mean about figuring out your work?"

"Oh, with Franklin, you mean?" I nodded. "Every time I try to sit down and focus on it, my mind drifts. It's almost like I am physically incapable of it. It's worrying, to say the least."

"Yes, but you're what, not even two months into motherhood? Come on. Time will make it easier."

"I hope so, Sarah. Because from around month four of pregnancy until now I have been coasting on God knows what in the business department. It's a miracle my company is still afloat. I think my partner has just about had it with me."

This did not bode well for me. At least Kate had a career at the moment of Franklin's conception. If I wanted to make this marketing-consultant thing work, I had to get started immediately, before I had even less energy to care.

"Does she have any kids?"

"Yes, but they're older. Eight and twelve. Different ball game."

"Well, at least she's sympathetic."

"You would think, but it's almost as though she's forgotten what the reality of having an infant entails. I've heard that all women function that way. We all forget, apparently. It's the only way to maybe want to do it again."

"Have you forgotten your labor yet?"

"Not one millisecond." She emptied the remains of the carafe into her glass. "Not one."

"And would you do it again?"

"Yeah, as crazy as that sounds. Did I tell you about my labor?"

"You hinted at some stuff, but you didn't really go into detail."

"I didn't?" She looked surprised. "That is very unlike me."

I laughed. "Tell me about it."

"Do you want to know?"

"Do I have a choice?"

"No, not really. I feel like it's my duty to share this knowledge, because not one woman could even come close to describing the experience to me when I was curious, and it really pissed me off. Seriously, not one woman!"

"Maybe they all blocked it out."

"Bullshit. It's more like this secret-society crap. But I am not an elitist, and I think everyone should know what it feels like." She lowered her voice, grabbed both of my hands and stared me directly in the eyes. "You ready?"

"Jesus, Kate, should I check the telephone poles outside for a flock of perched black crows? This feels very ominous."

"Labor feels like a Mack truck pushing a piano out of your asshole," she said, careful to enunciate each word. I recrossed my legs under the bar. "And not just in one fell swoop, either. The truck, like, backs up and charges forward again, over and over." She nodded and drained the rest of her glass.

"Your asshole?" I whispered.

"Yes. Your asshole. And you know what else no one told me about?" Winona approached and let us know our table was ready.

"I think I may be okay not knowing," I answered as we gathered our things. We followed the hostess through a maze of tables. Kate hung her purse on the back of her chair and sat down unsteadily, rocking the chair dangerously to the left as she did so.

"Okay, I'm drunk."

"You don't say." I poured her some water.

"But I need to tell you something about the postpartum sexual experience and then I'm done."

I raised an eyebrow. "Promise?"

"Promise. Okay. Here goes." She took a deep breath. "So, Ben and I finally had sex the other night. Our first time since Franklin was born." The waiter delivered a basket of warm bread and I greedily plunged my hand inside of it as Kate ordered the charcuterie plate to start.

"So, my vagina," she continued, not missing a beat as he walked away. "I had a vaginal birth, which is all well and good, and I wouldn't change it for anything, believe me. But." Her eyes widened. "My vagina is just not the same."

"Well of course it's not, Kate! Give the ole girl a break."

"Now, when I have an orgasm"—she lowered her voice to an almost undetectable decibel level so that I was forced to lean across the table to hear her—"it sounds like my vagina is eating fried chicken."

"What?" Water shot out of my nose and I covered it with my napkin.

She nodded somberly. "I'm not exaggerating. Not even a little."

I threw my head back and laughed uproariously as she cracked a small smile. "Are you serious?" I wheezed. "Fried chicken?"

"Start doing your Kegels now is all I'm saying. Now, pass that bread basket over here, I am fucking starving."

"I don't think I'll be ordering the chicken tonight," I said as she bit into her slice.

"Seriously. Man, that feels good to get off of my chest. I've been dying to tell someone about it."

"Could Ben hear it? Did he say anything?"

"Are you kidding? He was so grateful to be having sex that a humpback whale could have swum out of there and he wouldn't have said a word. Anyway, let's change the subject, shall we?" She paused to chew. "How's Mona?"

"Her attitude is incredible."

"Is it?"

"Yeah, she's fully faced the reality of her situation, she's admitted to being pissed off about its unfairness, and at the same time she's trying her best to be mindful of her luck."

"What luck?"

"They caught it early, and she doesn't have to endure chemo or radiation. To her, that's lucky."

"Wait, what about this boyfriend who's totally in the dark? That doesn't sound like facing the reality of her situation to me."

"True." The waiter deposited our platter of cheese and meat on the table and Kate clapped her hands appreciatively. "That's the only glitch."

"It's a pretty big glitch," said Kate as she wrapped a piece of prosciutto around a hunk of Gruyère. "Although I can understand her position."

"You can? I think she's nuts. He really cares about her."

"I'm sure he does, but does he care enough about her to handle not only her cancer but a hysterectomy to boot? That's pretty heavy for a new relationship if you ask me."

"Right, but what's heavier is lying and telling him that you're going to Paris. That's a relationship ender in my book. *'Oh, how was Paris, Mona?' 'How was where?'* You know?"

"Wait, she told him she's off to Paris instead of telling him the truth?" asked Kate.

"Yeah, for work. It's her way of explaining being gone for two weeks."

"Wow. That's pretty creative. He buys it?"

"Yeah, I guess so. You know, I wasn't a huge fan of his at first, but he's grown on me. And I know for a fact that he's crazy about her. I think he would really be there for her if he knew. She deserves that kind of support."

"Well, what can you do? You can't force her to tell him. Maybe it will all just work itself out on its own."

"How often does that happen?" I asked.

"Less often the older we get, it seems."

"Exactly." My phone vibrated in my pocket. Josh. "Hey, Kate, do you mind if I step out for a second? It's Josh."

She waved me away. "Of course not, go on. I'll just finish this platter." She smiled devilishly, her lips purple from the wine.

"Hey," I answered, moving as quickly as I could through the mass of hipsters in tiny peacoats and oversize glasses crowding the bar.

"Hi. Sorry it took me so long to call you back. Hectic day. How are you?"

"Good, good." Out in the fresh air at last, I shivered. I had left my own jacket inside.

"You with Mona?"

"No, actually. She's with Nate tonight. I'm having dinner with Kate."

"Just the two of you?"

"Yeah. She was desperate for a little girls' time."

"Nice! Good for you guys. How's she doing? Ben says she's—"

"Josh."

"Yeah?"

"Josh, I'm pregnant," I whispered, my heart racing.

"Wait, what?" His voice cracked. "Did you just say what I think you said?"

"Yeah." My eyes welled for what felt like the thousandth time that day.

"Oh my God, Sarah! Wha— Are you sure? Of course you're sure, what am I talking about? Sarah! We're having a baby?"

"Looks like it." My smile was so wide that my face hurt.

"How do you feel about it? Are you okay?"

"I'm surprisingly happy. Happy and terrified, but not one bit remorseful."

"Sarah, I am overjoyed. I really am. God, I can't believe we're not together to celebrate this!"

"I know, it's ridiculous."

"Do you feel okay? Are you taking care of yourself? Are you getting enough rest?" His questions came at me rapid-fire.

"Yes, I'm fine." I laughed. "Not even that nauseous, really. Just stunned."

"Have you told anyone?"

"Mona."

"Oh God, that must have been hard."

"It was. I'll call you later, Josh. I should get back to Kate."

"Does she know?"

"No, no idea. I'd like to keep it to ourselves for a little bit, if that's okay with you."

"Sure, whatever you want, Sarah. I love you so much. I know you weren't exactly prepared for this, but I think you're gonna be great at it."

"I love you, too. And thanks. I think you're going to be a wonderful dad."

"Dad!" He laughed. "Oh wow."

"Bye."

As I pushed back through the crowd to my table, I placed my hand over the lower part of my stomach, no longer protecting just myself, but us.

16

I crept out of Kate and Ben's apartment in the morning, careful not to wake them. Brooklyn was quiet save for the click-clack of early-bird work heels, the soft thuds of runners' feet, and the garbage trucks rumbling by like disgruntled rhinoceroses.

Mona and I had not even discussed the possibility of something going wrong with her operation. I knew the odds of that happening were slim, of course, but what if? What if they found more cancer? I willed myself out of that negative spiral and vowed to only focus on Mona's wellness.

On the train, I sat down and closed my eyes, visualizing a smiling, cancer-free Mona floating in a swimming pool come summer. *But wait, Mona really isn't a fan of getting her hair wet. How about the roof of the MoMA sipping wine? Okay, much better. What about a demure Mona hand in hand with Nate in Prospect Park? Nice, although will Nate still be around, all things considered? For my purposes I'll assume that he will be.*

At her stop, I climbed the subway stairs to the street. I shivered slightly, thinking of how much I missed the curl of Josh's body around mine, even the way he would get heavier and heavier as he fell asleep, until at last, feeling like a giant boulder had collapsed on top of me, I shoved him—sometimes gently and sometimes not—off.

I buzzed Mona's apartment and took a deep breath. Would she be pretending that everything was the same as always, that this wasn't the day they were going to remove much of her insides, or would she be facing it head-on? I had no way of knowing, but whatever mood she was in, I would match it.

She buzzed me in and I ascended the stairs slowly. Her door was ajar, and I pushed it open tentatively to find her suitcase splayed open the way, well, the way I imagined she would be in about six hours.

"Do you think I need more than one pair of pajama pants?" she asked, walking out of the bedroom and holding up two to show me.

"How long will you be there?"

"They say I should be in and out in twenty-four hours."

"One is probably fine then. And something to go home in." She draped one pair over the couch and folded the other with careful precision. "And won't you be in one of those hospital gowns for most of your visit anyway?"

"You're right. I hope not, though. What about shoes? Do you think I need to bring another pair?"

"Other than the ones you're wearing?" I glanced down at her black flats. Like everything she owned, they looked expensive. Not garishly expensive, but the kind of expensive that good taste and a well-paying job afforded. "Those are nice, by the way."

"Thanks. I got them on sale."

"Remember that time you let me borrow your Prada loafers?" I asked, smiling.

"Oh my God, I had forgotten about that. I came out of the bathroom and you were wearing them with white ankle socks!" She shook her head, laughing. "The horror!"

"You almost had a heart attack," I said.

"Who wouldn't? People should go to jail for that sort of fashion offense."

"I was worried about blisters! Anyway, I'm better now. No socks with flats."

"I'm so proud. And to answer your question, yes, these are comfortable. I don't need another pair. I'll just bring these."

"Hey, Mona, you haven't stopped moving since I arrived. You okay?"

"I'm scared, Sarah. What can I say?"

"You don't have to say anything," I replied softly. "Just let me know how I can help you." I walked over and hugged her, and she rigidly returned my embrace. "Everything is going to be okay."

"Is it?" she asked. "Will you make some coffee? Oh wait, I keep forgetting that I can't eat or drink anything."

"You can't? Will you hate me if I have some?"

"Can you?"

"What do you mean?"

"Can pregnant ladies drink caffeine? I think that's a no-no."

"You're kidding." No soft cheese, no raw sushi, no wine, and now no coffee? I slumped against the wall dejectedly.

"I guess it depends on your doctor?"

"Well, I'll just make a weak cup, then. Wait, should I? Never mind. Forget it. What time did Nate leave?" I asked.

"Around two this morning, I guess. He didn't want to, but I insisted. I just needed some time alone to process what's happening today."

"Instead of pretend to be excited about Paris, you mean?"

"Exactly. I don't know if I'll ever be able to think about Paris the same way. It will always be a code word for 'hysterectomy' now."

"We should use the word 'Paris' as a stand-in for everything shitty we have to endure from here on out," I suggested.

"Like what?"

"I don't know. Idiot bosses, for example. Instead of saying your boss was riding you about something insignificant, you could say that she was sending you to Paris."

"I like that. Or when you go away for a weekend, have a great time, and somehow manage to gain three pounds, you could say that the doughnuts you inhaled gave you the Paris."

"Or when your man is irritating the crap out of you, you can say that you're sending his ass to Paris."

"I'm sending this doctor to Paris if he screws up."

"With a six-hour layover in Frankfurt."

"Okay, I think I'm all packed," Mona announced.

"Let's sit down then. Take a load off." I made myself comfortable on the couch while Mona perched on the edge of it nervously.

"What time do you think we should leave?" she asked, fidgeting with her waistband.

"You have to be there at eleven?"

She nodded.

"We're taking a cab?"

"Well, I thought about driving, but since I probably won't be able to drive back, I decided against it." Mona had inherited her mother's 1984 BMW. She used it for menial tasks like going to the grocery store or traveling upstate whenever she had an itch for greenery. She called it Gus.

"I can drive Gus!" I shrieked, my heart immediately racing at the thought. "I can drive now, thank you very much."

"Virginia back roads are one thing, Sarah, but New York City is quite another. Let's be real about this."

"Mona, I can drive, damn it. Whatever you need, I can do. I have Ray on speed dial in case I need any guidance."

"Sarah, that's very sweet of you. I'll take you up on it next time. For now though, let's just take a cab."

Thank you, Jesus, I uttered in my head to the rug. Why I had railed so passionately in my own driving defense I had no idea. What would I have done if she had accepted my offer? "Okay, if you're sure."

"So let's leave at ten, just to be safe," said Mona, settling back against the cushion at last. "We'll leave at ten," she repeated.

"Sounds like a plan," I replied uselessly.

"Have you started on Ray's campaign yet?" she asked.

"Yes. Well, no. I haven't yet."

"Sarah! Come on! This is a great starting point for you." She scowled at me.

"I know, Mona! Geez. I'm planning on working on it while you're in surgery."

"Okay, good." She looked at her watch. "Shit, it's nine forty-five. How did that happen? Maybe we should leave now, just to be safe."

She looked at me with an expression of panic on her face. As she got up, I closed my eyes and uttered a silent prayer. *Please, God, let this operation go smoothly*. It wasn't much, but it was all I had as insurance. I turned to Mona, who was rummaging through her wallet.

"You ready?" I asked, trying my best to sound calm.

"I guess so," she whispered. "I wanted to be all tough today, but it doesn't look like that's going to happen."

"Who do you need to be tough for?" I asked.

"You."

"Me? Are you kidding? I'm the biggest wimp on the planet. I practically crapped my pants a moment ago just thinking about driving a car."

"Maybe I wanted to be tough for me," she said, reconsidering.

"Mona, you are the strongest person I know, hands down, no contest."

"I am?"

"The way you've handled this—the way you handle everything—you are incredible. To be nervous about this operation does not make you weak. If anything, it makes you stronger."

"How's that?" She closed her wallet and pulled her shirt hem down over her waistband.

"Embracing vulnerability is strength, I think. Not feeling like you have to apologize for it is strength."

She reached down to help me up from the couch. "I like that," she said. "Thanks."

The waiting room smelled like pepperoni. I crossed my legs and my foot shook against my will. A teacher had reprimanded me loudly once in middle school, in front of the entire class, for my endlessly vibrating appendage, and the embarrassment stayed with me still. I stood up to stop myself, and the man sprawled out on the couch across from me opened one eye in annoyance. Fidgeting was not encouraged here either, apparently.

I glanced at my watch. The doctor had told us that Mona's laparoscopic hysterectomy should take about forty minutes, which blew my mind. You could get a manicure and pedicure in forty minutes, commute to work in midtown in forty minutes, wait in line for brunch on a weekend in Manhattan for just forty minutes if you were lucky. It seemed like an impossibly short amount of time to enter someone through an incision the size of a keyhole, scoop out some vital organs, and close her again. Impossibly short in that context, but impossibly long for the person waiting on the other side.

I ambled over to the wall directory, curious where the nursery was. I'd never seen one in real life, only on television. All of those freshly scrubbed pink babies wrapped in their blanket burritos with those tiny paper bracelets circling their wrists. It was on the third floor. On second thought, it seemed unfair to Mona, to go look at babies while she was having her chance to have one removed. I would stay put.

My phone vibrated in my pocket. It was a number that I recognized, but I couldn't remember from where.

"Hello?" I asked tentatively.

"Sarah?"

Oh, that voice. That unmistakable, nicotine-edged, blunt voice. The kind of voice that would ask you if that was what you were wearing when you had already commuted in to work and were tucking into breakfast at your desk. It was Meghan.

"Oh, hi! Meghan, how are you?" I began to perspire despite the fact that the hospital's temperature rivaled that of a meat locker.

"Oh God, this Petals launch is officially dead in the water. Five years of blood, sweat, and tears and sayonara. Utter bullshit."

Petals was a tween makeup line that the company had been trying to launch for what felt like forever. Every time we had been ready to unveil our plan, either the celebrity spokesgirl ended up in rehab or a focus group of twelve-year-olds ripped our packaging ideas to shreds with their tiny manicured nails. It had been the bane of my existence while I worked there.

"Good riddance, I say." I walked outside into the fresh air. The smell of pastries from a nearby coffee cart tickled my nostrils. My eyes lit up as I realized that I could have one, minus the guilt. Point one for pregnancy.

"I suppose. Although, at the moment we're focusing on men's makeup. Kill me now."

"Men's makeup?"

"Oh yes, it's all the rage, didn't you know? The bastards lose weight at ten times our speed, look better as they age, and now can pat a little concealer onto their under-eye circles to salt the wound even further."

"What on earth are you calling the line?"

"Not a clue."

"What about Bastard Balm? For the lip balm, at least. Assuming there is one."

"That's actually not bad." A pen scribbled furiously in the background. "Listen, I got your e-mail. Of course we can grab lunch. What's your week like?"

"This week is out, but next week works. Are you free on Tuesday?" I heard the *tap-tap-tap* of her keyboard.

"It's a miracle, I'm free. How about one o'clock at that sushi place around the corner?"

"Around the block from work?"

"Yes, that's the one. Sushi Den. See you then."

"Okay, see you then. And, Meghan, thanks a lot, I really appreciate it."

"As long as you aren't begging for your job back. You aren't, are you? I'm just about to hire someone remotely acceptable and can't deal with any more setbacks on that front. You should have seen the candidates I had to interview. One woman came in with her thong hanging out of her pants, for chrissake. It was all I could do not to kick her out of my office. Anyway, I have to run. See you next week."

"See—"

Click.

Mona looked so fragile in her hospital bed, as though her vigor had been surgically removed as well. Her arms, once brown and strong, now appeared almost twiglike to me, and gray, like the bark of a birch tree. Her hair had not lost its luster, however. It spread across the pillow like a sea of dark chocolate. She blinked against the glare of the fluorescent lights.

"Hi," I said quietly.

"Hey," she replied hoarsely.

"Want some water?" I stood up too quickly, and my asleep foot shot pins and needles of pain up my leg.

"Yes, please."

"Okay, no problem, you got it." I dragged my foot with me to the small kitchen that I was already a frequenter of. I didn't even like Gatorade, but there were three bottles of it in my bag. If it was free and not nailed down, I was taking it. I filled her glass with ice and shook my foot in an attempt to speed up its recovery.

"Here you go," I announced breathlessly as I handed her the cup. She turned her head and smiled at me.

"Sarah, take it easy. I'm not going anywhere."

I sat on the bed. "Can I sit here?"

"Sure, why not?"

"I'm a spaz. Forgive me. I'm the world's worst nurse."

"You're not my nurse, you're my friend. And you're an excellent friend."

"No, you are."

"No, you." Mona's laugh morphed into a cough.

"You okay?" I asked, panicking.

"Yeah." She finished coughing. "The doctor told me that everything went really well. I'm just a bit hoarse I guess, from the breathing tube." She sighed and held the cup on her lap. "I'm sad," she confessed.

"I'm sure," I answered, since I had nothing else to say. "Is there anything I can do to make you feel better?"

"No." She sat quietly and I began to get up to comfort her. She waved me away. "No, no, please. No hugs or anything right now. I just need to be sad."

"Do you want me to get lost?" I asked. "I can wander the halls, no problem."

"No, I want you here. Just don't speak or anything for a while, okay?"

"Okay."

"You know, before this, I kept trying to imagine what it would feel like after it was done. Would I feel differently with so much of me gone? Would I be relieved that it was over? Would I look different?" She rubbed her eyes. "Remember the first time you had sex, and afterward you just laid there, wondering if other people would be able to tell just by looking at you that you were someone that had sex?" She looked at me and I nodded. "I remember my first postcoital moment in the mirror so clearly. I was literally examining my face, as though the words 'just had sex' might be etched into it somewhere. Of course I looked exactly the same, but to me, I didn't. I looked older. Wiser. At any rate, that's the way I feel now. Like I must look different now that so much of me is gone."

"Want a mirror?" I asked.

"You have one?"

"Sure, a compact."

"When was the last time you wore the sort of makeup that required a compact, Sarah?"

"That's beside the point. I carry it for emergencies. You never know in this day and age of reality television when a camera crew might appear on the scene."

I dug into my bag and reached my arm across the blue blanket to hand it to her. She opened it tentatively, as though she was afraid it might explode.

As she lifted it to her face, I found myself holding my breath. Of course she looked exactly the same, but fact and fiction were often impossible to separate in times of emotional strain. She tilted her face to the left, and the right, and then lifted her chin up and moved it back down before snapping the compact shut.

"Well, I look the same," she declared. "For better or worse. Definitely tired, though."

"You always look tired," I said, teasing.

"Thanks a lot. Who are you, my mom?" She stuck her tongue out at me. "Sarah, I'm never having kids. It's official."

"But you know what else you're not having?" I said.

"What?"

"Cancer."

"God, I hope you're right. I really hope you're right."

"Okay, honey, time for me to check your vitals," announced a nurse, wheeling a cart in behind her.

"Want me to pick you up some dinner from the outside?" I asked as she wrapped a blood pressure cuff around Mona's arm. "Hillstone?"

"You would do that?" Mona beamed. "For me?" I gave

her a thumbs-up and grabbed my jacket. On the street, I headed south as I dialed Josh.

"Sarah," he answered. His voice sounded like home.

"Josh. I miss you."

"I miss you, too. How's Mona?"

"The operation went well, but she's very sad."

"The doctor says everything looks good? The cancer is out?"

"Yeah."

"That's the most important part."

"You're right, it is. I think the reality of her situation has just really hit her now, though."

"The not-able-to-have-kids part, you mean?" he asked.

"Yeah. The timing of our situation and hers, it's just crazy. I feel terrible about it."

"Tell me about it. What's it like, both of you knowing that you're pregnant while she can never be?"

"She's been incredibly supportive, but I'm sure it's hard. I'm trying to keep a low profile."

"You feeling okay? Nauseous or anything? Should I come up there, Sar?"

"Oh God, no! I'll be home soon enough."

"Okay. You sure?"

"I'm sure."

"How's New York treating you, anyway? Are you still feeling over it, or has she got you in her claws again?"

"No, I'm still of the same mind. I can't imagine having a

baby here." A woman with half of her head shaved wearing a very expensive suit and stiletto heels emerged from a cab in front of me. "I mean, some things I'll always miss. Sophistication, for one."

"Sure, that's a given. The best-looking, most sophisticated people in the country are in New York."

"They really are." I entered the restaurant and approached the hostess.

"But think about it this way. In New York, we were invisible, but in Farmwood, we're at the head of the sophistication-and-attractiveness class. Right?"

"Speak for yourself! I am not invisible here. Hold on a second." I placed my order and then took a seat at the bar between two balding fraternity guys dressed in identical black suits and blue button-downs, their shined black loafers reflecting the overhead light like mirrors. "Okay, I'm back."

"No, of course you're not invisible. My point is that the bigger fish/smaller pond scenario has its advantages."

"Right. Hold on again." I motioned to the bartender. "Could I have a seltzer, please? Thanks."

"A seltzer!" exclaimed Josh. "Never thought I'd see the day when my wife ordered a seltzer from the bar."

"The day has come." We sat in silence for a moment as I took a sip.

"I should get going, Sar. I have about a million tests to grade. Please give Mona a hug from me and tell her I'm thinking about her."

"I will."

"And you—take it slow."

"Roger that, doc."

After the hostess brought me my food, I settled my tab and walked out into the chilly air. Here, my feet knew where to go. I could close my eyes and find my way back to the hospital easily if I wanted to.

Would I ever feel like my internal compass was hardwired accordingly in Farmwood? Could I actually get behind the wheel and know where I was going?

In the distance, the hospital loomed in front of me like a giant honeycomb. I quickened my pace, eager to serve my injured queen.

Morning, sunshine," I announced groggily as I pulled back the curtain to greet Mona. She was sitting up, her mouth set in a determined line.

"Oh, Sarah, don't tell me that you spent the night here."

"Okay, I won't tell you that I spent the night in the pepperoni-infused waiting room." I collapsed onto the foot of her bed.

"There was really no need, my dear. I'm fine." She smiled unconvincingly.

"Yeah, but the idea of taking the bus to the subway and then going all the way back to Brooklyn just to wake up at dawn and do it again seemed like a miserable one, anyway. What's one night?"

My explanation was partially true. Yes, the one-two punch of bus and subway transport had been a bear to consider at ten P.M. on a Wednesday night, but the real truth was that I was scared for Mona.

She had cried throughout dinner and when pressed, refused to talk about anything. She'd ask me to go, told me that she just wanted to be alone, really and truly, and so I had made myself relatively comfortable two hundred feet away.

"Did the doctor give you the green light?" I asked, shuddering as I caught a whiff of my own breath.

"Yep, all systems go."

"Did he tell you what to expect? What to be wary of in terms of symptoms?"

She reached over to smooth my furrowed brow. "Yes, Florence." The nurse wheeled in a breakfast tray.

"What's on the menu?" I lifted the silver dome to find congealed eggs and damp toast, with what appeared to be beef jerky passing for bacon alongside it. "Ew."

"My thoughts exactly." Mona pushed her covers back. "Let's get out of here."

"You sure you're ready?"

"As ready as I'll ever be, I guess." She began to stand up and I reached out to help. "My scar is so tiny, Sar. You wouldn't even know it was there if you weren't looking."

"That robot is a hell of a surgeon, huh? Somebody give that guy a promotion."

Mona smiled. "Ooh, feeling a little woozy." She stretched slightly and rocked on her toes with her eyes closed.

"Take it easy." I stood up myself and grabbed her. "You need some help?" I asked, handing her her clothes.

"I didn't wear this in the hospital bed like I was supposed to!" she exclaimed, unfurling her folded sweater and draping it across the bed. "You called it, though. Who can be bothered when they give you the gown?" She reached around to untie it. "To be honest, this thing is actually dangerously comfortable."

"Should we steal a few?" As I opened my mouth to forecast my own expanding girth and potential use for them, I thought better of it and snapped it shut.

"Oh my God, Sarah, me wearing these at home as nightgowns would be the end of my libido. Let's at least pretend I'm going to want to have sex again."

"What do they say about that, anyway?" I asked. "Can you? Physically, I mean?"

"Physically I should be fine. The doctor said I could even resume sex in a month or so. Emotionally, well, that's a different story."

Ten minutes later, Mona's nurse wheeled her down the hall as I walked beside them. The elevator opened and a new mother cradling her swaddled, tiny infant sat in a wheelchair with her husband and a nurse behind her.

"There's room, come on in," said the new dad.

"Oh no, we'll wait for the next one," I answered.

"No! No, we'll get in," barked Mona. And then quietly, "Thank you very much."

We got in and I glanced at Mona, expecting to see her staring at some imaginary something on the floor. Instead, she peered down into the bundle, a look of wonder and sadness on her face.

"He's so sweet," she whispered.

His mother looked over at her, her eyes bright. "Thank you. We think so."

His eyes were shut, the delicate pink lids and sparse eyelashes reminding me of a baby bird. Suddenly, his mouth puckered into an O and we all giggled appreciatively. "He's hungry, I guess," she announced. "Everything is so new now. I can only guess."

"We can't believe they're letting us take him home," murmured his dad.

"Believe it," said the nurse, sounding bored.

"Good luck," said Mona as we parted ways on the ground floor. The parents smiled graciously before being whisked away. In nine months' time, that would be me and Josh. I couldn't believe it.

"What's that Robert Frost poem?" asked Mona as her nurse deposited her by the door and she stood up.

"Which one is that?"

"Something about the road less traveled?"

I took Mona's arm and we walked slowly into the crisp air. The sky was as blue as the Caribbean, with not a cloud in sight. "Oh of course, his famous one. 'Two roads diverged in a wood, and I—' "

" 'I took the one less traveled by, and that has made all the difference,' " finished Mona. "That's how I feel right now. Sad, but somehow a little optimistic at the same time." She took a deep breath. "Mostly sad, though."

"You're incredible," I said, grabbing her hand.

"Thanks, Sar. Let's go home."

17

No right turn on red in New York City.

I stared at my blank computer screen. How could I take Minnie's Driving School to the next level? Did we lose the mouse ears altogether and start from scratch, or did we capitalize on the publicity the cars had already created for themselves? There was something comforting about the fact that no matter what, even the most reserved student could not take himself too seriously behind a furry wheel.

I brainstormed quickly, feeling enlivened by the *click-clack* of the keys. Mona was taking a nap. It was day three of my nursing duty, and really, it wasn't bad at all. She seemed to be recovering nicely, and for the past two nights we'd eaten ice cream in bed as we watched back episodes of *Mad Men.* It was kind of lovely, actually.

Other than the very occasional wave of nausea, I felt perfectly normal and had even found myself wondering if that pregnancy test had been wrong. Two more tests had disproved that theory, however. It was official, and I was grateful for the—so far at least—easy ride. Mona didn't ask, and I didn't tell. We had an unspoken, and smart, in my opinion, agreement not to bring my uterus up again until she had sufficiently mourned the loss of her own.

"Sarah?" she called.

"What's up?" I asked from her doorway. "How may I assist you, madame?"

"Could you pour me a glass of orange juice?"

"You got it." I hustled into the kitchen.

"Shake the carton first!" she yelled.

"I did!" I brought the glass to her and she leaned back against her pillows.

"Can you fluff these, please?" she asked, leaning forward immediately.

"You serious?"

"Yes, I'm serious. They're flat. Please, Florence?"

I rolled my eyes and complied. "How are you feeling?"

"Good. Just tired." She closed her eyes. "God, I hope I'm not depressed. That's the last thing I need."

"You just had major surgery, Mo. Your body is exhausted." I sat on the bed and smoothed her comforter.

"I know, but it's weird to be in bed for this long. Despite my best efforts, my brain is spinning like a hamster wheel."

"I know what you mean. But try your best to just surrender to your recuperation. In a few days' time, you'll be back in the functioning world and wondering why the hell you were so anxious to jump back in."

"What are you up to?"

"Just brainstorming about the driving school."

"Cool. Any winning ideas yet?"

"Not really. But I feel like I'm getting there, you know? Which is good. I really think this consultant idea could work."

"I know it can work. And it seems like it would be the perfect solution for the whole return-to-work-after-the-baby-comes dilemma."

"Yeah," I replied flippantly, not wanting to dwell on the subject. "I'm eager to hear what Meghan thinks."

"I bet she's going to be really supportive."

"I hope so." I stood up. "You want to take a slow walk around the block before we leave for your appointment?" Mona and I were due at her doctor's office for a follow-up visit later in the afternoon. She grimaced in response. "Come on, the doctor said you needed to do that at least once a day."

"Really? In the rain?" She looked out the window and sighed. "Can we go to Tart and get cupcakes?"

"The ones with the vanilla frosting piled about eight inches high?"

"Those are the ones."

"Done. Just throw on some rain boots and a jacket over

your pajamas. No one will be the wiser." On the street, I held the umbrella over our heads as we shuffled through the mist.

"You know, it would be nice if that umbrella actually kept the rain off of us," whined Mona.

"What? It's hard to keep it in the middle!"

"Oh God, give it to me." She yanked it out of my hand.

"Man, what is with you today? You're lucky I don't quit. Just put it over your own head, I don't care about the rain."

"No, here, I'll hold it over us."

"Mona, we'll have the same issue. Seriously, it's fine. Just go ahead."

"Sorry, Sarah. I'm just feeling tired and sore and sorry for myself today."

"It's okay. You're entitled." We walked past an abandoned and sodden love seat on the curb. "Hey, remember that time I made you help me move one of these into my apartment?" I asked.

"I do. That was when you were in that place on Henry, right?"

"Yep. I loved that place."

"I was on my way to meet an Internet date when you called."

"It was perfect timing! You were practically right outside."

"Sarah, I was dressed up. I had blow-dried my hair, for chrissake."

"Since when does moving a couch mess up your hair?"

"Since always when it's eighty-five degrees out."

"Well, who else was I going to call? You're the brawniest woman I know, Mona."

She smiled at me. "Thanks a lot."

"Man, we really had to wrestle that thing through the door. Didn't we end up having to screw the legs off?" I asked.

"Yep. A solution that we only came up with after an hour of attempting to get it through in one piece, mind you. My date ended up bailing."

"Wasn't he the one who played the drums in some no-name band?"

"Yeah."

"I did you a favor."

"You're probably right. Where is that love seat now, anyway?"

"Rescued by another broke twentysomething and currently residing in their apartment, I'm sure."

"Right, and I bet some other best friend got suckered into helping."

"It's the circle of life." I reached to grab the pocket of her coat. "Hey, in case I haven't said it enough, thank you."

"For what?"

"For being such a wonderful best friend. You've always been there for me, no matter what."

"As you have for me." She grabbed my pocket with her free hand in return and we became a walking human pretzel. "You know, a lot of people fall in love, get married, and forget all about their single bestie. Not you. That says a lot about the kind of person you are."

"Yeah, but a lot of people don't have the history that you and I have," I replied. "We spent our twenties together in New York. That's a lifetime in other cities. And besides, I wasn't always so great about it. Every time I met a guy who was even remotely into me I would inevitably disappear for a month or two."

"That's normal. Part of the girlfriend code. You're allowed three months max. I did it too," said Mona.

"Yeah, you did. Remember Indigo?"

"Oh my God! Indigo! Jesus, he was hot."

"And ridiculous."

"So ridiculous!" She laughed. "The actor who moonlighted as a nude model at Cooper Union! I forgot about him."

"I didn't. I thought you'd been kidnapped."

"And look at me now, dating a comedian paralegal. I don't exactly shoot for the stars, do I?"

"Yeah, but Nate is different. There's more to him than what he's currently doing." I bit my tongue, not wanting to spill the beans about his teaching aspirations.

"That's a change from your first impression of him."

"Yeah, he's grown on me. I actually miss having him around. Or rather, I miss seeing you when he's around. He seems to make you really happy."

She nodded. "He does. I miss him too. I've been thinking—I may tell him." We stopped in front of the bakery, admiring the goodies glistening in the window.

"I think you should." I took my hand out of her pocket and put my arm around her.

Okay, I'm ready," announced Mona, walking out of her bedroom dressed in street clothes for the first time in days. "Does this look okay? I may have cupcake-induced body dysmorphia."

"You look great."

"The headband isn't too much?" she asked, her back to me as she gazed at herself in the mirror.

"It's not my favorite look."

"Okay." She ripped it off and threw it onto the chair beside me.

"You feeling okay about this?" I asked.

"Nervous, but relatively okay," Mona answered. "I feel pretty good, you know? Hopefully everything checks out down there."

"Fingers crossed." I followed her down the stairs.

"Yuck. Now it's truly disgusting outside," said Mona. We stood in the foyer of her building and frowned at the curtain of rain waiting for us on the other side of the door. "We're never going to get a cab in this weather, and the subway is going to be slow as molasses."

"That's a given." Whenever it rained in New York, all forms of transportation took a predictable and incredibly frustrating hit.

"That's why you're going to drive Gus." She reached into her pocket and retrieved her keys, which she dangled in front of me like a fishing lure.

"Very funny."

"I'm serious, Sarah."

"Get out of here, Mona. Don't be crazy."

"Why is that crazy? You said that you know how to drive, so let's go."

"Why can't you drive?"

"Because I don't want to." She put the keys in the palm of my hand and closed my fingers around them. I stared at her in disbelief.

"Mona, come on. It's raining and your doctor's office is across a fucking bridge and in a different borough. I've barely driven to the grocery store in a town called Farmwood, for chrissake. I can't do this. I won't. You're nuts." I lowered my voice to a desperate whisper. "Plus the stress on the baby."

"So how come you were all gung ho to drive me to my surgery the other day? No excuses. You're doing it." She took the umbrella from me and opened the door. "Let's go." She charged ahead, forcing me to keep up or get completely soaked.

"Mona, do you want us all to die?" I asked. "Seriously, do you? Because our chances of doing so are pretty good if I'm behind the wheel. And I wasn't actually serious the other day when I offered to drive. It was temporary insanity brought on by my concern for you."

"Sarah, enough with the whining. So far this month I've survived cancer and a hysterectomy. I think my chances of three for three are pretty good."

"You just jinxed us! You said it out loud! Spit on the ground! Spit!" I was on the verge of hysteria.

"Sarah, get ahold of yourself." Mona turned around to

face me. "You can do this. Whatever you set your mind to, you do. You wanted to work for Glow a long time ago—"

"God knows why," I interjected.

"That's not the point. The point is that you made it happen and happened to be very good at what you did. You wanted to fall in love and marry a good man. You did. You were over New York and wanted to make a change—you did that too. You wanted a new sense of self, so you're on your way to finding it with your new business plan. The thing with the driving is, I know that you know you have to do it, but I don't think you quite want to do it. There's a small part of you that likes being immobile and dependent on other people, because then you can use your phobia as a convenient excuse not to have to make an effort."

"Mona, I—"

"Shush. You know I'm speaking the truth. This fear of driving isn't about driving at all, it's about starting over in a new place and embracing change. Besides, that kid is going to have to go to the doctor and on playdates and all sorts of shit. You need to be ready."

"I'm not ready," I whimpered, referring to both the baby and driving.

"I love you and I know that you're ready for this, even if you don't believe it yourself. You came up here to fix me, and now it's my turn to fix you." She pointed to the keys in my hand. "Let's go."

I nodded slowly. "Okay."

"Okay?" asked Mona.

"Okay." We approached Gus. I stood before the car, taking it in.

"Speed it up already, I'm going to be late!" yelled Mona. I opened her door and then ran around to mine.

"I'm sitting in the driver's seat," I announced, my heart beating rapidly. "I think I may have to say everything out loud, to calm my nerves."

"I know I gave that impassioned speech back there about three for three and all that, but I really would like to survive this drive. Whatever works for you, do it." I put the key in the ignition and then immediately removed it.

"Mona, I can't do it. I just can't."

"Drive. The. Fucking. Car. Sarah."

"Okay, okay." I took a deep breath. "You know what? I'm going to call Ray." I dialed his number. *Pick up, please pick up.*

"Hello?"

"Ray!"

"Yeah?" He sounded confused.

"It's Sarah!"

"Sarah?" I could hear the television in the background.

"From driving class? Your marketing guru?"

"Oh yeah, of course, of course. How you doin', girl?" Mona tapped me on the shoulder and pointed to her watch impatiently. I started the car.

"Do you have a minute?" *Windshield wipers?* I mouthed to Mona. She leaned across and flipped up the lever.

"Sure, I got a minute."

"What about a half hour?"

"Uh, yeah. What's up?"

"Well, long story short, I'm about to drive into Manhattan from Brooklyn, and I was just hoping that I could have you on speakerphone, you know, for comfort purposes. And also to make it less likely that I'll, I dunno, veer off into the East River." Mona looked at me with alarm.

"All right, you got this. No problem. You parallel parked?"

"Yes."

"Okay, well, just take your time gettin' out."

"You know what, Ray, I'm just going to lay the phone between the seats, and if I need you, I'll holler. Just knowing you're right here if I need you is really what counts."

"Okay, so I can watch TV?"

"Yeah, just listen out for me. If you don't mind, that is."

"Fine by me."

"Hi, Ray," said Mona.

"Oh hey, who's that?"

"That's my friend Mona."

"Nice to meet you, Mona."

"The pleasure is mine, Ray."

I wiggled the car out of its space, grateful that I wasn't wedged in completely. Once angled optimally, I waited for every car in a ten-mile radius to pass before tentatively turning onto the street. I plodded slowly, sitting so far up that the wheel and my sternum were practically one.

"So wait, I just stay in this lane until we hit the bridge, right?" The rain was lessening now, and I adjusted the wipers accordingly.

"Yes, that's right," answered Mona.

"Say what?" asked Ray.

"Nothing, Ray, we're all good for the moment."

"Cool. What's it like in New York today?"

"Cold. Rainy. Gray," I answered through clenched teeth.

"No shit. It's sunny and blue skies in Farmwood. The kids and I just got back from the park."

"Okay, Ray, that's nice and all, but I can't really talk and drive at the same time yet. That's advanced."

"God, Sarah, that was rude," said Mona.

"Yeah, it was rude, Sarah," agreed Ray. "But it's all right, I know how she gets behind the wheel, Mona. Like a little old lady."

"She does look like a little old lady!" exclaimed Mona.

"I know, right? Ain't it crazy?"

"Hello!" I said. "I am trying not to kill us here! Can the two of you focus, please?"

"Sorry," mumbled Mona.

"Yeah, sorry. I know you're nervous, Sarah," said Ray.

"And sorry I was rude, Ray. That was unnecessary. I'm not myself."

In front of us, the bridge loomed like a dinosaur skeleton in the mist. The Brooklyn Bridge was one of my favorite places in the world, and my collection of memories surrounding it was too huge to catalog. I would walk it before I left, in order to give it its proper respect. At the moment, I could only focus on one thing, and that was making it across in a vehicle. Alive, preferably.

"Good work, Sarah," said Mona. "See, it's not so bad."

"Where y'all at?" asked Ray.

"Sarah's driving across the Brooklyn Bridge," Mona informed him.

"Get out! The Brooklyn Bridge! I've never seen it in person. What's it like?"

"It's beautiful, Ray," answered Mona. "Stunning, even."

"Someday the family and I are gonna get there. Eat some pizza at that famous joint underneath it. What's it called? Maybe see a basketball game."

"Grimaldi's. And that sounds great, Ray," said Mona.

The rain had stopped, and the sun peeked out ever so slightly from behind the dense clouds, casting a yellowish filter on downtown Manhattan. I was coasting down from the apex of the bridge, my heartbeat elevated by the thought of finding my way through the hectic streets below. I imagined my cartoon fetus navigating the churning waters of my agitated insides. *Don't worry. We're okay, baby.*

"Okay, now at the bottom, you're gonna make a right," Mona informed me.

"No shit, Sherlock," I replied.

"Oh ho ho! Look who's cocky now!" said Ray.

"Seriously," agreed Mona.

As I left the bridge and drove toward the light, a bike messenger suddenly swerved in front of me, causing me to slam on the brakes.

"Watch your ass, fucknut!" I yelled.

"You're fine," said Mona calmly. "No damage done."

"What happened? What happened?" asked Ray anxiously.

"Just some moron bike messenger. Sarah handled it like a pro."

"Good work. You definitely don't see a lot of those in Farmwood."

"No you do not."

I took a deep breath as we waited at the red light. Mona's doctor was in SoHo, which wasn't far. I had taken us three-quarters of the way through the journey, we were still alive, and the car was intact. All good things. I couldn't believe that I was doing it. *I was driving.*

Mona's technique had been a brilliant one. Instead of swim lessons, she had just thrown me into the deep end. Not without floaties, of course; in this case the floaties were both the lessons I had taken with Ray and, literally, Ray himself—if only in audible form.

We ambled along through Wall Street, the suited-up men and panty-hosed women who walked its sidewalks trotting along ever so efficiently in the post-rain air. With a left turn into SoHo, the scenery changed significantly—impossibly willowy models and trust-fund twentysomethings in cashmere ski caps even though it couldn't have been less than sixty-five degrees out sashayed down the street, barking into their cell phones as poorly dressed tourists cluelessly held up the foot traffic. Mona rattled out driving directions patiently, and before I knew it, I was parking in a garage and the entire ordeal was over.

"She did it, Ray," said Mona proudly as she beamed at me. "She fucking did it."

"Aw, I knew she would. Good job, girl."

"Thanks." A lump formed in my throat. It had been a long time since I had been this proud of myself.

"See you when you get back, Sarah. Lookin' forward to talking shop about the business. I got some good ideas, I think."

"Me too, Ray. Thanks for being my safety net."

"You're your own safety net. Mona, best of luck to you. I hope everything works out with, well, you know."

"Thanks, Ray. I appreciate that."

I hung up and looked at Mona. "Mona, I cannot believe that I did that."

"Believe it! I knew you could do it."

"You did? Really? You weren't even a little bit nervous?"

"Well shit yeah, I was nervous, but I knew you could do it."

We got out of the car and I handed her the keys. "Mona, I could have killed you."

"But I was with you! Worst-case scenario, we would have gone out like a modern Thelma and Louise."

I reached over and hugged her tightly. "Mona, I love you so much. You called me out. I needed that."

"That's what best friends do, silly. I love you, too."

"But I haven't called you out about Nate."

"Are you kidding? You've been calling me out on it since you arrived."

"Not really."

"Sarah, you really have slammed me over the head with your opinion already." I held open the door for her. "And trust me, I appreciate your *You deserve a man you can be honest with* bit." She nodded to the security guard as she scribbled into the guest book. "The fact of the matter is that Nate totally is the kind of guy that I can be honest with. It's me that's the problem. I don't want to get too close to anyone, so in order to avoid that I sabotage it myself."

"Do you think it's easier that way?" I followed her into the elevator.

"Well, I used to. Like I said earlier, I'm getting more comfortable with the idea of telling him."

"So you're going to tell him now, after the fact?" We got out on our floor.

"Oh, hell no. But I'll be honest with him going forward."

"Mona, that's cheating. That's like me driving to the bridge instead of across it."

"Yeah, I know. Maybe I'll change my mind, but I doubt it. What's the difference between pretending I had a hysterectomy years ago and having one last week?"

"Well, a lot for you emotionally. You could use some support."

"I have you for that."

I shook my head at the back of hers as I followed her into the office.

18

In the car on the way home, I relished the comfort of the passenger seat like I never had before.

"For me, driving is like getting waxed," I said to Mona, who was perched happily behind the steering wheel. Her doctor had given her a great report, and both of us were feeling especially pleased.

"How's that?"

"You don't want to do it, it hurts like hell, but once it's done there's no denying that you feel better. Also, you can go months without doing it and be just fine."

"Interesting analogy. And gross—months without doing it? How does Josh stand it?" She pulled into a parking spot.

"Let's pick up something delicious to eat," suggested Mona as we began to walk toward her apartment. "Today calls for a celebratory something."

"Sounds good to me."

"Oh fuck," said Mona under her breath.

"What? Are you okay?" Her face was red. "What?"

I looked up. In front of us stood a very sweaty and perplexed-looking Nate, who appeared to be walking off the end of a vigorous run. He looked at Mona and then at me and then back at Mona in disbelief.

"Hi, Nate," said Mona finally. She folded her arms in front of herself defensively.

"Uh, hi? Or should I say *bonjour*?" He wiped the sweat off of his forehead with the back of his hand and for a moment I thought he was going to hurl it at us. "What the hell, Mona? That was a short trip." I pretended to be fascinated by my phone.

I heard sniffling and looked up to find Mona crying. Now it was my turn to play people Ping-Pong. I looked at Nate and then at Mona and then back at Nate as I stood awkwardly to the side.

"I'm going to take off, Mo. I'll call you later," I said, not knowing where I was going but making the executive decision that it needed to be somewhere else, and fast. She mumbled something unintelligible in response. I rounded the corner and tried to determine what exactly I was going to do with myself. I called Kate.

"Good afternoon," she answered. "How's it going? Wait, don't tell me that Mona is already having sex again!"

"No, not exactly. Can I come over?"

"Naturally. Price of admission is a bottle of red, though."

"Done."

Franklin lay on his play mat, occasionally gurgling and batting at the brightly colored jungle animals that hung from its overhead bar.

"Sarah, I can't believe that you drove into the city. That is incredible. Did you tell Josh?"

"I haven't yet, actually." I grabbed a napkin off the coffee table and attempted to stuff it through the lid of an empty to-go coffee cup that lay beside it. Kate reached out and put her hand over mine.

"Please stop. You're reminding me of what it felt like trying to get back into my regular jeans the other day."

"What! Why would you do that? It hasn't even been three months yet!"

"I know, I know, but I couldn't help myself. Sarah, what's happened to my abdomen is straight out of a horror movie. It looks like melted candle wax."

"Kate, please. You grew a human being for what, nine months? Don't rush things."

"What are you doing now?" she asked. I looked down to

find myself tearing the napkin to shreds. "What's going on with you?"

"Oh, nothing."

"Doesn't look like nothing to me. You're acting like some sort of crazed goat."

"Really, I'm fine."

"Franklin doesn't believe you. Look at him." I looked down and he was giving me an *mmmm-hmmmmm* face. I laughed.

"Isn't that face hilarious? He started with it a few days ago. I would be talking to Ben or whomever but then look down and there he'd be, giving me that."

"It's pretty awesome."

"So, what gives? Besides the obvious."

"What's the obvious?"

"Duh." She smiled mischievously. "You're pregnant."

My face warmed. "Am not."

"Are too."

"How did you know?" I squealed.

She leaned forward and enveloped me in an eager hug. "Honey, please. You think you had me fooled the other night at dinner? Your glass of wine sat untouched, and now, after a run-in with your best friend's supposedly duped boyfriend, you refuse one altogether? What am I, dumb? Oh, Sarah, I'm so happy for you guys! And for me! Franklin will have a cousin!"

"You're not going to tell Ben, are you?"

"Honestly? Yes. But I swear that neither of us will leak the news to Sylvia. Scout's honor. Word to the wise, keep the wee one under wraps from the ole mother-in-law as long as you possibly can. Lots of advice, that one. How far along are you now?"

"No idea. A month, maybe? I need to make a doctor appointment when I go home."

"Well, you look the same. No fat face or anything."

"Thanks, I think," I replied. "It's all been so surreal, what with Mona's predicament and the fact that I'm here and Josh is in Farmwood."

"I can't even imagine. Just peering down at the word 'pregnant' on that stick was probably the most surreal moment of my life." She picked up Franklin from the floor. "I'm going to go put him in his crib. I'm attempting to start nap training." As she walked toward his room, she sang over her shoulder, "All of this glamour is waiting for you!" For no apparent reason, my eyes began to well.

Kate came back out and shut the nursery door softly, muffling Franklin's whimpers. She handed me a Kleenex. "You okay?"

"Yeah, just overwhelmed at moments, I guess. It's been so hard, what with Mona's situation and all. Talk about shitty timing."

"Seriously. Have you told her?"

"She was actually with me when I took the test. In the Barneys bathroom, of all places."

"What?"

"Yeah, crazy, right? But Mona insisted. She's been an amazing friend, and I mean that in the truest sense of the word."

"Well, you're a pretty amazing friend to her, too, coming up here to take care of her and all. You guys have something really special. I wish I had a girlfriend like that."

"You don't?"

"Not really. I met Ben in college, you know? He was my best friend from the beginning, which is all well and good until you need to talk to someone about stuff like your postpartum vagina. Thanks for listening the other night, by the way. I hope I didn't scare you."

"You did a little, but that's okay."

"I've loved having you here, Sarah. I hope we can stay close like we've become, even when you go back to Farmwood."

"I've really liked getting closer to you too, Kate. I wish we had done it sooner."

"Why didn't we do it sooner?"

"I dunno. To be honest, I was pretty intimidated by you."

"Me?" She pointed at herself. "Are you serious?"

"Yeah, of course! Why wouldn't I be? You're younger than me and you've got your own thriving business going, plus you dove headfirst into the baby pool and made pregnancy look like no big whoop. That's intimidating."

"No big whoop? Sarah, I think I was pretty candid about the fact that pregnancy is indeed a big whoop."

"Well yes, you were—you are—incredibly candid, but that's just what I mean. Your openness makes it seem less terrifying somehow, even though you would think it would have the opposite effect. I think it's because even if your labia were blue or labor felt like a piano coming out of your butt, or your postpartum vagina has a penchant for fried foods, you're still *you*, without any apologies."

"Is that your way of saying that I should apologize for who I am?"

"No, not at all!"

"I know, I'm just messing with you. And thanks, I guess. Although I was intimidated by you too, you know."

"Why?"

"You were a ball-busting businesswoman!"

I laughed. "Kate, that couldn't be farther from the truth."

"No, you were! Working for a big company, always on your phone putting out fires. You always seemed to have your shit together in a way that I just didn't."

"Kate, I definitely did not have my shit together. I may have worked like a dog, but I was miserable."

"Yes, but you would never have known it from the outside looking in. I was shocked when Ben told me that you guys were moving and that you were quitting your job. Absolutely shocked."

"Why, because it seemed like such a cop-out?"

"Not at all. Because it just seemed so out of character for the you I thought you were."

"The me you thought I was."

"Yeah. And by the way, I'm not an open book about everything. My labia is one thing, but inside my head is quite another."

"What's happening inside your head?"

"So much. My entire identity has been forever changed by Franklin. My priorities, my work ethic, my marriage—everything. Figuring out how to put the pieces into this new puzzle is fairly exhausting."

"I'm sure. But he's still so new. I think you need to give yourself a break. There's no way to have it all figured out at this stage in the game."

"But that's the thing! America basically tells you that you have to have it figured out at this stage in the game. How else do you explain the standard three-month maternity leave? It's nuts!" She shook her fists in the air, looking remarkably like Franklin in the process. "And I don't even get three months, since I'm the one paying myself essentially. My partner, Kim, is dropping hints that she wants me back sooner rather than later."

"Oh wow, that's tough."

"It is. Although I guess I shouldn't complain so much. I can do a lot of the cooking here if I need to, or bring Franklin with me. Those are the pros of my line of work. Then again, how the hell can I expect to focus on making a quiche when he's around? I haven't figured out how to quiet the mommy part of my brain yet."

"That's the thing. Do we ever quiet it, once we become part of the club? I just found out that I was pregnant—I'm not even a mom yet, officially—and already my brain is going ninety miles a minute."

"It's crazy. You know, I don't think this happens to men in the same way. Yes, they become fathers, but it doesn't seem to overwhelm their every waking moment the way it does for women. Take, for example, Franklin's nighttime feedings. I mostly do them all, but sometimes Ben gives him a bottle. After I feed him and get back in bed, my mind races, and I mean races, for a good hour, cataloging all of the various Franklin duties and questions and milestones, blah blah blah. No matter what I do, I cannot shut it off. Ben, on the other hand, gets back in bed and, no lie, is snoring again in two minutes. It's unreal."

"Yeah, they do seem to be able to shut things down in a way that we're biologically incapable of. On the rare occasions that Josh and I get in an argument, I'm stewing over it for days, and he's back to himself in a half hour."

"Maybe it's not a man thing but a Simon thing."

"Maybe. Although Sylvia can hold a grudge."

"That's for damn sure! Do you remember when she lost her shit because my wedding thank-you card to her cousin was late?"

"I do! She practically threw the Seder plate across the table." We both laughed.

"All gender differences aside, Ben is an amazing dad." Kate smiled. "Just overhearing him talking to Franklin melts my cold, cold heart, much less seeing them together. It's incredible. I didn't expect to be such a sap."

"I think Josh will be great too. He's so patient."

"I have a feeling you won't be so bad yourself."

"You do? How come?"

"You just have a way about you. Remember that time,

right before Ben was, unbeknownst to me, about to propose? I called you up, crying, because you were the closest thing to family I had here and I didn't know who else to turn to. I was convinced that he was seeing someone else."

"I do! We went for drinks and I tried to talk you off the ledge. You thought he was cheating because he was making all of these secretive phone calls and going on vague appointments, when really he was finalizing your ring design."

"I was beside myself! And ridiculous in retrospect. But you were so patient with me that night, listening to me go on and on and not once patronizing me."

"I was so nervous that I would ruin his surprise. I think I drank a bottle of wine myself."

Kate laughed. "Yeah, we were both pretty tipsy. On the way home, we made the cabby pull over for pizza."

"He refused to let us eat in his cab! Kept the meter running as we inhaled it at the counter. I forgot about that night."

"Well, it meant a lot to me."

"I'm glad I helped. That was a fun night. Our first date without the boys."

"And our last, until this visit. Here's to many more." She smiled and raised her glass. "You really are gonna be a great mom, Sarah. Welcome to the club, sis."

19

I climbed the stairs slowly, careful to move out of the way of the runners skipping down them, sweaty and focused. Although there was a crisp edge to the air, it was subtle, and the strap of my messenger bag had created a horizontal line of sweat across my chest and abdomen. I shifted it now, frowning at the giant wrinkle it had also created. I was on my way to meet Meghan for lunch in the city and had decided to follow through on the vow I had made to walk the Brooklyn Bridge.

I began what was a laborious climb up the bridge's initial slope, wondering whether my pregnancy was slowing me down or I was just woefully out of shape. I looked out onto the water and park below, a montage of photos that didn't actually exist and in which I looked effortlessly beautiful flashing through my mind. From twenty-one to thirty-six I had trekked back and forth across this bridge for one reason or another, and always it was cathartic. Something about its architecture, the sun in the sky, and the clouds on the horizon always cleansed me in a very specific way.

Early in our relationship, I had met Josh on the Manhattan side of the bridge after work to walk home, and we had bonded over our mutual respect and affection for it. That had been the first time we had held hands. Like so many things I was scared of, I had scorned all hand-holders until Josh came along and took mine sweetly into his own.

I paused for a moment by a bench and then quickly moved on. I was not a lingerer, even when I wanted to be. I wasn't sure if that was the New York in me or something ingrained from birth. Josh was the opposite. He was a bona fide stop-and-smell-the-roses person, which was, although at times infuriating, exactly what I needed in a partner. Without him, I'd never notice anything. I wondered whom the baby would take after in this regard. I hoped Josh. It seemed like a nicer way to be.

I couldn't believe that I was going home in three days. *Three days.* Two weeks away had felt like months, and although I was excited to return, I was nervous. We had so much to do.

I forced myself to stop for a moment, holding my phone up with the rest of the tourists and snapping what I hoped was my head and the water behind me. I surveyed the photo, approved it halfheartedly, and texted it to Josh with the words: *Missing you.* As I pressed send, I began to tear up again. These hormones were no joke. I put my phone back in my bag and began the descent into Manhattan.

As I adjusted the waistband of my pants, I thought of Mona, mostly because they were her pants. She and Nate were a bit wobbly, but they weren't over by any means. Mona had told him everything that day, and by the time she was finished the sweat from Nate's run had long dried. He hadn't known what to say at first, so he had asked for some time, and then, to her surprise, he returned a few hours later showered and shaved with Italian takeout and a bottle of wine under his arm. He had come clean to Mona about his plans to go back to school, much to her delight. Now there were no secrets between them. He was understandably wary but open.

In Manhattan, I turned around to get one last look at the bridge before heading down into the subway station. Being on this side made me want to scamper back across its slopes at lightning speed, but I continued my journey. Hopefully, lunch would be free, and that was always worth the trip.

Sarah."

I looked up from my seat to find Meghan smiling wryly at me, her impossibly white teeth beaming out from her immobilized face like headlights. She was a Botox fanatic but swore to the public that her wrinkleless visage was all due to the company's most expensive moisturizer, a bottle of which cost about as much as my round-trip plane ticket to New York.

"Hi, Meghan." I stood up to bestow an air kiss on each of her unlined cheeks.

"Well, the southern air must work for you, my dear. You look fresh as a daisy," she replied.

"Oh, it's just sweat."

As soon as the words were out of my mouth, I regretted them, but this was how our conversations always went. She paid me some vague compliment that she didn't really mean, and I responded with the verbal equivalent of a burp.

The Japanese hostess escorted us to a low table surrounded by pillows, indicating that we should remove our shoes and sit on the floor, but Meghan's pursed taupe lips said no in any language.

"How have you been?" I asked when we were seated at a regular table.

"It was a hell of a summer," replied Meghan, cupping her mug of green tea. "Don't look at my fingernails. They're an abomination. I haven't had a manicure in two weeks." I curled my own fingernails, which hadn't seen polish in months, into my palms under the table.

"I couldn't find anyone decent to replace you for the longest. Every person I interviewed was worse than the last. I told you about the woman with the whale tail, didn't I?" She rolled her eyes.

"You did." I took a sip, burning the roof of my mouth on contact. "I'm sorry I left you in the lurch, Meghan. That certainly wasn't my intention. I did offer to work remotely, you know."

"Yes, and I offered to stand in for Beyoncé at the Super Bowl. Some things just aren't realistic, my dear. Anyway, enough about that. It's water under the bridge." She blew on her tea before taking a ladylike sip. "I mean, a month's notice as opposed to two weeks would have been nice given our, I don't know, zillion years together, but you did what you had to do." I nodded. "The good news is that I've got someone now who seems like a proper fit. Not as smart as you, but smart enough."

"That's good. I'm glad."

"Literally, I was steering the ship with only Emily on deck. Can you imagine? Emily. Brainstorming with her was like working with a ventriloquist minus the dummy. Every question she asked me she answered herself." I giggled, and Meghan followed suit, leaning back against her chair in relief.

"She is pretty bad about that. It used to drive me nuts," I said.

"I finally had to tell her about her habit. Poor thing, she had no idea! I couldn't believe that no one had told her sooner." Our plates of sushi appeared in front of us, mine minus the raw fish. "Enough about poor Emily. That's not why you're here. Talk to me, Sarah."

"Well, I'm at a crossroads of sorts. I've been trying to figure out what it is exactly that I want to do with my life, and nothing really seems to appeal. Or at least, nothing did until recently."

"How old are you, Sarah?"

"Thirty-six."

"That's a little old to be looking for that proverbial pot of gold at the end of the career rainbow, don't you think?"

"It is a little pathetic, I know, but with Josh's job offer and the move, I figured I finally had a chance to figure out what it was that I really wanted to do."

"And it wasn't marketing, I take it? Or at least you hoped it wasn't?"

"Well, no," I answered. Meghan chewed thoughtfully and I seized the opportunity to shove my first piece of California roll into my mouth.

"Well, that's a shame, Sarah," she said finally. "Because you were really very good at what you did. Very good."

"Thanks, Meghan. I appreciate that. I'm starting to realize that it wasn't the marketing itself that burned me out, though."

"It was working for me?"

"Well, not you, per se. More like Glow as a corporation."

"I can see that. I think that was because you weren't cut out for makeup marketing, my dear. To be honest, it never seemed like a match to me."

"True. I'm not exactly an advertisement for the brand." I waved my hand in front of my bare face.

"Right, but that doesn't mean you didn't have a knack for it. In your e-mail you said that you were thinking about starting up your own consulting business down there in—what's it called?"

"Farmwood."

"No, it's not. You're kidding me, right?"

"I'm not kidding."

"Good lord. Your first item of business should be changing the name of the town. Do people there even know what marketing is, or do they assume it's some version of grocery shopping?"

"Meghan, come on."

"Oh, I know! I'm ridiculous and that was a terrible joke. Forgive me. I love playing the catty New York snob role. Actually"—she peered around furtively before lowering her voice—"I grew up in Arkansas."

"Shut up."

"If you tell anyone, I'll kill you." She placed her chopsticks neatly on the plate. "Back to you. Do you have any clients lined up?"

"There's one. He's looking to rebrand his driving business."

"Driving as in limousines to the airport and whatnot?"

"No, driving as in driving instruction."

"Like driver's ed?"

"More or less."

"Oy. Wait, is that how you met him?"

"Yes, actually."

"Well, I don't blame you for taking lessons. The last time

I was behind the wheel I think the first Bush was in office, and I am not exaggerating."

"Thanks."

"You're welcome. Okay, so you've had the real sit-down with him? Asked him about his vision for the company? Where he wants to be in two years? Five years? The standard spiel?" I nodded. "Does his company have a name?"

"Yes, but I'm thinking about some new ones." I told her about the mouse ears.

"Oh God, that's awful."

"Well, in theory it sounds terrible, I agree, but somehow in person it's charming."

"Seriously?"

"Yeah, I can't explain it. Anyway, I'll keep brainstorming and if anything else comes to mind that really sings, I'll suggest it. Speaking of names, there's also this jewelry store that could use my help."

"What's it called? Bauble Head?"

"How did you know?"

She threw her head back and laughed. "Sarah! I love it. Farmwood is screaming for your help. It was meant to be. You came up with that fantastic men's lip balm name in less than three seconds the other day. You could single-handedly rename every business in town if you wanted to. For a fee, of course." She motioned to the waitress to bring the bill.

"Sarah, you should go for this. Take this town by the balls. These people are practically begging for your expertise. You know what I'm saying? Get excited about this next phase of your life. You're free of all the New York, hierarchical bullshit that was bumming you out." She brushed nonexistent lint off of her sweater. "By the way, hello—do you have a company name? What about your branding? Please tell me that you have a business card at the ready." The waitress brought Meghan's credit card back; she signed and tipped and slid it back into her sleek wallet.

"In the works," I lied.

"And if your business doesn't pan out immediately, what's the big deal? Just get pregnant and focus on that for a while."

I cleared my throat uncomfortably.

"What, you're not pregnant right now, are you?"

"No, no," I replied, squirming in my seat.

"Oh, okay." She smiled suddenly—a real smile that lit up her blue eyes like candles. "Did I tell you that my partner and I are adopting a baby girl from Ethiopia next month?"

"No! That's incredible."

"It really is. God help me, I'm going to be a mom." She looked at her watch. "Listen, I have to dash. Great to see you. E-mail me your address and I'll send you a giant box of goodies. We have this new cream that's supposed to take ten years off in ten days." She air-kissed each cheek and was gone in a flash of black cashmere.

I walked out and stood on the sidewalk dumbfounded. A baby girl from Ethiopia? I had worked with this woman for over ten years and this was the first I was hearing of any maternal inclination. All of this time, I had thought regular Botox injections were the extent of her outside interests.

A fine mist started to descend from the sky. As I moved to retrieve my umbrella from my bag, I found a red ladybug politely planted across the teeth of its zipper.

"Hello," I said softly, choosing to soldier on, damp be damned, instead of disturbing its journey. A little rain wouldn't kill me.

20

How long have you been up?" asked Mona groggily as she padded into the kitchen.

I lowered my laptop screen to get a better look at her and raised my cup of tea in greeting. "For some ungodly reason, I was wide awake at five."

"That's terrible," she grumbled.

As Mona went about making coffee, I repositioned my screen and continued to divide my time between googling every pregnancy question under the sun, fleshing out Ray's business proposal, and brainstorming new store names on Mitzi's behalf. It was my last day in Brooklyn, and I was feeling purposeful and optimistic about my return to Farmwood. If this was the pregnant version of me, the next nine months didn't look so bad.

Mona sat down beside me and eyed me warily from behind the rim of her mug. "Okay, I'm human again. You may speak."

"Oh, I don't have anything to say," I said, continuing to type. "Same shit, different day. Just working on stuff. What do you think about the name Gem de la Crème?"

"Are you kidding?"

"What! It's cute!"

She frowned. "I guess. Maybe for like, a mall chain in—"

"Farmwood?"

"Yeah. Maybe you're onto something."

"No, you're right, it is cheesy. I want a name that will attract a younger demographic."

"That ain't it." She pushed my laptop lid down.

"Hey, watch out!" I pushed it back up and saved the document. "What's your deal this morning?"

"You're leaving me tomorrow." She made a sad face.

"I know, but let's be honest. Nate's a clear upgrade. He gives you back rubs, for God's sake."

Mona grinned and took another sip of her coffee. "He does give a fine back rub. He really commits, you know? None of that measly two-minutes-of-halfhearted-kneading business."

"He's a keeper. How are you guys doing, Mo?"

"We're doing pretty well, all things considered. Emotionally, I'm all over the map, so he has a lot to deal with. Sometimes I feel this sort of ache, like I can actually physically feel that a part of me is missing, and that makes me melancholy and sad. Then sometimes I'm angry, as in why me, and, no offense, why you with your spiteful fertility—I know it's not spiteful, but that's the way I feel when I'm at my least compassionate—and then there are good moments when I'm grateful that my cancer was caught early and I have friends like you and a boyfriend like Nate to get me through this."

"Did you just say *boyfriend*?!" I scooted my chair over and it screeched angrily against the wood floor. "Whoops. I hope that didn't leave a mark. You know I didn't mean to get pregnant right now, Mo."

"Of course I know that, Sarah. And I really am happy for you. Honestly. It's just, you know, hard at this point to not feel at least a touch sorry for myself."

"I know."

"But every day, it gets a little better. A little easier. And with Nate, we're just taking it day by day. The fact that he stuck around through all of this says a lot about him."

"He's crazy about you. As he should be."

"I'm pretty into him, too." She stood up. "So we'll see where it goes. Speaking of, he's coming over with doughnuts in a few minutes."

"Doughnuts!" I clasped my hands together in glee.

"Yes, didn't you know that artisanal doughnuts are the new cupcakes?"

"Ah, the fickleness of the Brooklyn hipster baking curve."

"Great band name. The Brooklyn Hipster Baking Curve." She leaned against the counter. "How are you feeling about returning to Farmwood?"

"Pretty good, actually. I can see my future there now, you know? I think I'm finally finished with New York."

"That's what you said last time."

"No, this time is for real. Coming back here was like getting back together with an ex you know isn't right for you just because you're bored. Now it's really over. I'll always come back to visit, though."

"Damn right you will." Mona smiled. "Are you excited to see Josh? I can't believe he hasn't seen you since you found out you were pregnant."

"I know, it's crazy, right? Do I look different to you?"

She cocked her head, surveying my face. "Pretty much the same." Her buzzer rang and she got up to let Nate in.

"I'm gonna go put on a bra," I announced, giddy with pastry anticipation.

As I fastened the clasp, I looked down at my stomach. It did seem mushier, but then again, I had been indulging with abandon. I wondered when I would pop, or rather, *how* I would pop. Common sense and a hate/hate relationship with my abdomen told me that I would not be one of those women who just looked like they had a basketball shoved under their shirt. *Que sera, sera.*

Suddenly, a hand pressed against the small of my back. I gasped, turning around so quickly that for a moment the room spun.

"Surprise," whispered Josh, a huge smile on his face.

"What are you doing here?"

It felt so good to see him, so familiar in all of the right ways. Just to see his brown eyes twinkling at me and feel his stubbly salt-and-pepper beard scratch against my cheek as I hugged him filled me with unmitigated joy. I released him long enough to plant a giant kiss on his lips and then jumped on him again. He stumbled backward, laughing.

"I flew up for the day," he whispered into my ear. "There was no way I was going to let my pregnant wife fly home alone."

"Get outta here!" I replied, pushing him playfully. "That's ridiculous."

"I know, but I was worried for some reason. Plus, I just wanted to see you. To celebrate with you here, in the city where we met."

"You mushpot." I kissed him. "God, it's good to see you."

"You too. You look beautiful." He stepped back, looking me up and down. "What do they always say about pregnant women? That they're glowing?"

"I guess."

"That's exactly what you're doing, Sar. You're glowing."

"I think that's probably just my excitement about the doughnuts Nate was bringing. He's here, right? With the doughnuts?"

"He's here. Seems like a nice guy."

"He is."

Josh lifted up my shirt and put his hand to my stomach.

"I can't believe there's a baby in there." He looked at me in wonder, and in that moment I knew what our little boy would look like, if that was indeed who was in there.

"Me either." I took his hand. "I love you so much. Thanks for coming up like this. It's very romantical of you."

"Romantical?"

"Yes." I kissed him again.

"All right, you two, break it up," announced Mona, striding through the door. "Making out is bad for the fetus."

"Mona, you sly fox." I walked over to hug her. "How long have you known about this?"

"Only a day or two. I think Josh was keeping a low profile, trying to spare my feelings." She peeked around me and smiled at him. "What with my recent hysterectomy and all." Nervous silence filled the room. "And that was sweet of you, Josh, really. But like I told Sar, the rest of the world's procreation certainly isn't going to come to a standstill while I get back on my feet. I love you guys and am really happy for you."

"I love you too, Mona." Josh walked up and took her hand. "I'm so sorry that you had to go through all of this. You're a hell of a lot stronger than I am."

"Thanks, Josh. Your wife has been a huge help, save for the whole stealing my thunder with the pregnancy thing."

They laughed, and I cried, which was par for the course these days.

You're feeling okay?" asked Josh as we walked through Prospect Park. "You sure?"

"Josh, for the thousandth time, I'm fine. I swear, my pregnancy is bringing out your inner Woody Allen. Don't be so neurotic. I promise, if I feel less than great, I will let you know."

"Sorry, I know I'm a little much. I just want to be here for you. It seems so unfair that you have to do all of the heavy lifting while my life continues on as usual."

"That's pretty enlightened of you to say." All around us, the leaves were beginning to explode into vibrant hues of yellow, orange, and red. A new mother walked past with her infant strapped to her chest, his tiny legs curled like parentheses.

"Yeah, well, you know me."

"So what did you think of Franklin?" He had flown in the night before and spent the night with Ben and Kate, almost as eager to meet his nephew as he was to see me.

"He's pretty adorable."

"Isn't he? Did he smile for you?"

"He did indeed. It was pretty wild to see Ben as a dad. I can't believe it's taken me so long to get up here."

"Well, with teaching it wasn't like you could just take off any time you liked. Plus, we had the move and everything. Honestly, I think they were grateful for some time to adjust to parenthood before being deluged with well-meaning guests."

"Probably." We rounded a corner, nearly colliding with a sprinting man clad head-to-toe in red spandex.

"That's a lot of look," I commented as we recovered.

"Is that what you think you're going to want to do?"

"When?"

"When the baby comes, are you just going to want it to be me and you? Like in the delivery room and everything?"

"Oh hell to the yes. Me, you, and the doctor. That's it." Josh was silent in response. "What? You want a party?"

"Not a party, but I just thought our parents might be there." He stole a glance at me. "But it's whatever you want, obviously."

"Thanks." I exhaled, realizing that I had been holding my breath while he voiced his opinion. "There's so much we have to figure out!"

"I know, right? It makes our previous worries seem so trivial, you know?"

"I do." I grabbed his hand. "For now let's just enjoy this walk though, okay? I'm so happy you're here."

"Me too." We ambled on, and I tried my best to take my own advice and just enjoy the moment. It was the kind of idyllic fall day captured on postcards from Vermont.

"I'm happy to be leaving," I said.

"You are?"

"Yeah. The romance is officially over. I'm ready for Farmwood."

"You sure this time?"

"I really am. My business idea and this baby—both have revitalized me in a really nice way. I mean, I'll always have love for New York, but this visit has confirmed what I knew in August when we left. It's time to move on."

"Good." He squeezed my hand.

Franklin is really going to miss you," declared Kate.

"You think?"

Kate nodded. "Yeah, he really likes you."

"Kate, come on. How on earth can you tell if Franklin likes me? He's not exactly vocal."

"A mother knows." She picked him up and cradled him in her arms. "Sometimes I get pissed when he likes people other than me. Isn't that terrible?"

"It's not that terrible." I reached over and touched his knuckle-less hand. "It's understandable, actually. You work your ass off twenty-four/seven to keep the kid alive; the least you could expect is a little favoritism."

"Thanks for indulging me, Sarah." She handed him back to me. "Here, hold him while I get some water. You want anything?"

"No thanks." I stared at Franklin. Already, in just two weeks, he had changed. His limbs had gone from noodles to gnocchi, and there was a focus to his gaze that suggested the personality he would soon embody.

"Sarah, did you speak to Mona? Are she and Nate on schedule?" Josh asked me from the kitchen, where he and Ben stood together drinking scotch.

"Yep, just about. Running about ten minutes behind, but they should be here soon."

They were coming over for my good-bye dinner, which would feature delivery from my three favorite restaurants. I had hesitated to bring everyone together at Kate and Ben's apartment, fearing discomfort for Mona because of

Franklin, but she had insisted that it was fine. Franklin gurgled.

"Hey, little guy, try not to be so cute when Mona is here," I whispered. The doorbell rang and he flailed for a moment in distress. "It's okay, buddy," I cooed, picking him up and pressing his stomach against my chest. His head fit perfectly in the space between my clavicle and ear, and it was all I could do not to shudder in delight at the warmth his compact body provided.

Mona and Nate entered in a flurry of cold air and hugs, with nervous compliments flying between Kate and Mona like confetti.

"You look amazing!"

"No, you look amazing!" Hugs were exchanged and Ben took their coats to the bedroom. As I held Franklin and waved to Mona, I felt terribly self-conscious and naïve. How could we have thought that exposing her to a baby so soon after her surgery wouldn't hurt?

"Sarah, I never thought I'd see the day. You look downright maternal over there," she said as she slowly made her way over to me.

"Sit," I commanded. She obeyed and looked at Franklin hesitantly.

Kate came over and sat on my other side. "Mona, you can hold him if you like," she offered.

"No, that's okay." We sat in silence as Mona observed him. "Well, okay," she said, reconsidering. I handed him over and she held him stiffly, as though he was made of papier-mâché.

"Bring him into your chest," said Kate encouragingly, getting up and returning to the kitchen. Mona slowly brought him closer until he was snuggled into her like a cashew.

"This feels nice," whispered Mona.

"Mo, is this—is this okay? Are you sure? We can change the plan and go out; Kate and Ben will understand."

"Shhhh. He's almost asleep, I think." She shifted slightly to answer me. "It was pretty silly of me to think that I could hang out with Franklin and not feel sad, I suppose." She sighed before continuing. "But what can we do? I'm here, and that's it. I mean, what do I expect? To just not see babies until I feel emotionally ready?"

"I know, but still. I brought you right into the belly of the beast."

"No, you didn't. I came willingly." She readjusted him gently. "You know, before I had the operation, I would close my eyes at night and see cancer. Those little flashes of light when you close your eyes tightly? To me, that was the cancer inside my body. Now those flashes of light are just flashes of light."

"That's great," I said. "Less scary."

"Yeah, it is."

"Mona, I'm in awe of you, really and truly. You've been such a trouper through all of this. I don't know how you've done it."

"Thanks, I guess. You've been a huge help. And Nate, too."

"I'm so glad that you let him in."

"What can I say, you were right." She rolled her eyes. "As

usual. He's such a good person, Sarah. Like, authentically good. And kind. And patient." She stroked Franklin's head tentatively. "He told me that he spoke to you about going back to school."

"He did. Pretty impressive, huh?"

"It really is. I was worried about that, for sure. Can you imagine him as a sixty-five-year-old comedian paralegal?"

"I'd rather not. And apparently, neither would he, which is terrific."

"Thank God."

"What does he think about kids, Mo?"

"He said he wasn't sure he wanted them anyway."

"No kidding."

"Yeah. We even talked about adopting for, like, a minute before I changed the subject. I'm not ready for that discussion yet. But you know, just that he even entertained the idea is fairly huge."

"I'd say more than fairly." I kissed her cheek. "Mona, you're the bravest person I've ever known. You always have been."

"I am?" She looked me in the eye, and I could see hers brimming with tears.

"No contest. You inspire me, you really do." I geared up to hug her and then pulled back. "I don't want to squash Franklin."

"Probably not a good idea." She smiled at me. "You inspire me too, you know."

"Get out of here."

"No, you do. You always pull yourself up by the boot-straps."

"I do?"

"Sure. Remember when Clark broke up with you and you gained thirty pounds and wallowed in self-pity for a year?"

"You call that pulling myself up by the bootstraps?"

"You knew yourself well enough to take the time you needed to get over it, and then one day you just up and registered for the marathon and joined Date.com. When you were ready, you were ready."

"What a year that was. Each guy was worse than the next, and my nipples were in a constant state of chafe." I shook my head, remembering.

"So, you've done the same thing now. You wallowed for a bit, but when you were ready—bam! Driving lessons; a new career; a baby. I really admire you."

"Come on, I certainly dragged my feet enough on all fronts."

"Not true."

"Thanks."

"And I think you're gonna be a great mom."

"Really?"

"Really."

"What's happening over here?" asked Kate, approaching us with three flutes of bubbly beverages.

"Just getting mushy," I answered.

"I don't want her to leave," said Mona.

"Join the club," said Kate. "For you, Sarah, some delicious sparkling apple cider, and for Mona, champagne."

"Will you guys come visit?" I asked, braced for the "Of course we will" but knowing that they most likely would not. When you lived in New York, the America outside of it didn't really exist, unless of course you were talking about Los Angeles.

"Well I guess we have to now," answered Mona. "What with the baby on board and all."

"Really?" I asked, excited. "Good." I raised my glass. "To your visit." Mona and Kate followed suit, and we clinked over Franklin's head.

21

When you approach a roundabout, slow down and watch for signs and/or pavement markings that prohibit certain movements.

Morning sunlight filtered through the blinds as a ladybug crawled across the sheets toward me. I picked it up gently—after all, this was the new, maternal me, lover of all of God's creatures—but despite my best intentions, I found myself crushing it to a pulp within seconds. *Oh well. Rome wasn't built in a day.*

Josh rolled over and laid his arm across my stomach, burying his head between my collarbone and jaw. It felt good to be back in my bed, although leaving New York had proved to be unexpectedly emotional for me. In the cab, I had held Josh's hand and cried quietly, overwhelmed by the realization that when we returned to visit, it would be with our child in tow.

"Morning," he mumbled.

"Morning," I replied, snuggling into him. "I missed this."

"Me too." He reversed onto his back and yawned loudly. "That was the best sleep I've had in weeks. The bed is too cold without you in it."

"Come on, I know at least the first couple of days I was gone had to be nice. You could stretch out as much as you liked, hog the blankets, not make the bed . . ."

He smiled, his eyes closed. "Maybe the first two days or so."

"Mmm-hmm."

"But it got old quickly."

"Yeah, so did sleeping on Mona's couch."

"I bet. Hey, you hungry?"

"Yep."

"Let's go out to breakfast."

"Ooh la la." I threaded my fingers through his. "That sounds nice. Can we go somewhere that serves biscuits? Real biscuits, not the frozen-and-reheated kind?"

"Yeah, there's this place that Curtis told me about down by campus. Biscuits and bacon as far as the eye can see, supposedly."

"That's a great name for a restaurant that only serves breakfast. Biscuits and Bacon. Who's Curtis, by the way?"

"One of my TAs, remember? I told you about him before. He came to taco night."

"A fellow math nerd?"

"Yeah. I'd love for you to meet him."

"How old is he?"

"I dunno, twenty-three, twenty-four?"

"Oh my God, twenty-three. Can you even remember what being that young felt like?"

"Yeah, itchy. Those were not my finest years."

I laughed as I slowly unwound myself from the sheet. "Guess I'll go take a shower."

"Can I come with you?"

"Josh, you know I love you, but the showering-together thing is not for me. Especially with the baby. I could slip or something."

"Fine." He rolled onto his stomach and pulled the comforter over his head.

As I massaged conditioner into my scalp, the door opened. On the other side of the mottled glass, Josh's blurry frame appeared. I closed my eyes and continued to relish the warmth of the water, hoping that he was not going to pull a fast one and attempt to join me.

"Oh, hey, I forgot to tell you something," he said as he squirted toothpaste onto his toothbrush.

"What's that?"

"Iris and Mac filed for separation."

I slid the door open, my mouth agape. "What?"

"Yeah, crazy, right?" He began to brush his teeth.

"Shit, don't stop there! What's the scoop?"

He pointed to his mouth with his free hand.

"Fine, I'll wait." I rinsed my hair quickly, wondering

about the cause of their split. Had Mac wanted to go to Madrid and Iris to Johannesburg? Or had Iris been keen to run a marathon and Mac set on the Ironman? I was being an asshole, but based on what I knew of both of them, I honestly couldn't think of any other viable options. Unless I had been right about the cracks in Iris's no-baby-for-us façade. I turned off the shower and got out, pulling my towel from its hook.

"Hey, wait, let me look at you," pleaded Josh. I put the towel back hesitantly, feeling embarrassed. "You're uncomfortable being naked in front of me now?" He looked at me mournfully.

"No. Yes. I don't know. I've gained some weight."

"I would hope so! You've got a baby in there." He moved closer. "You look beautiful, honey. Honestly. I can't wait until you're showing."

"Really?"

"Yes, really." He hugged me, and I relaxed into his embrace, his minty breath cold on my shoulder.

"So what's the story with Iris and Mac?" He handed me my towel, and I wrapped myself in it.

"Nobody knows for sure. I haven't spoken to either of them; it's just hearsay at this point."

"Wow. I feel badly for them."

"Me too, but at least there are no kids involved."

"Yeah. Makes it a little easier, I suppose. You know, Iris told me on our coffee date that they didn't want any." We both moved into the bedroom.

"Really?"

"That's what she said."

"I don't understand how that could be. With both of them being so good-looking, it's sort of their genetic obligation to procreate."

"Maybe she wasn't telling the whole truth. Maybe one of them wanted kids and the other didn't. That would be grounds for separation, I would think."

"True. Kids change a marriage, that's for sure," Josh remarked as he watched me put lotion on my legs.

"Are you ready for that?" I asked. "The change?"

"I think so. Are you?"

"Ready or not, here we come." I pulled on my underwear. "But that doesn't mean that it's going to be easy. We can't be scared of each other's changing perspectives throughout all of this."

"No, we can't. We have to vow to communicate. No walking on eggshells and hoping that things iron themselves out," Josh said. "Like before."

"Right, although I think with some things we can just sort of wait and see. There are going to be epic mood swings on my end over the next eight months. It's probably best if we don't dissect each one."

"Yes, but no more being scared of honesty. Especially with a baby coming. She's not a Band-Aid for our problems."

"Of course not. Did you just say 'she'?" I raised my eyebrows.

"Did I? Huh. I'd love a little girl. Girl babies are so cute."

"Really? I think I'd be more into a boy at this point. Teenage girls are murder. Karmically, I'm screwed. I was the absolute worst to my mother," I said, shuddering. "I think I told her that I hated her at least three times a week."

"Geez. That's terrible, Sarah."

"I know. Hormones, what can I say? Speaking of my mom, I was being too hard on her, I think, blaming her for my own parenting fears. Now I'm more comfortable taking ownership of them myself. How could anyone possibly feel like they've done everything they wanted to do with their own life by the time they're ready to have kids?"

"And if you do, then isn't that sad?" said Josh. "Shouldn't you always want to be expanding and growing, regardless of your kids?"

"Right, but I think physically it's much harder to chase your dreams when you have a baby suckling at your breast."

"True," Josh conceded.

"At any rate, I'm feeling good about the baby. Hopeful and excited."

"You know what's cool?" asked Josh.

"What?"

"That you put your marketing-consultant wheels in motion before you found out that you were pregnant."

"What do you mean?"

"Well, just that figuring out an appealing career path probably would have been a lot harder with a baby around, or even with a baby in there." He patted my stomach.

"Okay, really, Josh, I love you, but enough with the hands

on the stomach until, you know, it's an actual pregnant stomach and not a bowl of oatmeal."

"Fine. But do you know what I mean?"

"Of course. I'm excited about this new venture. Although, who knows if it has true potential."

"I think it's a no-brainer."

"Thanks, Josh." I laid my damp head on his shoulder.

"Have you told your mom yet, by the way?"

"Not yet. I want to keep this ours until we have our first doctor appointment and see the baby on the big screen."

"I can't imagine what that's going to feel like," said Josh.

"Incredible, overwhelming, and surreal for starters."

"I can't wait."

"Me either."

I backed out of our garage, looking in my side mirrors maniacally as I squeaked out of the narrow opening. On the road, I turned on the radio—a first for me—and rolled down the windows. I relaxed my grip on the wheel. I was almost enjoying myself. Almost.

I pulled awkwardly into a parking spot at the coffee shop that Ray and I had agreed on. Realizing I was crooked, I reversed out and reparked, only to find myself in the same position. "Okay, breathe, Sarah. Take your time," I said aloud. I backed out and did it again, landing in exactly the same position. *Screw it.*

As I reached over to grab my bag, a knock on my driver-side window made me jump. I looked up to find Ray beaming at me through the glass. He stepped out of the way and I opened the door.

"Look out, Miss New York is back!"

"Hey hey," I replied, blushing under the crush of his enthusiasm. "Did you see that?"

"See what?" He went in for a hug and I returned it, temporarily submerged in a sea of cologne that smelled like black licorice and tobacco. Not an unpleasant smell by any means, but Ray seemed to have bathed in it.

"My parking mess." I locked the door and smiled, taking him in. He truly was a human teddy bear—tall, sturdy, fuzzy, and somehow in a constant state of grin despite the fact that he put his life in jeopardy each day by teaching people like me to drive. And in a car that looked like a mouse, no less.

"Naw, that wasn't a mess. You went in a little crooked, but you took your time and straightened out. That was a pro's work."

"Get out of here."

"Naw, for real. You're serious now. You drove into Manhattan! Hell, I don't even know if I could have done that."

I reached out and grabbed his elbow as we made our way into the shop. "Thanks, Ray. I was pretty proud of myself. And thanks for your help, too. Having you there, so to speak, was incredibly helpful." He held the door open for me and we approached the counter.

“Yeah, that was something. I don’t think I’ve ever given a driving lesson on the phone. This is on me,” he said, pointing to the menu.

“No!”

“I mean it. Give me your order and take a seat. I’ll bring everything over when it’s ready.” I threw up my hands in surrender, ordered a decaf latte and an oatmeal raisin cookie, and slid into a booth.

“So, you movin’ back to the big city?” Ray asked, taking a bite of his Danish.

“No. I’ve been cured of my New Yorkitis.” I shook some sugar into my latte.

“Ooh, that’s good to hear!” declared Ray. “I was nervous there for a minute.”

“You were?”

“Sure. You seemed pretty sweet on that place. I didn’t think ole Farmwood stood a chance.”

“I’m back, baby.”

“Yeah, you are.” He took a sip of his sweet tea. “My marketing guru.”

“I hope so. Ray, I’ve got to thank you. Your reaching out to me really got me thinking. I’m going to use our work together as a springboard to launch my own consulting firm.”

“Now, that’s a good idea, Sarah. Farmwood needs some urban sophistication.”

I choked on my cookie. “That’s a phrase I didn’t expect to hear from your mouth, Ray.”

"What? 'Urban sophistication'?"

I nodded, grinning.

"What can I say? I'm full of surprises. Don't think that ole Ray is easy to figure out." He took a dramatic pull from his straw. "I am a complex man, you know."

"I know." I winked at him. "So, do you want to take a look at what I've come up with so far?"

"Sure do."

I pulled my laptop out of my bag and we spent the next half hour going over the ins and outs of what I was proposing.

"Sarah, these are some great ideas," said Ray when we had finished up.

"Thanks, Ray. I think Minnie's has a lot of potential to grow in ways we're only beginning to imagine." I paused. "Oh God, I sound like a hedge fund manager or something."

"It's all good. I know what you mean." Ray glanced at his watch. "All right, boss, I should get back to work. I'm giving an eighty-seven-year-old man a lesson in twenty minutes."

"Shouldn't he be turning in his license at this point?"

"He refuses, and his daughter threatened to take it away if he didn't take a refresher course. I guess he backed through their garage door last week."

"Ay ay ay."

"Exactly. Wish me luck." We stood up together. A wave of queasiness washed over me, and I held on to the table for a moment. "You all right?" Ray's brow furrowed with concern.

"Yeah, fine." I took a deep breath. "Just a little light-headed." I smiled as convincingly as I could, crossing my fingers in the hope that my thus-far-pleasant pregnancy wasn't taking a turn for Vomitville.

"You sure?" I nodded and walked slowly out in front of him.

"See you later, boss," said Ray as he unlocked the mouse car's doors. "You sure you're okay?"

"Positive. Just heading to work."

"Okay." He opened his door as I waved and began to walk away. "Sarah?"

"Yes?"

He closed the door and jogged over to me. "You pregnant?" he asked.

"What?" I replied, shocked.

"Sorry, that was rude. But I have three kids. I know pregnant when I see it." He smiled supportively. "You need any advice, you call Vanessa, you hear? She's a pro."

I nodded, embarrassed. "Thanks. I'm really not that far along though, so it's, you know, private."

"You got it. You won't hear another peep from me about it until you're ready, and then I'll talk your ear off. Take it easy." He patted my arm gently.

"Thanks, Ray."

I waved and continued on toward Bauble Head, wiping my eyes. It had been sweet of Ray to offer his and Vanessa's much-needed wisdom but a little too premature for my taste. I was barely a month along. Hopefully Mitzi lacked the fetus sonar that Ray seemed to possess. I wanted to keep my pregnancy quiet until I couldn't button my pants anymore. Which, unfortunately, looked like it would be sooner rather than later. Already my waistbands were beginning to leave angry red indentations in their wake.

A new display featuring a stuffed turkey with a rhinestone tiara perched atop its head greeted me as I pulled open the door to Bauble Head. I wondered for the thousandth time if Mitzi even *wanted* to make more money here, or if she was perfectly fine with bejeweled tchotchkes in her windows and, oh wow, were those bedazzled gourds at the register?

"Sarah?" Mitzi's perfectly coiffed head popped out from the back-room door. "Hey, honey!" The sound of a box hitting the floor startled us both. "One second, I'm just goin' through some new inventory!"

"No problem!" I called back. I realized I was grinning ear to ear as I took off my coat.

"Darlin', how was New York?" she sang as she skipped toward me on purple kitten-heeled mules. "How is Mona?" She reached out to give me a hug and then pulled back, observing me with wide eyes rimmed with mascara and purple liner.

"She's feeling good, thanks. Day by day, you know?"

She pulled up her stool and gestured for me to have a seat on my own. "I do know. Bless her heart. And did you say that she was single?"

"She was, but she actually reconnected with somebody a month or two before the surgery . . ."

Mesmerized by Mitzi's unwavering interest, I surprised myself by launching into a thorough rendition of my trip, complete with tales about Franklin and even my drive into Manhattan. Throughout, she laughed and mmm-hmmed and hand-patted in all the right places. I imagined it must have been what talking to Oprah felt like. When I was finished, I felt terrific. *Rhinestone therapy. Oh my God! Rhinestone Therapy! Of course!*

"Mitzi?" I said, barreling through my reservations about challenging her current business model.

"Hmmm?"

"Have you ever thought about trying to bring in a new demographic of customers?"

"Sure I have. I mean, who wouldn't want to turn a better profit? Although I would hate for Bauble Head to overwhelm my life. This is really just fun for me, you know? Sorta like my playhouse." She looked around. "My big, gaudy playhouse. Why? Did your New York trip get that brain of yours buzzin'?"

"It did, actually. I just, well, first and foremost, I wonder about the name."

"Bauble Head?"

I nodded.

"Why? You think it's tacky?"

"Maybe a smidge."

"I can see that. To be honest, I don't love it, but Clyde and I came up with it over a bottle of Dom Pérignon the night we officially leased this space, so it's got some memories for me. Why? Did you think of somethin' better?"

"I did. Just now, actually, although I've been racking my brain over it for weeks."

"Well, go on, what is it?"

"Okay, it's just a thought, but what about Rhinestone Therapy?"

Mitzi tilted her head as she considered it. "Rhinestone Therapy," she repeated slowly. "I think I like it." She drummed the counter with her fuchsia fingernails. "You think that will bring in new customers? A new name and a new sign?"

"Among other things, yes, but that's a good start. I'm actually starting up a marketing consultant business—"

"Are you leavin' me?"

"Oh no, not at all. I'd love to stay on part-time if you'll have me. I'm just letting you know that—"

"If I like your ideas I'm gonna need to pay for 'em?"

"Well, yes. But at next to nothing, of course. I'm just starting out and you're a friend, and also I work for you, so you would have me at a rock-bottom rate."

"What's *your* business name, smarty pants?"

"I actually don't have one at the moment."

"I have an idea for you, free of charge."

"What's that?"

"Big Mouth Marketing."

"Mitzi, I'm sorry, did I offend you with all of this? If that's the case, please just disregard it. It was just a thought."

She stood up and put her hands on my shoulders, seeming

to take particular delight in the fact that, from this angle, she was actually the taller one for once.

"Sarah, I love your idea. I'm just givin' you crap." I smiled, relieved. "You think I'm thin-skinned enough to get my feelins hurt over a name change? Come on, now. You're not givin' southern women enough credit. As far as workin' with you, let me think about it."

"Oh good. I'm so glad. And of course, take your time. Although, your suggestion is actually pretty great."

"What suggestion?"

"Big Mouth Marketing. I kind of like it."

"Of course you do. That will be fifty dollars. Pay up." She laughed and walked out from behind the register. "Now, we have a ton of unpacking to do. I just got a bunch of winter crap in." She glanced back at me. "Rhinestone Therapy, huh? It's growin' on me, missy."

22

As I locked up the store, I was suddenly seized by an urgent need for iced tea. I had never craved it before, but now every taste bud I possessed yearned for it. My first official craving. Sure, I had indulged in some decadent foods since finding out I was pregnant, but that was just gluttony. This was different. This was a *Somebody in this parking lot is going to die if I don't get that iced tea* situation. Ah, the coffee shop. They had to have it, or at the very least, a beverage that came close enough.

I made a beeline for it with the focus of an Olympic speed

skater, practically breaking a sweat in the process despite the fact that it was, finally, cool outside. Inside, it was all I could do not to squeal with delight upon seeing the very words that were flashing neon in my brain scrawled on the chalkboard menu behind the register. I closed my eyes as I took my first sip through the straw. Sweet Sally, it was good. I thanked Bonnie, who was no doubt a bit taken aback by my show of gratitude.

On my way out, I surveyed the early-evening crowd, almost draining my cup in the process. *Oh God, Iris.* Common decency said that I had to go over and say hello, but I was not in the mood. Besides, how was I going to address her and Mac's separation? I could play dumb—after all, I had been out of town for two weeks—but knowing me, my nerves would reveal themselves in some predictably ungraceful form, e.g., dropping my to-go cup on the floor, choking on an ice cube, or somehow managing to unscrew and upend the table's saltshaker, which I had actually done before in similar predicaments. Twice. Naturally, at that moment, she looked up and saw me. She waved hesitantly and I returned the gesture. *Showtime.*

"Hi, Iris," I said a little too cheerily as I approached, in an attempt to mask my discomfort. She was as beautiful as ever, but beneath her eyes was the telltale gray of lack of sleep. And was that a pimple on her cheek? So she was human after all.

"Hi, Sarah." She gazed up at me plaintively. "How was your trip?"

"Good, thanks. I—I went to help my best friend recuperate from surgery. She had a hysterectomy." Why, why had I just told her that? Me and my stupid mouth.

"Oh, I'm sorry to hear that. Josh mentioned that you were going to help a friend, but I wasn't clear on the details."

I nodded, unsure of how to see my way out of the awkward fog I had created. "How are you doing?"

"Eh." She shrugged her shoulders. "I've been better."

"Josh told me about you and Mac. I'm so sorry, Iris. Can I sit?"

"Of course! Sorry not to have offered sooner. My head is all over the place lately." She removed her bag from the other chair. "Here. And thanks. I'm still in a bit of a state of shock about the whole thing."

I nodded. "Please don't feel like you have to open up to me about anything. I just, you know, didn't want to avoid the elephant in the room." I rocked my ice-filled cup back and forth on the tabletop. "And wanted to tell you that I'm sorry."

"Oh no, I'm fine to talk about it. I could use an ear, actually. I don't have a lot of girlfriends in this town. Or anywhere, for that matter. Mac has pretty much been my sole sounding board for fifteen years." She sighed. "Which I'm regretting now, obviously."

"What happened? I know this sounds cliché, but you guys seemed so happy."

"We were, for the most part. Something happened."

I raised my eyebrows. Who would cheat on Iris? Or did

Iris cheat on Mac? The pickings around here seemed slim on both ends considering their presumed standards.

"Sarah, I'm pregnant."

"Shut up. I thought you said—"

"Yes, I did. Neither of us thought we wanted kids. It was an understood agreement, just like I so self-righteously told you." She laughed curtly. "I can only see the self-righteousness now that I'm on the other side, mind you."

"But how?"

"Do you know that antibiotics can cancel out birth control?"

"You know what, I do, actually."

"How did you know that? I mean, I consider myself a fairly informed woman, and I had no idea."

"If I tell you how I know, do you promise not to judge me?"

"I promise."

"*Teen Mom*."

"What's *Teen Mom*?"

"It's a ridiculous show on MTV that follows the lives of these teen moms. One of them got pregnant the same way you did."

"Wonderful. I'm in great company." She laughed again, this time a little more authentically. "I guess there is something redeemable about the show though, if you actually learned something."

"That's what I say to Josh every time he catches me watching it." I laughed too. "Although it's hard to be taken seriously."

She smiled. "Thanks for that, Sarah. I can't remember the

last time I laughed. Anyway, I had this horrible sinus infection, which led to the antibiotic prescription, which led to this." She put her hand on her stomach. "We were both shocked, obviously, but Mac was actually outraged. Saying we should sue the doctor and ranting like a caged tiger."

"Wow. That must have been really stressful."

"It was. I was shocked and worried too, but when Mac suggested that I terminate the pregnancy, I just couldn't do it. It seemed so selfish of me, when so many women can't even have children to begin with. Like your friend in New York." She sighed. "I deliberated over it for days, with Mac breathing down my neck all the while, and finally, I told him that I wouldn't. That I was going to have the baby with or without him."

"Whoa."

"So now I'm without him."

"I don't know what to say."

"Yeah, me either. It's been an eye-opening couple of weeks, let me tell you. I mean, had you asked me a few months ago what I would have done should I get pregnant, I wouldn't even have courted the possibility of being pregnant in the first place. I guess circumstance changes everything."

"Everything. So where are you living? What happens now?"

"I'd be lying if I said that I wasn't holding out hope that Mac will come around. I know that he loves me, it's just the 'us' bit I'm not certain about. For now, I'm still in the house and he's in an apartment close to the hospital."

"Are you still talking?"

"Yes. Although it's awkward. If he doesn't come around, of course, there's the whole question of financial support. It is his child, even if it wasn't part of the grand plan."

"Are you feeling okay? Physically, I mean?"

"I'm okay. I've had some nausea, but nothing too awful. I'm living on a steady stream of crackers and Sour Patch Kids."

"Sour Patch Kids?"

"Oh yeah, they really cut the nausea. Something about the sourness. Just for future reference."

On cue, I tipped my cup over, sending its top and an avalanche of ice cubes across the table. "I am such a klutz! It never fails. Sorry." I pulled some napkins from the dispenser and attempted to sop up the mess.

"No worries. I better get used to messes, right? No more white jeans for me."

"You do wear the hell out of white jeans." I held the cup under the rim of the table with one hand and pushed the ice back into it with the other.

"Thanks."

"Iris?"

"Yes?"

"I'm pregnant too." I hadn't planned on telling her, but it felt right to share my news. As sad as her situation was, there was something infinitely more likable about her in this vulnerable position. Her hands flew to her mouth in surprise.

"No!"

"Yep." I laughed nervously.

"This is fantastic news! Congratulations!"

"Thanks. It's still really new and hush-hush, but I figured since you were sharing, I would too. Plus, you know, if you want to, we can commiserate about stuff."

"Sarah, I would love it," she gushed as her cheeks flushed peach with excitement. Whose cheeks flushed peach? "I can't tell you how giddy it makes me feel to think that I could, that we could, lean on each other for support throughout this process."

"I'd like it too. The whole thing has been quite a roller coaster for me thus far. Not like your roller coaster, granted, but you know, lots of twists and turns."

"Hence the analogy," Iris teased.

"Right. Thanks."

"You know, I've been going to these amazing prenatal yoga classes, maybe—"

"Nah, not for me."

Iris nodded. "Got it."

"Maybe we could go walking together, though? Early mornings before work?"

"I'd love that." We smiled, content in the knowledge that we were newfound allies. "Well, I better get going. Josh has your number, right?"

"Yes, and my e-mail." She gazed at me wistfully. "Have a nice night."

"You too. And I really am sorry about Mac. I hope things work out."

"Thanks, Sarah. Me too. Going through this alone isn't exactly preferable." I reached over and squeezed her shoulder because I didn't know what else to do. Without Josh's support, I would have been a wreck. I turned to go but stopped in my tracks.

"Hey, do you want to come over for dinner?" I turned around and asked. "Josh is making macaroni and cheese."

"No way." She beamed at me.

"Yep, and not the box kind either."

"The kind with a bread-crumb top?"

"Yep."

"I'd love to. Are you sure I'm not imposing?"

"Not at all. Just come over when you're finished here. Do you remember where we live?"

"I do."

"Okay, see you soon."

"Thanks, Sarah. See you soon."

As I drove away slightly dazed, I thought about what had just transpired. Never in a million years would I have expected to be inviting Iris over for dinner and baby talk, but I guessed stranger things had happened. As much as it was a surprise, there also seemed to be something slightly fated about our intertwined destinies. Neither of us was the baby-crazy type, and yet here we were.

Mona and I had become friends in much the same way,

actually. On paper, we had nothing in common. She was fresh out of Princeton and the impossibly sophisticated daughter of globe-trotting parents, while I was head-to-toe New Jersey and the scrappy product of an even scrappier single mom. We'd been introduced by a mutual friend—the woman who shared my cubicle wall, to be exact—because she knew that both of us were desperate to vacate our current Craigslist-roommate apartments. Voilà, best friends. Maybe that was the key to everlasting friendships—a humbling dose of intimidation at the outset. After all, Kate and I were now much more than sisters-in-law. We were friends as well.

I was probably getting ahead of myself. There was always the possibility that Iris really did suck as much as I had first surmised, but something in me doubted it. Talking with her tonight, I had gotten a glimpse of the real her, without the shiny façade, and I liked what I saw.

I pulled into the driveway and as I went to pull the key out of the ignition, I realized something. Something huge. Something I never thought I'd have the pleasure of realizing. I had driven home. No nerves, no chattering teeth, no sternum glued to the steering wheel. Just me, driving a car. Getting from Point A to Point B without so much as a second thought.

A knock on my window made me jump. Josh stood on the other side, wearing the apron that I had received as a wedding gift and never worn. MRS. SIMON, it read in white letters across his chest. He smiled at me.

"Don't you look pleased with yourself," he said before giving me a peck on the lips.

"You know what?" I turned the car off and opened the door.

"What?" He took my hand to help me out.

"I am."

Insights,
Interviews
& More . . .

About the author

Meet Zoe Fishman

Karen Shacham

ZOE FISHMAN is the author of *Saving Ruth* and *Balancing Acts*. She lives in Atlanta, Georgia, with her husband and son.

On Writing *Driving Lessons*

THUS FAR IN MY CAREER, my novels have largely been based on my life and personal experiences, for better or for worse. Someday I'd love to write a story that takes me outside of my immediate experience, but at this point, writing what I know has proved to be an emotionally challenging and cathartic experience that I treasure deeply. There is no better feeling for me as a writer than when a reader tells me that they related to or took comfort from the journey of one of my characters. That's exactly the kind of connection that made me want to be a writer in the first place.

Driving Lessons is no exception. In the spring of 2011, two things happened. First, after thirteen years in New York, I was over it. And I mean *over it*. I was tired of the constant hustle, fed up with my tiny dust-ridden apartment with its thimble-sized bathroom attached to our kitchen, and exasperated by the foodie-cum-hipster invasion of the Brooklyn neighborhood I had called home for ten years. Second, I got pregnant. Not a whoops-I'm-pregnant moment or anything, but more of an ovulation-tracking-and-fist-pump-of-joy pregnancy moment. I was thirty-four, my husband and I had been married for two years, and we were ready.

The idea of having a baby in Brooklyn overwhelmed me. Peering into a future that I could only imagine at that point, I knew that with the juggling of my ▸

full-time job and motherhood, something was going to go. And that something would no doubt be my writing. I had worked too hard and loved it too much to give it up. We had to move, and quick.

We decided on Atlanta for a number of reasons, the most prevalent being that my husband grew up and still had family there, and my family was close by in Alabama. He got a job and two months later I sat in a lawn chair on the sidewalk in all of my lumpy, pre-popped pregnancy glory and watched movers carry out our Saran Wrapped belongings while I sipped lemonade through a straw. It wasn't until the cab ride to the airport that I bawled. What was I doing? How could I leave New York? I had grown into my skin in New York, and now I was leaving it? How could I survive outside of it? How could my baby not know what it meant to take the subway or eat a real bagel or play in Prospect Park? I was a mess.

And so, the initial idea for *Driving Lessons* was born. As I began writing, however, my pregnancy became much more real to me—physically and emotionally—and then, of course, I actually had my son, Ari. Although the story was still focused on that move and all that it entailed, it changed dramatically. I longed to write about both the idea of pregnancy before it became absolute and the blurry day-to-day of new motherhood. I also thought it would be interesting to present other points of view as well. What if you made no apologies for not wanting a child, as Iris does? And how does that look juxtaposed against someone who does want a child but cannot have one, like Mona?

When I moved, it was August, and I was about four months pregnant. I had no job lined up in Atlanta and was thrilled to focus on writing. Excited about the prospect of daylong stretches of creative genius, I promised to deliver the first draft by December. I am laughing now as I write this, thinking back to my naïveté. Needless to say, that didn't happen. Ari was born in January, and December turned into the following September in the blink of a sleep-deprived eye.

I wish I could blame my tardiness solely on the fact that I had a baby to keep alive, but my lack of focus was probably never more tangible than during my pregnancy. I would sit down to write and then inevitably spend hours researching cribs and nursery rugs online. I'm certainly not proud of my truancy, but looking back, I'm grateful that I allowed myself that time.

Although I had only been told by new mothers to treasure the months before the baby arrived, I could never have imagined what being in the trenches truly felt like. Days upon days of zero sleep; cracked nipples; tears for no reason at inopportune moments, along with pockets of sheer joy—those were ▸

the things I learned about firsthand and, although I had been warned, was not prepared for. How can you possibly be prepared for such unselfishness when prior to delivery your biggest concern was whether or not to invest in ridiculously expensive eye cream or just go for the drugstore brand? Yes, I'm speaking from experience.

At any rate, where was I? Oh yes, the genesis of *Driving Lessons*. Ari is now fifteen months old, and although I do sleep more, it is still not nearly enough, and my brain can certainly wander. For the most part, though, I've gotten the hang of it. With the help of wonderful babysitters a few hours a day, three days a week, I've learned to focus again, and it feels really good.

Like Sarah, I worried that any sense of my own lack of fulfillment would translate into my day-to-day with Ari. That's not the case—I literally don't have the time to deliberate on that or beat myself up about what I have or haven't done in terms of personal goals—but I am sincerely grateful that I was able to call myself a writer before he was born. The sacrifices you make as a parent, especially as a mother, are exponential. I know that had I not had a head start with *Balancing Acts* and *Saving Ruth*, I would have had a hell of a time putting pen to paper with a baby in tow.

It's May now, and about two weeks ago I heard from my editor that, finally, after I'd submitted my third draft,

Driving Lessons was going into production. I promptly burst into tears upon reading her e-mail conveying this happy news. It's been a tough road, the writing of this novel. The hormonal shifts alone, not to mention all the demands of new motherhood, made me feel at times like some of my plot and characterization obstacles were absolutely insurmountable. To hear that I had overcome them anyway was an overwhelming feeling of accomplishment.

After reading the e-mail three times for good measure, I placed my phone on the counter and turned to Ari, who was sitting in his high chair and eating his banana slices with unbridled gusto. He swallowed, cocked his head, and pointed at me.

"Mama," he declared.

"That's right," I replied, wiping my eyes. "Mama." I paused to squeeze his delicious, knuckleless hand. "Mama and writer."

Reading Group Guide

1. At the beginning Sarah seems lost, despite the fact that she can claim a successful career. Can you relate to this? Would you be able to walk away from lucrative stability in pursuit of emotional fulfillment?
2. Sarah feels guilty because of her maternal uncertainties and is unable to be truthful with Josh as a result. She feels as though she is letting him down, despite the fact that she will be the one carrying the literal load for nine months. Do you think most women feel pressured by society to play the role of eager mom?
3. In the same vein, what did you think of Iris's unapologetic stance on children? Were you put off or did you admire her chutzpah?
4. Sarah agrees to move to Farmwood despite the fact that she has some serious driving fears. What are these fears analogous to?
5. Sarah has led a fairly workaholic lifestyle prior to Farmwood. This left some time to pine for a career she was more passionate about—without actually allowing her the time to pursue it. Ironically, when she's unemployed and with nothing but that kind of time, she's paralyzed by the opportunity. Has this ever happened to you?

6. Sarah is plagued throughout the novel by ladybugs. Is there a metaphor here? If so, what is it?
7. Did you find Sarah's relationship with her mother to be realistic? As you approach the idea of motherhood, or as a mother yourself, what things about your own mother do you find yourself trying to emulate or avoid?
8. Sarah and Mona handle Mona's diagnosis and pending hysterectomy with a lot of humor, despite the fear and vulnerability they feel. How do you think you would react in a similar situation? And do you think Mona's fears pertain more to the diagnosis or to the results of the surgery?
9. What did you think about Kate's unabashed frankness about her pregnancy, delivery, and postpartum sex life? Could you relate or did it make you uncomfortable?
10. Do you think Sarah and Iris will indeed be friends?

Recommended Reading

The following are some of Zoe's favorite books:

Olive Kitteridge, by Elizabeth Strout
State of Wonder, by Ann Patchett
Middlesex, by Jeffrey Eugenides
Prep, by Curtis Sittenfeld
The Secret History, by Donna Tartt
Plainsong, by Kent Haruf
Bird by Bird, by Anne Lamott
Heartburn, by Nora Ephron
The Girl in the Flammable Skirt,
by Aimee Bender
The History of Love,
by Nicole Krauss

Have You Read?
More by Zoe Fishman

SAVING RUTH

Growing up in Alabama, all Ruth Wasserman wanted was to be a blond Baptist cheerleader. But as a curly-haired Jew with a rampant sweet tooth and a smart mouth, this was an impossible dream. Not helping the situation was her older brother, David—a soccer star whose good looks, smarts, and popularity reigned at school and at home. College provided an escape route and Ruth took it.

Now home for the summer, she's returned to lifeguarding and coaching alongside David, and although the job is the same, nothing else is. She's a prisoner of her low self-esteem and unhealthy relationship with food, David is closed off and distant in a way he's never been before, and their parents are struggling with the reality of an empty nest. When a near drowning happens on their watch, a storm of repercussions forces Ruth and David to confront long-ignored truths about their town, their family, and themselves.

Have You Read? *(continued)*

BALANCING ACTS

With beauty, brains, and a high-paying Wall Street position, Charlie was a woman who seemed to have it all—until she turned thirty and took stock of her life—or lack thereof. She left it all behind to pursue yoga, and now, two years later, she's looking to drum up business for her fledgling studio in Brooklyn. Attending her college's alumni night with flyers in hand, she reconnects with three former classmates whose postgraduation lives, like hers, haven't turned out like they'd hoped.

Romance book editor Sabine still longs to write the novel that's bottled up inside her. Once an up-and-coming photographer and Upper East Side social darling, Naomi is now a single mom who hasn't picked up her camera in years. And Bess, who dreamed of being a serious investigative journalist à la Christiane Amanpour, is stuck in a rut, writing snarky captions for a gossip mag. But at a weekly yoga class at Charlie's studio the four friends, reunited ten years after college, will forge new bonds and take new chances—as they start over, fall in love, change their lives . . . and come face-to-face with haunting realities.